When the feeling is effortless, "Love conquers all!". When we are blinded by emotion, "Love makes people do crazy things." After that, we're making excuses when someone who is supposed to love us hurts us. Love is complicated, and it makes the imagination go wild with possibilities. Life is too short to wonder what if or be stuck in a bad situation. Life is an adventure, and love is the fuel on which we drive.

Love is not complicated. It's the people, their lives, and their pasts that make it complicated. Understanding that person, their life, and history is what makes love stronger. The problem is no one wants to put effort into understanding anymore. The dating rules of the new generation have changed the value of love. I believe in the old-school notion of one and one only. Love is hard enough with one person. You complicate the situation and destroy others when there is more than one.

For the love we want but afraid to go after, we want but don't want us back, want but can't have, and dreaming of having!

Thank you, first and foremost, to you, the reader that decided to support my first work. I appreciate the time taken to venture into my world of fiction.

To my five beautiful daughters, who can be a handful but keep me on my toes and give me the inspiration to put stories to paper for their support, I love you!

To all my friends and family that have been background rooting every step, I thank you so much for being the crowd of cheers I heard until the finish line.

To some special individuals:

Charles Graham- I appreciate sifting through my lousy grammar and being the first to read and see potential in my work. Thank you for being my biggest fan and encouraging me to go further than a blog. Thank you for helping bring together all the components of this finished works. If not for you constantly telling me I could make it, none of this would have been possible. I love you dearly and hope you continue to push me to be great!

Serena Elvery- I appreciate you taking the time out of your primary business to return to the world of editing for me. Without you, my confidence to publish and go forward would not have been so high. You are my guardian angel and make sure I come out looking great! I hope the next book won't be so much work for you, but no promises!

Kareem Williams- Gosh, just thank you! You've been in my corner since way before the print work. Since my blog, you have been one of my longest fans and another to push me to my goal. I love you for holding my hand through this journey and being there for me when I was at my worst. I thank you for being such a good friend!

Cody Hubbard- When I was down and out for artwork, you came in the last minute and hit the buzzer-beater! I love the work you did for me and appreciate you dealing with my many alterations and request. I so hope we get to do another cover for my next book! Thank you so much for coming in when you did and putting the perfect final touch on this work!

Elton King II- Coming aboard late meant nothing. I value your input and suggestions. I appreciate your giving me the advice I needed for my point of view. Thank you for being another great inspiration on this journey. I definitely appreciate you taking the time to help me be great. I cherish your friendship!

JB Stewart- Words cannot express how much I really appreciate you. You got me pointed in all the right directions and never asked me for anything. The help you gave took me higher than I was. I love everything you did for me, and I hope to do more business in the future.

CHANCE ENCOUNTER

The terminal was packed for it just being a Wednesday. I got my bags checked in and had about thirty minutes before my plane departed for Chicago. While getting checked by security, something bright red caught my eye. I turned and saw the most beautiful woman I've ever seen. She was short, dark-haired, brown eyes, about five foot six, "C" cups, and a phat ass that called your name. Everything about her screamed classy from how she walked; switching her hips seemed to come naturally to her. She KNOWS she is sexy.

For an entire thirty minutes, I couldn't stop thinking about her. I closed my eyes, trying to imagine what she looks like under that dress. In an instant, my sense of smell went haywire with an intoxicating melody of what smelled like berries. I glanced to my right to catch her figure over my shoulder. I opened my eyes and almost lost all composure. *Butterflies in my stomach? Am I actually nervous?* "Get yo shit together nigga! We don't get nervous. This is what we do!" I tell myself. "Now boarding flight 069," I heard over the intercom. As I grabbed my bag, I hesitated to catch one last look and started walking towards the gate. I handed the attendant my ticket, then it hit me hard like a punch in the nose. Peeking over my shoulder, I saw her again. *Wonder if she noticed me?*

I stowed my bag, and as I was about to take my seat, the sweetest sound hit my ears. "Do you mind if I have the window seat?" I turned to look the woman in red in the eyes. That was a bad idea. They were brown, not light but not dark, with a unique grey ring to outline. They twinkled in the sunlight, and I was captivated. "Not at all," I replied. I stepped back so the lady could get the seat and I caught a view from behind... *Damn!* I wondered if I said that out loud.

Even though she had a dress on, I could see the shape of each ass cheek like two crescent moons put together. My mind was envisioning the shapes and colors of our bodies intertwined. She sat down and giggled a bit as she pushed her hair behind her ear. “What is so funny?” I asked.

“You think it will be enough room for you and uh… your friend?”

“My friend?” I asked questioningly, looking down, and then I saw it. I had a half-hard dick stretching its way down my pant leg. I had to catch myself from showing embarrassment. “Don't worry,” I started with a half-smile and innocent look on my face. “He doesn't bite.”

“Neither do I,” she replied, blushing. My mind took off! The thought of my tip gently sitting on those soft, luscious lips, then sliding between to feel the warmth and wetness of her mouth. I had to calm myself because I did not want to make a more significant scene. I quickly adjusted myself and proceeded to take my seat.

Staring at her reflection, she sat looking out the window with stars in her eyes. As the plane started moving, the attendants came up front and made their takeoff speech.

“Please fasten your seat belts.”

“Please stay seated during takeoff.”

“The regular exits are here... And the emergency exits are there.”

“Enjoy your flight!”

I settled in my seat and tried not to show how excited I was...I admired her movements, from putting on her seat belt, pulling papers out of her bag to the way she sits back and slightly slouches in the seat. I tried not to stare so this does not become a long, creepy flight.

After about an hour and a half into the flight, I needed to adjust in my seat. I placed my arm on the armrest. Not knowing that the mystery woman's arm was already there, I pulled back my arm and looked up at her. “I'm sorry,” I quickly said, “You can have it.”

“No. I’m sorry,” she said. “I forgot we have to share these things.”

“How about you keep that gorgeous smile on, and we can call it even.” My heart pounded so fast, and even though it was only seconds, in my mind, I thought it was more like twenty minutes. I played every scenario of what the reaction could be: I imagined everything from a simple “OK” to the lady being offended and slapping me. However, I found myself shocked by the actual words.

“OK. Deal!” she replies. “Only if you give me a reason to, though.”

I think my shock reflected on my face because she let out the most joyous laugh I’ve ever heard. Feeling embarrassed, she covered her smile. I adjusted my face and raised a suspicious eyebrow. “So do I get bonus points if I make you laugh like that again?” I asked.

“If you make me laugh the entire flight, I will buy you a drink when we land. But what do I get if I can make you blush again?” the lady replied.

My damn! What a woman! She is snappy but keeps her class. I like her spirit. She is not afraid to say what is on her mind. She does not back down either and wants to have the last word I see. The aggressiveness is what I was drawn to. It was a complete turn-on to meet a woman who can keep up mentally. I wanted to know if she really could, so I took it a step further. “Oh, OK,” I started, “So smiling, laughing, blushing.... Anything else I could try to make you do?”

The woman in red's eyes got wider to the point where you could really see the brown in her irises. She sat back as if her body was ready to respond to a challenge. She lifted a hand and placed a finger to her temple and thumb on her chin. I could tell her brain was firing up for a spirited comeback. The look on her face said, "Come get some!" and it made my dick jump. She licked her lips and said, "Well, you could try just about anything you like. The real challenge is getting me to respond."

Goddammit! She did it again! That was sass I have never encountered before. It's almost as if she has her own little ego. I leaned in closer to her as if to imply an intimate situation. Before I could say what was on my mind, an attendant stopped by us to ask if we wanted drinks. I took a scotch, and the woman in red took vodka and cranberry. As I brought my drink up to my face, I watched her over my glass. I watched her plump lips pressed up against the rim of her cup and how she pursed her lips when she sipped. I waited until she put her drink down to speak. "So," I began, "I don't get any hints as to what would make you respond?"

"A person can respond to anything," she said with a cocky smirk. "However, what you are looking for, Sir is the correct response.

"And how does one get this correct response?"

"By touching all the right buttons. And those are yours to explore and find."

I sat for a minute staring into her dark eyes, pondering what was in there behind them. Ideas were bouncing off the walls of my brain, and then I thought, *OK*. I stood up and reached into the overhead compartment and pulled down a blanket and got comfortable. "Oh, my bad. Did you want me to get yours?" I asked, and she gave me that smile again.

"No. I'll just take half of yours," she said as she scooted closer to get underneath the cover.

"Damn. Do you always take what you want?" I said, allowing access to my blanket.

"Depends on what it is and how bad I want it."

I gave a chuckle and a smirk, and I replied, "Roger that." I got close to her, and she reclined her chair. I slid my hand down to her thighs. I felt stockings, and for a minute, I was like, damn, because I would have to work around them. As my fingers kept venturing further up her thighs, they turned out to be knee-highs. My dick instantly got hard. I massaged her thigh as a tease before I touched her pussy. I noticed she was a bit ticklish on her upper thigh, so I played a little: poking and caressing, squeezing, and pinching every sensitive spot I found, her body would flinch a little. The heat between her legs became hotter as I moved towards her pussy.

She took a hand and started rubbing my leg. She moved her hands up my thigh toward my already rock-hard dick. My adrenaline starts pumping more as I got closer and realized she was not wearing any panties. I took my hand and rubbed it against her lips up and down, then took a finger and slowly rubbed her clit. She let out a sigh of anticipation like she was ready for me to touch her there. As she moved to grab my dick, I looked at her and saw she was biting her lip. I slid two fingers inside her wet pussy and slowly began to move them in and out. I could tell it was hard for her to hold her composure. She was very expressive.

I moved my fingers faster, making sure I hit her clit with every move, all while she stroked my shaft. I went for her forbidden spot, and her legs squeezed my arm as if to say, "Don't stop!". They started quivering, and I could see her fiercely biting her lip now. She lifted slightly, and a shoe fell off. I could see her toes begin to curl. Her breathing became heavy and fast-paced. Her body was contorting like she was dancing in her seat. Her hips moved seductively in a slow circle. She placed her hand on mine to reassure me that I wouldn't stop. Then came a low delectable moan, and her body jerked in a way that made it look like she was trying to do a backbend sitting down.

I could feel her little tender box squeeze and wrap around me almost until it was tough to move. I forced my finger deep in her and picked up the pace. When she came, I found my fingers to be covered in hot nectar flowing down her legs, past her thighs, and into the seat. Her breathing was hectic and heavy, and I just stared at her. After she caught her breath, I felt compelled to ask, “Did I just push some of your buttons?”

She looked up and replied with rapid breaths, “You got a few, but you still got a long way to go, Sir.” She sat up and tried to compose herself and moved her hands down her body, seeming to straighten herself. “However, you do seem like maybe you could give me what I'm after one day,” she said. I raised an eyebrow. *Interesting,* I thought.

She sat up in her seat, went for her bag, and came back up. Her eyes started at my shoes, and then followed my pants up to my pelvis. She stopped and sat correctly in her seat and said, “Um...you might wanna go to try to calm him down.”

I looked down and saw that my pant legs had risen to the bottom of my calves. My erection had. stiffened my pants to the point where I was a little worried about circulation. I got up to go to the bathroom with my briefcase out in front. Alone in the bathroom, I let loose a heavy sigh. "Damn," I said, looking down at myself.

As I was getting myself together, I heard that we were getting ready to land. I left out and hurried back to my seat, and what I saw next hurt my feelings and made my stomach drop. The empty space where my lady friend was sitting was very empty. I looked up and down the aisle and could not see her. The attendant came by and asked me to take my seat because we were landing. I took her absence like a toddler who had just been told no and flopped down. I looked over at the seat and noticed something in it. I reached over to grab it. I instantly smelled the mixture of raspberries and a feminine odor, and I stared at that spot before taking what was purposefully left on the seat.

It was a business card for the Weston Hotel in downtown Chicago. It had the address on the front with the Weston logo, and on the back was no name, but handwritten was a room number. I saw this, and I gave a smile that was similar to the Grinch. *This woman has my wheels turning*. I thought about things that she may like, favorite food and music, and hell, her name. I had never been so intrigued by a woman before. I looked down at the card again and noticed she didn't leave a date or time. I laughed out loud and tried to figure out the game she was playing.

The plane landed, and passengers were exiting. At my turn to exit, I looked back once more to see if I could catch sight of her, but no dice. Like the many other passengers, I left the plane, went through gates, waited for luggage, shuffled through crowds, and got a taxi. My colleagues had set us up at the Holiday Inn. I ordered room service and planned to sit in the room for the night.

As I finished up, I pulled the card out of my pocket and stared at it. I kept thinking about why there was no date or time and no name. I couldn't stop wondering about her. I got up quickly and grabbed my coat. I left the hotel, not knowing what I was doing. I hailed a taxi and asked for the Weston Hotel. When I got there, I made it out of the cab, and I stood at the door racking my brain. *What if she is not there? What if this is a set up?* I thought to myself. I shook it off and told myself that I would never know unless I actually go in. *Fuck it! Let's go.*

I walked through the door and studied the busy lobby. People were sitting in chairs on the left reading newspapers, and right was an entrance to what looked like a lounge. The entire hotel was built like a palace. I saw people at the desk as I went right to the elevator. I ran to catch one that was closing. I pulled the card out of my pocket for the room number. "436." I said the number under my breath, then pushed the "4" button and leaned against the wall. It stopped on the second floor so the little old lady and her little black Pomeranian dog could get off. The elevator moved again and stopped on the fourth floor. I stepped off and looked around for signs on which direction I was supposed to go and saw that I needed to go right. I walked down the hallway with my heart beating so hard and loud it sounded like someone was bouncing a ball.

I finally found room 436. I got ready to knock, but the latch clicked, and I opened the door with a slight push. I peeked around the wood, half expecting someone to be there, but there was no one. I slow-walked inside to see a suite with a living room. I saw a love seat with an almond coffee table sitting in front. The room was dim, so I tried to find the light. I stumbled a bit, looking at other things in the space. I stopped thinking about the lights and approached a cart in the middle of the room. It had a bottle of champagne and two glasses.

As I picked up the bottle, the phone rang, and it scared the shit out of me. I looked at it, hesitant to pick it up, but after a while, I picked up the receiver and put it to my ear. I didn't get a chance to say hello before a voice I recognized said, "Welcome. Make yourself at home and please do not touch anything yet," and then a click. She hung up. I couldn't tell you what I was thinking at that exact moment. I was amazed that she was there. She knew I was in the room. *But how? This woman is something the hell else.* I've never encountered such aggression and confidence.

I took off my jacket and hung it on the coat rack. I turned around and started unbuttoning my cufflinks. I wasn't sure what to do or expect. The uncertainty of what was to come was making me sweat heavily. I took my shirt off and dropped it on the love seat. Walking towards the bathroom, I glanced at the bedroom part of the suite. There was a queen-size bed with a chocolate headboard and bed frame. The black and scarlet comforter set made it almost look like chocolate-covered strawberries.

I got to the bathroom, and I stood in awe. There were boxers, a robe, and a note that said,

> "I meant to really make yourself at home. Take a shower to wash away the worries."
>
> XOXOXO

My mind was not in this room. It was outside of my body trying to put together this whole situation. But all I could really see was that I was having the best fucking day of my life! I liked this take-charge attitude. I wanted to know where this was going. *I just hope she is not expecting too much submission from me. I do as she asks.* I took a shower and put on the boxers, which fit (to my surprise), and the robe laid out for me. I opened the bathroom door and stepped out into the bedroom area, and it hit me like a monkey wrench to the senses. Her scent drives me nuts. I have smelled raspberries before, but there is another sent there that I can't put my finger on. Maybe it's her natural smell fused with the sweetness of the fruit. Whatever it was, it had me deadlocked.

I walked out of the bedroom area into the living room part. My eyes could not take what they were looking at, but my brain immediately processed the sight. My arousal said enough because there she stood with the glasses now with champagne in them. I walked over to her, she smiled that smile again. She wore black cheekies, and her bra looked like a comic strip cut out, outlined in black. Her confidence came off strong, and it was damn sexy. I took a glass, we clinked them together and shared a drink. All I could do was stare at her. I didn't know what to say. I pulled myself together and started to say, "My name is…," but she put a finger to my lips and shook her head. "No."

She took the glass from me and set both down on the cart. She grabbed my arm, led me back to the bedroom area, stopped me at the foot of the bed, and took place in front of me. She took her soft hands, gently removed the robe, and let it fall to the floor. She got closer to me, and I could smell cocoa and shea butter. It was as if the raspberry is the scent that draws you in and when you get there, waiting just for you is a nirvana of aromas.

She stood so close I could feel her body heat. The look in her eye was vividly burning. It made my dick solid, and I went to grab her. But before I could make my move, she pushed me, and I fell to the bed. *This woman just might give me a show.* I scooted backward and watched this prowling vixen crawl towards me with an insatiable look on her face, hungry with eyes locked on her prey. It was such a turn-on to see a woman so in control of her sexuality. She was even confident in the sheets, which I found so interestingly fucking sexy. She came for me and went right for the boxers. Surprised by my excitement, she smirked a grin that was deviously angelic, and I had a moment where I thought to myself, *I may love this girl.* I was not expecting her to change the face to angel cakes and mildly slide off my boxers with such care and ease. I felt there was more to this woman. *Who is she?*

After she removed my boxers, she got closer and grabbed my cock and I sat up to watch. She took a gentle approach and stroked me first. Slow up and down movements with a little bit of squeezing was her choice of ammo. Her hands were warm and smooth, and I began to enjoy myself. She stopped and moved closer. It was almost a tease that she was that close, and I could not touch her. When her breath hit my skin, my heart pounded like it was trying to jump out of my chest. Anxiously, awaiting the next touch, I got tiny kisses that sent electric currents through my body. I tried to stay calm, and I let her run her show. She took her tongue and ran it up my penis before enveloping me inside her mouth. I felt my dick slide against her moist tongue and hit the back of her throat. As she released me, I felt the walls of her mouth wrap entirely around me. It felt like a tight embrace from a long-awaited visitor.

She continued at a tamed pace, and I let my eyes close to enjoy this serenity. She started to speed up and added a hand to stroke my shaft. I was trying to hold back from moaning, but as she pushed her throat down on me, I thought I would lose all control. It started out with just enough room, and as she goes further, the walls of her throat tighten and the hug around my dick, and it gets tighter. As she came back to my tip, she dragged her tongue along the side of my dick, and made it pulsate every few centimeters.

I couldn't hold back anymore, and I let her have what I think she has been after all along. I moaned and let my arms go and fall onto the bed. She started picking up speed, and my hand moved to her head like it was metal attracted to a magnet. She started to moan, and the hum vibrated against me and sent chills up my spine. I noticed that her mouth was getting wetter as my hand moved around her head. I wrapped my fingers around some of her dreads, and I pulled just enough to pull her up some and look me in the eye. I slowly pushed her head down as far as she would allow. I let her go, with a handful of her hair still, and she released me to catch her breath, and I pulled her head backward by her hair. I'm astounded at the fact that she is enjoying the dominating.

I let her go completely, and she composed herself. She crawled further towards me, then stood up and straddled me. She reached both hands out to me, and, as if I already knew, I gave her both my hands. She took them and put them on either side of her hips. She made my hands slide her panties down, and I caught on and took over. I slid her panties down, and she lifted a leg to kick them off, then the other. This woman never forgot her confidence for a minute, and she reminded me of it when she gave no warning and sat on my face.

My mysterious lady took a hand and moved her mahogany lips, glistening from a tiny trickle of juices. She directed herself, now showing the treasure box to my mouth. I welcomed her. I lunged at her like a lion preparing to sink its teeth into prey. She let out the most tantalizing moan. Her head fell back as my tongue went from inside her to her clit. Her hair fell further down her back as she let her head hang. I flicked at her clit, and she jumped with the jitters. I grabbed both her thighs and proceeded to show my attention to her bean. I take my lips and wrap them around her clit, slowly sucking on it.

She rubbed a hand on my head as she moans with pleasure. I took my time. I wanted to enjoy having her in my control. Watching her move with every lick, suck, and flick. I started moving my tongue faster, and her moans got intense. My voluptuous vixen started moving her hips to move away from me, so I locked my arms tighter around her thighs. Her response was like hearing a bird's song in the early spring morning for the first time. The tone went up an octave, and she slightly rocked back and forth. She started to sing that song that I know all too well.

They were nonstop now. I went crazy from the reactions, and again like the hungry lion, I dove right for the glory spot. Ravenously mad, I did not hold back. I hungrily ate her pussy like I was trying to win a watermelon eating contest. She couldn’t stop moaning, and she grabbed the headboard and closed her eyes tight. Her moans went higher, and her body started moving like she was a cobra. All of a sudden, she made a deep gasp, and I heard nothing for about three seconds. She grabbed my head with one hand and let out the loudest delectation of vibrant sound, and I could taste the nectar she let free when she succumbed to me. She wasted no time, and neither did I.

Me at the ready, she slid back and positioned herself right above my tip. She slid down easily and made sure she had it all. The warmth alone was enough to make me pulsate while entering. The feeling of her pussy wrapped around my dick was like a key made for a lock. All the grooves fit in the perfect place to unlock the next level of intimacy. She placed two hands on my chest and started to bounce not too fast, not too slow, but just goddamn right. I grabbed her by the waist and held on for the ride. She started shaking more quickly, and I felt chills run through my body. I stopped watching her and let my eyes close to enjoy the moment. I made sure I responded to every bounce, and once in a while, rocked slowly. Then it was almost like her persona changed.

She stopped bouncing and took her hands from my chest and seized hold of the headboard. Her thighs were brought in closer to my sides as if she was getting ready for the next show. She rocked slowly to start, and very carefully, she rose up. When she came back down, her ass was tooted up, and about halfway, she brought her hips to me. It was like she was rocking on air, but she reminded me again that she is aggressively confident. When her lips reached about the bottom of my shaft, she let me have the rest of her with force. This made my body jerk upright with the sudden urge to reciprocate, an opposite and equal reaction, if you will. She caught this, and I swear I saw her smile. She started going faster, and I tried to keep my composure. Her every move made me twinge, then I couldn't help it.

Out of sheer automatic response, I sat up and wrapped my arms around her to hug her body. Her response to this was a cocky chuckle and quickening the pace. As she moved, I moved with her, and we flowed into each other like two pieces of ribbon intertwined, blowing in the wind. I felt the need to show off a bit. I flipped her over, still inside, and laid her down. I'm pretty much hip to the fact that she likes it rough, so I took this time to play with her emotions. I left her on her back, and I began to move slowly. She welcomed it, and her body responded accordingly.

I moved my hips in and out then, faster. Her moans told me what she liked, and she said harder. I got closer to her and let her put her arms around my neck. I lifted her legs and spread her ass cheeks. I started pounding at her so hard the headboard started banging against the wall. Her moans got rough and loud. I sped up and thrust harder. I could feel the struggle in her hands to scratch or not to scratch. I dug deeper, and I found her spot. The spot I reached made her sweet nectar flow uncontrollably, like an endless waterfall. I felt the warm trickles of her juices run down my dick. I could feel the walls contract around me as if it were trying to say stay. So, I did.

I lifted up and grabbed her legs. I pushed her legs back, so her knees were touching her ears. I wanted that spot again to explore her boundless depths. I started off fast and hard, and her moaning became an exotic outburst of euphoria. The harder I fucked her, the more of her she gave to me. I stopped and turned her over with force. She obliged and scooted towards me like she was ready for me to take her. I slid into her and grabbed both her arms. I fucked her like I was trying to keep my tip on her brain for real. I kept pounding her pussy all while she screamed out with intoxicating jubilation.

I looked down and saw my dick moving in and out of her dripping wet pussy, and every time it brought out more of her glistening juices. I let her arms go, and I pushed her head down so she arched her back. I grabbed hold of those curved hips and gave her all I had. She clenched the sheets and screamed out in a way that sounded almost as harmonicas in a choir. The look on her face told me she was again reaching her climax. I pulled her up, so her back was against my body.

I put a hand around her throat and squeezed but not to the point of choking. At the same time, I helped her move up and down on me. I wanted to cum with her. I could already feel the build-up like before. The tightness accelerated my climax. She grabbed my arm, and blissful lyrics came floating through my eardrums. As she came, so did I. The intensity of my orgasm made me hold tighter as I erupted. She dug her nails into my arm, and the continuous pulsing sensation coming from inside her made me more sensitive with every throb.

We fell down together with panting breath. We rolled over, and I looked at this woman, whom I have yet to know, sweating yet still a radiant face. I wanted to speak, but I think she knew that because she turned right over. She scooted back into me and put my arm around her. I followed suit and pulled her closer in and hugged her tight. We fell asleep that way. The following day when I got up, the spot next to me was empty. There was a note that read,

"Sorry, I had an early start.
Please feel free to call for

breakfast. And when you are ready, there is a car downstairs to take you anywhere you'd like."
XOXOXO

I didn't know how to process this. I was actually kind of speechless because this has never happened before. I didn't stay for breakfast, but I did use the car to get back to my own hotel.

When I got to my room, a cart of breakfast was waiting and still steaming. I walked over to the cart, removed the newspaper from the top, and a Fortune 500 magazine fell to the floor. I picked it up and put it back on the cart and walked away. It took my brain a while to comprehend what was seen. I stopped mid-walk and almost ran back to the cart. I stared at the cover and still couldn't believe what I was seeing. On the exterior, the headline read, "Guaranteed to Cater to You." The caption by the photo read, "Meet the New Executive Officer for the Weston Hotel!" The picture was that of my mystery woman.

BUSINESS ENCOUNTER

Him

I couldn't believe my eyes. My heart was pounding so hard I could feel it trying to break out of my chest, and it hurt! I felt lightheaded and needed to sit down. *A drink! Yes, a drink. Never mind that it's eight in the morning.* I needed calm. I stopped myself halfway to the minibar. "My presentation," I started to think out loud, "And alcohol on the breath would kill my reputation." I forgot about my stash. I went to my small business bag and pulled out what looks to be a giant bottle of aspirin, but it's hollowed out and coated in lead to get past the x-ray detection at the airport. I opened it from the bottom and instantly smelled the sweet dank of a very potent marijuana strain. *I have a business meeting at noon, so I got plenty of time to read this five-page article on my mystery woman.* I rolled a fat joint, grabbed a towel to stuff under the door, put on the very comfy hotel robe, and picked up the magazine. I grabbed the ashtray and flopped on the couch. I lit the joint, opened to the article, and tried to learn more about my undercover vixen.

Her name is Zora Desiree Humphreys. She grew up on the streets of Chicago and made sure she didn't end up there. The article said she went to Illinois State but ended up switching to Berkeley after attending two years. Zora noted that she initially got a scholarship to Berkeley but ended up staying home to take care of her mom. The latter, at the time, was riddled with cancer. Zora's mom passed just five years before our meeting. After that, she contacted Berkeley. They accepted her on half a scholarship for the remaining two years of her four-year college term. She graduated top of her class in Business Communications.

She graduated top of her class in Business Communications. The article tried to touch on her personal life, but she replied, “That is private.” The reporter asked if she could just say if she is taken or single. My eyes got huge here. I wanted to know, too! I took a big hit off the now half of a joint and put it out. I returned my eyes to the article where I left off. It said that she laughed, crossed her legs, and with confidence said, “I belong to no man. But if a man were lucky enough to enjoy my company you guys would never hear of it.” *My God, what a woman! She is ruthless in every aspect of her life.*

I finished the article, learning that she has been at that hotel for eight years and has worked her way to the top. She takes care of all the high-level executives and handles the big complaints and problems personally. All I could do was keep repeating her name in my head. *Zora Desiree... Miss Zora… My desire indeed.* I felt my dick throb. I'm getting a hard-on from just saying her name. Couple that with the heavy flashbacks I was having, and I ended up at a full salute. I had to get myself together for my meeting. This is going to be the biggest deal I close.

I got in the shower. I should have taken a cold one, but I stood, letting the warm water hit my back. I couldn't get that woman out of my head. The perfect chocolate tone with that golden glow made her skin look forbidden to touch. I could still hear her moans in my ear and feel her breath on my skin. Damn! I didn't have a choice now. My thoughts lead me to reach for my dick. It was hard as a rock.

As the water hit me, I stayed to the drops' rhythm as I moved my hand up and down my shaft. As I rolled down, the grip tightened, and moving up, I loosened the grip. I did this for about five minutes before switching hands. My mind kept getting flashes of the night before. How she smiled when she thought she had me. How she rolled her hips to make me moan. How she dominated the entire session and still let me have her my way. I could still smell that smell... my chocolate-covered raspberry.

Eyes closed; I could feel the eruption about to happen. My hand moved at a steady pace, from the bottom to the tip, and then the sticky cum oozed out the end onto the shower floor. I caught my breath and got myself together. I still had a meeting to go to. I took my shower, shaved, and suited up. As I'm trying to get the knot right for my tie, I walked past the article and stood there and stared. I wondered what it would take to tame a wild but mild-mannered beast like her. I wanted her, not just for sex. I wanted her mind, body, and soul. The energy she brings with her makes me feel like a kid watching fireworks up close and personal. I grabbed the magazine and stuffed it in my briefcase and called downstairs to have them get a cab ready for me.

The hotel did like I asked and had a cab waiting for me. I partner with a company that specializes in catering to hotels. We provide the cleaning service if a room is destroyed by something like a fire, we come to rebuild and redecorate. We make the hotel look presentable, and at the same time, offer to merge and do business with some other companies. For example, a specific restaurant that doesn't deliver will, but only to our hotels. The same for cable T.V. services in the rooms, and their conference areas where certain events can be guaranteed to be held.

We call ourselves The Source. I started this company with a few college buddies. We were a bunch of fraternity boys being drunk and disappointed with the hotel we were staying in. We started talking shit about what kind of services a hotel is supposed to have and the customers' experience. Me being the nerd, wrote it down in a drunken rage. When I came to, I couldn't remember the name of the girl that was lying naked next to me. I tried to roll out the bed and found paper stuck to my arm. I looked bewildered, yet I was intrigued. More paper was stuck to the sleeping girl, so I gently rolled her over and collected them. Through some robust coffee, I read the pages. By the time I was done, I was convinced that we were actually onto something in a drunken stupor. So, I got the boys sober, and we went to work. Four years later, here we are.

I was about to try and close a deal with a Hyatt Regency of Chicago. They had been looking to add a bar or lounge to the lobby. I thought we could get a Leona's in and tie it as a restaurant merger. I was waiting on a call from Alex to see if he got in good with the owner yet, but no answer. The cab pulled in front of the Leona's on Taylor Street. It still had the “Sorry! We’re Closed” sign out front. The plan was to get the hotel manager to allow the restaurant owner to have their empty lounge space. The food was great, and the wings were the hottest I've ever had. This way, the restaurant's kept open, the hotel gets more than what they were looking for at an even better price.

When I walked in, Alex and Courtney, my business partners, were already there. With them was Clara, the owner of Leona's, and two other gentlemen I did not recognize. I assumed that they were there to represent the Hyatt. I approached the table with a smile, hearing the laughter. Then I smelled it. Raspberries....... I stopped dead in my tracks and froze like a kid on stage for the first time. I saw her walk out of the bathroom. Her walk was flawless as she approached the table and glanced at me like we didn't have the best night last night. My eyes followed her and only her. I stood there staring as if seeing her for the first time.

"Um... Keith, are you gonna join us or stare all day?" asked Courtney, jerking me back to reality.

"Yes. I'm sorry. Yes," I said, and continued to my seat.

"How is everyone this afternoon? This mid-August weather is different from what we're used to in Seattle," I addressed with a slight laugh. I was trying to shake my nerves off and warm up the room. "My name is Keith Jefferies. And it looks like my colleagues already introduced themselves." Alex sat upright in his chair and said, "Yes. We were getting acquainted while waiting on the brains of the operation," making a hand gesture towards me. "This is George Harris, the representative from the Hyatt, and we are joined by Miss Zora Humphreys and Freddy Graham from the Weston Inn. They heard about what we do and were interested in sitting in to see if we can do future business." I made a surprised face at the sound of future business. I nodded at everyone as Alex introduced them, and I stopped and stared at Zora. I couldn't help it. She gave the sweetest glance that said, "Not here," and I took it as a sign that she did not want to acknowledge the night we had in front of her co-workers. I smiled even though I tried to fight it.

After the pleasant greetings, we got down to business. We went over what our company does and how we make connections. Courtney touched on why we are needed instead of going directly to the owners. We explained how to bring the ideas, the good ones, and help save a business and create more revenue. We deal with the paperwork, oversight to the remodeling if needed, so they do not have to hire extra hands. The projects are entirely our responsibility in the event something goes wrong. We deal with the headache of the deadline. We bring people together to further their future business. Courtney goes into the numbers, and we wrestled papers and answered questions. Alex gave them our fees and cost. Both representatives looked happy.

By the end of negotiations, we had a signed contract for a Leona's lounge in the Hyatt on the lobby floor, and the remodeling will start two weeks following this meeting. We also had a signed contract for Leona's food to be present in the Weston Inn kitchen. Clara would put three of her chefs in the kitchen to oversee the menu change and training on making the dishes. We closed two deals when we were expecting one.

As everyone was leaving, we shook hands and said our goodbyes. I looked back to see where my desired Zora went, but that woman is elusive. Just like on the plane, I blinked, and she was gone. Alex asked if I needed a ride back to the hotel, but I declined. I wanted to obsess about Zora some more. I reached in my pocket for my phone to call a cab. Suddenly, I was forcefully grabbed by my arm and towed away to the back.

The double doors to the kitchen area flew open as Zora pushed her way through. She turned and looked at my half-shocked, half confused expression- and smiled. She stopped right in front of a counter. The counter was where they plated the food and put it in the window to go out to the customer. Behind her was a chrome table that held the pots and pans. She forcefully pushed me up against the plating counter and dropped her bag to the floor. She squatted down in front of me and started to undo my pants. I took in a deep breath to calm my excitement. *This woman has again caught me off guard, and I am not disappointed.*

She got my pants undone and slid my boxers with my pants down to my ankles. I tried to keep my dick from jumping too hard, but this woman's confidence aroused me so. She put one hand on my rigid member and licked the side of my shaft before taking my tip into her mouth. My head fell back, and I moaned as if I've been waiting my entire life to feel her lips wrapped around my dick. She kept it slow, her mouth getting wetter with every thrust. I dropped my bag and reached around to her hair. I pulled it back in a ponytail and directed her head to go a little faster. With every thrust, the slurps got louder. I could feel slob dripping from her lips, gravity pulling it to hit my leg. She started moaning with pleasure as my cock hit the back of her throat. Moans of supreme ecstasy escaped my lips as I succumbed to the warmth of her mouth.

I pulled her, by the hair, off me. I grabbed her by the arms and straightened her up. I pushed her back on the chrome table and yanked up her dress. Ready to chew through some panties, I was surprised when I saw she wasn't wearing any. My face said, “Oh yea?”, and I dove right in. The taste of her wet pussy made my dick throb. She already was leaking sweet nectar down her lower lips. I licked the outside of her lips and proceeded to her clit. She let out a spectacular moan of pleasure as if she had not been touched there before, and her excitement showed through the body trembles as I sucked, licked, kissed, and devoured her pussy. She grabbed my head as if to say, “Don't stop!” but I disobeyed.

I turned her over and kicked her legs open with my feet to get her in the proper position. As the tip of my dick slid into her dripping wet pussy, she arched her back and made a long moan in anticipation for the rest. I slowly slid the rest of me into her and grabbed her by the hips. I did not give her the chance to brace for me. I immediately started drilling her. She grabbed the sides of the table as if holding on for dear life. She shrieked when I dug deep into her. I made a crooked smile when I heard it. I smacked her luscious ass and started fucking her harder. Her moans echoed throughout the empty kitchen and bounced off the walls, almost sounding like an orchestra hall. She started saying things like “Shit,” “Damn,” “Fuck me,” and “Oh my God” in between catching her breath. She pounded her fist on the table and moaned, “Fuck!” I started to feel the juices come from inside her. I took the opportunity to be cocky.

“What's my name?” I spoke. “Let me hear that “Daddy” moan off them lips.” She lifted off the table, and through her broken breath, she responded, “You gotta fight me for that word. I don't use it for just anybody. You have to earn it.”

Something in me snapped, and I went primal. I grabbed both arms and restrained them behind her back. I started going faster, fucking her harder and digging deeper into her box. She moaned louder and arched her back more, begging me to go deeper. So, I obliged. She made the shrieking noise again, and I felt her juices flowing heavier now. She was dripping like someone left the faucet running a little.

“Oh fuck!” I heard her breathe.

“What's my name?” I asked again. She moaned a succulent “No,” and I grabbed her by the throat. As I gave her a little squeeze, I felt a gush of liquid release on my dick. I looked down and saw it flow out of her glowing pussy. It stopped suddenly, and I felt her walls throb. She was trying to hold back; I smiled and sped up the pace. She started to shake and tremble. She jerked up, pressing her back against my chest, and whispered, “I'm cummin!”

“I'm cummin what?” I replied with my hand still around her throat, squeezing a little bit tighter. She hummed and then answered, “I'm cummin Daddy!” The phrase seemed to sing out of her mouth and was like music to my ears.

As I reached my climax, I felt the water gates open. There was a tremendous gush of liquid flowing out of her chocolate pussy. The sight of her squirting heightened my excitement, and I came harder than I ever have. We collapsed on the table, exhausted and out of breath.

After about two minutes, I pushed myself up and slowly slid out. Zora, still breathing heavy, stood up and pulled her dress down. She walked to the back of the kitchen and disappeared into the darkness. I pulled up my boxers and pants and peered towards where the shadows began. By the time I got my belt fastened, I saw her coming through the dark like a single candle lit in one of the deepest caves to be found. She was carrying a mop. I looked down on the floor and saw a small pool of her juices on the floor. I gave her the biggest smile and reached for the mop. She cocked her head to the side and gave me a look that screamed, “Nigga really?”. I put my hand on the mop and slowly took it from her. She was letting go but still had a grip on it like she agreed but didn't like it. I took the mop from her and cleaned up the floor. I started towards the back of the kitchen to put stuff away. I turned around to look at her, and she stood there glowing like she was in the happiest of places. I turned back around and smiled while heading into the darkness.

When I came back, Zora had again disappeared. I didn't even get to talk to her. I left the kitchen and went back to the dining room only to find it empty. I walked past the table we sat at for the meeting and found another card. It had her name, Zora D. Humphreys, and a phone number. I stared at the card with mixed emotions. I was furious that she kept pulling this Batman vanishing trick on me. I don't ever get to say goodbye or have a normal conversation. At the same time, this made me curious about her. The sex was amazing, so everything else must be too, or at least that's what I told myself. I felt sad because whatever happened to her made her be this elusive, never trusting, mysterious woman. I was also excited that she chose me to play her little game.

I heard the horn from the cab that I called. I walked out of the restaurant and stood on the streets, looking each way, hoping to see her before I took off. There was no telling if she gave me an actual number or if I would see her again. I entered the cab with a heavy sigh and told the driver to take me back to my hotel. I was ready for a nice spiff and a drink.

As I walked through the door of my hotel room, I kicked my shoes off, untied my tie, and flopped down on the bed. I laid there for several minutes thinking. Asking myself several questions, like what I was doing chasing this woman. I started wondering if this is just a game for her because I'm from out of town. A million things crept in my head as I lay there, staring at the overlapping crisscrossed pattern on the room's ceiling.

Finally, I decided I'm not myself when I'm sober and hungry. I stared at the room service menu, trying to figure out what the kitchen would or wouldn't cook right. Then it hit me. *I'm in Chicago, and I should be eating deep-dish pizza and*

Italian beef! I plan on being high anyway; might as well eat the right kind of munchies.

I spent two hours riding with a Haitian blunt from my friendly Uber driver, which offers rides using GPS and social app. We made three stops at three different restaurants, and $162.78 later, I was back in my hotel room finishing up my own nicely rolled joint. I ended up with both pizza and beef and some Italian ice off Taylor Street. I was stuffed and stoned. I was feeling better.

Taking a bottle from the minibar and flopping on the sofa in my room, I turned on the T.V. and tried to forget the woman of my dreams just gave me her number. I wanted to dial it, just to see if it was real. I wanted to hear that soft, monotone voice. However, I didn't want to feel like a fool if it wasn't real. I tried to force a laugh at "Archer," but my mind went back to her. "Fuck it!" I said and stumbled to my suit coat. I dialed the number and I listened intently as it rang. I heard a strange click and got excited. My eyes lit up, and I made a crooked smile at the sound of her voicemail. She didn't answer, but it was an actual number. I glanced at the clock and thought, "Holy shit!" It was one in the morning. I didn't want to be a creep either, so I left a respectable message and hung up.

Her

"Um. Hello, Miss Zora. This is Keith Jefferies. I was being rude and not paying attention to the time, so I will apologize and make this brief. I would like to see you again. Since we've been playing by your rules, I see no reason to stop. Besides, I kinda like them. My number is two, four oh, five, nine, nine, eighty-three, forty-two. Give me a call or text. Good night, Miss Humphreys."

A "click" sound was heard from a phone hanging up. I laid there staring at the phone for about five minutes, thinking it would ring. I rolled over back into my bed with a girlish smile on my face. The scent was still with me driving me insane. What they say is true. When they smell as good as they look, it's hard to forget them.

I tried all day, but the flashbacks kept taking me back. It sent chills through me like stepping on a jellyfish with a strong sting. It sends your mind flying through your memories, thirsting to relive the moment. I closed my eyes and tried to force it from me, but it only urged me more. Like a fed-up child, I got up with a huff and went for the phone.

Waiting was unbearable. Especially when it's something you want, it makes a minute feel like an hour. The questions I should have asked before picking up the phone came flooding into my brain. *Was it not understood? Was I rude? Should I be doing this? Is this inappropriate? Is it too early or late?*

Then I heard a knock at the door. All that worrying and I lost track of time. I nervously walked over to the door and froze when I grabbed the knob. I took a deep breath and opened the door. My heart jumped out of my body and followed the scent like a hungry child coming in for dinner. I heard the door close but didn't remember closing it. I felt my body moving but didn't remember where I was going.

My body had walked back to the bed by the time I snapped out of it. I felt a hand on my thigh, then another hand on my other thigh. I felt a soft caress leading up my back. I melted away from the feel of this gentle touch...it forced my eyes to close. When I opened them, we were spread over the bed, intertwined in a mass of ecstasy.

The caressing, the rubbing, the grabbing all played a part in my surrender. As we took a step further towards the awaited abyss, something started bugging my inner ear. I thought it was just my imagination until....

I awoke with a sweat-soaked tee. I reached for the phone that was buzzing on my nightstand.

"Hello?" I answered.

"Sorry to wake you, but you wanted to know if the presidential suite requested anything special, Ms. Humphreys," said the front desk attendant.

"No, it's fine. I'll be there in thirty minutes."

"Very good, ma'am. I will let them know." I hung up the phone and let off a huge sigh. I rubbed my face and laid there with my eyes closed. "What the hell was that?" I asked myself.

I stumbled out of bed and tried to gather myself. As I walked around my room, seemingly dazed but still functioning, my hand found its way to my neck, caressing the spot where he touched. Realizing this, my body quivered from head to toe with warmth. This chill was like a river's water heating in sunlight that had been disturbed by a pebble, and its ripples brought the cold water to the surface. My breathing increased as if I just came in from a run. I snapped myself out of that daydream and proceeded to get ready.

Steam roared from the bathroom as I opened the door. I ran in a beeline to my bed where cocoa butter lotion and my striped beige three-piece pants suit were already laid out. I oiled, got dressed, and let my hair dry, moving so fast I felt like Superman changing in the phone booth, but unlike him, I got a little dizzy. I stopped for a second and looked at the clock. While I thought I was faster than light, reality kept on ticking, and I was late!

Racing the lights and weaving through traffic seems to be what every Chicagoan is born to do, no matter what city they live in. But this is my city, and I know these streets like the back of my hand. When I first started driving, my dad told me that I can't just watch the road. I must watch everyone else too. He said to look two cars ahead just in case the vehicle in front of the car you're behind is driven by an idiot. That gives you time to plan a reaction. It's kind of like people living in New York City that take the subway and hold their belongings closer to them. When I was driving, I saw everything, and everyone was suspect. I could spot cop cars three blocks away in any direction. One's mind must be sharp when knowingly participating in ill acts.

As I power-walked through the hotel doors, my assistant, Ciera, handed me my vanilla chai latte with whipped cream and a caramel drizzle, and I gave her my bag. She handed me the reports from last night. But I wasn't interested in the news, I wanted to know about our guest in the presidential suite. "Tell me about 1600," I said as our pace picked up. "They asked last night for an 8:30 AM wake-up call, and for the kitchen to be alerted for an incoming order. She said it would be a big order and very personal and was very insistent on the chef paying the most careful attention to the special instructions," Ciera said in a frantic and broken voice. She handed me a printout of the most absurd breakfast order I have ever seen! I took one look at that order and shot Ciera a look that clearly said, "Oh my God!" I think she flinched. However, I didn't get to where I am by disappointing guests. "Sounds like a challenge. Let's get to work, CiCi!" I said to Ciera with a confident smile.

Like my bathroom, steam reached for the ceiling when I pushed open the double chrome doors to the kitchen. The smells that entered my nostrils could be traced, like flood lights guiding the way, in their route to my brain and pinpoint the moment it arrived by the blissful expression on my face. I took a tour down the rows of culinary wonders our chefs were in the process of starting or finishing. I stopped to check every few dishes, and the chef would hand me a spoon for the taste, one of the many perks of the job. I looked at the clock on the wall, and it was almost 8:23 AM.

"You guys know you're awesome, and I need you to keep up the good work by getting this top priority order out on time!" I yelled throughout the kitchen as I headed back to the front. My head chef yells back, "That order should be complete in three minutes!" I take the ridiculous order out of my pocket and walk over to the plate station. I approached the area where Suite 1600's food was being kept and warmed. I gave it the once over, and I read the order aloud:

- 2 orders of eggs Florentine
    - 1 with no tomatoes
    - 1 with no salt, just a pinch of garlic, half the usual serving of cream cheese, and extra butter
- 4 pieces of all wheat toast, no butter, and cut in triangles, NO CRUST
- A bowl of red, seedless organic grapes
- A whole grapefruit, cut 8 times.
- GOLDEN hash browns, no salt added when cooking.
- 8 slices of bacon cooked until crispy, but not burnt or too hard.
- 2 glasses of FRESHLY SQUEEZED ORGANIC orange juice
- A bowl of your FRESHEST ORGANIC strawberries
- A bottle of your BEST champagne, on ice."

I gave the dishes the once-over again and realized something was missing. I also checked to be sure. "Where are those hash browns?" I asked loudly. I heard footsteps coming from behind. I turned and saw a chef racing to the plating station with a skillet. He reached the table without acknowledging me and grabbed the plate needed. Then, he let the food slide out of the hot skillet onto the plate with ease and completed the work with a freshly chopped garnish. "Order for Suite 1600 is complete, ma'am," he said with pride. I made my way to the front of the kitchen, through the double doors, and back out towards the main lobby.

I turned the corner and saw the front desk. There was a line of about four patrons. I headed straight to the desk and asked to help the next person. A young woman with dirty-blonde hair approached and put her key card on the granite counter. She was ready to check out. I closed out her account and signaled for housekeeping to clean the room. I printed out her receipt and thanked her for staying.

As I asked to help the next person, the desk phone rang, and the screen indicated that it was Suite 1600. I apologized to the elderly couple now in front of me, politely asked for a moment, and answered the phone. "Front desk. This is Zora.

How may I help you?" I chirped. "Yes, this is Suite 1600. And I'm ready for my breakfast," a man said with a husky and raspy voice. "Yes, sir. It will be right up!" I replied proudly.

I heard the "click" sound that indicated he hung up, and I did the same. I smiled at the couple in front of me and asked the attendant to signal the kitchen to have the presidential order sent. He gave a slight nod, then picked up the phone next to him. I turned my attention back to the couple in front of me and gave them the biggest smile I could muster. They wanted a cab called for their opera event later that evening. I took their information, got the time and the place, and I threw in a hotel upgrade to one of the skyboxes for being so patient with me. They were so excited.

A few hours went by, and the lobby was picking up traffic between guests coming and going and guests going. I had already made my rounds, and everything seemed to be going smoothly. The guests seemed to be as lively as ever.: The usual happy sounds, laughter, or chit-chat amongst friends in the lobby. Regulars were shutting off to the world, curled in our corner recliners with a mountain of books or eyes intently focused on their laptop. It looked like I could take a break.

I was enjoying our lounge's homemade strawberry-flavored iced tea when I was paged for the kitchen. I stood up, rolled my eyes as I took my last sip, and walked behind the lounge counter to use the phone. The kitchen manager told me about the dishes from 1600. They had not come back down, and they had not been called for the lunch order they were told to expect. I told him not to worry, that I'd go and check on the room. I suggested that they just set the tray outside the room and stay alert for the lunch order, which could still come.

I left the lounge and headed towards the elevators. Our elevators had big brass doors, trimmed in a black frame that wove in and out of itself. They looked like graham crackers outlined in burnt twisty bread. Some elevators started on the first floor and only went to the seventeenth floor. Some of them started on the fifteenth floor and only went to the twenty-seventh floor. The rest started at the twenty-fifth floor, going up to the penthouse on the fortieth floor. I jumped the next elevator that goes to floors twenty-five and above. While the suite is on the thirty-eighth floor, we named it Suite 1600 because it is the presidential suite. I straightened my clothes out when I noticed the thirty-sixth floor being passed. The elevator stopped on the thirty-eighth floor, and the doors opened. This was one of the few floors with just one room. The hallway was empty and quiet. I was expecting to see someone outside the door, but it was utterly deserted.

When I walked up to the room door, it was slightly opened. I was about to knock, walk in, and grab the tray I saw sitting in the front foyer of the room, but I heard a scuffle and voices. I backed away and closed the door just enough so I could peek through. I saw my guest and his secretary half-naked, walking around the room. This six-foot-three, slightly built, with a chubby little stomach, salt- and pepper-haired white man had a hand full of his five-foot-six, black-haired, slim made with "C" cup titties proportionate, juicy assed Latina secretary's throat. She was panting heavily, standing there with just an open dress shirt on. He put his other hand on her face and brought it close to his.

"Are you gonna be a good little bitch?" he asked aggressively.

"Yes, sir. I'm gonna be a good little bitch, I promise," she replied submissively. "Let me show you, sir." She dropped to her knees, facing his already exposed member, and proceeded to take him into her mouth. He let out a satisfied moan and grabbed a handful of her hair as he forced more of himself into her mouth. She made a gagging noise, and he let her go for air. Slob flowed out of her mouth and ran down her cheek. He moved his hips towards her face and slowly inserted himself back into her mouth. He fucked her face slow, but with such force that she gagged after a few strokes. He started to pick up the pace while both of his hands were now directing her movements. He moaned with bliss, throwing his head back and moving his hips in and out. I could hear her gasping for air and moaning at the same time. My eyes were watching them both, but I kept a close eye on her. I could tell she really didn't want to do it. I recognized the look of "baring with it."

After a few more minutes of fucking her mouth, he stopped and snatched her to her feet by her face. He ripped off the dress shirt, the only piece of clothing she had on, and wrapped it around her neck while forcing her onto the circular table in the foyer. He thrust his throbbing penis into her exposed pussy and pulled on the shirt. He started at a fast pace, pounding her tiny, pink pussy. She made a noise that wasn't quite a moan, but more like the sound you make when someone bumps into you way too hard. She did that with every stroke as he pulled on that shirt. It looked as if she was the horse, and he was riding her good! He moaned and hollered,

"You like this, you good little bitch?" he asked, while choking her with every move.

"Yes, sir!" she gasped, "I'm a good bitch. Mmmmm.... More please, sir!"

"Yeah- that's right, bitch! Take this dick! Oh God! Fuck! You tight pussy bitch! Yeeeaaahhhh!" he shouted as he fucked her. His pace picked up, faster and faster. Her cries had turned into silent moans. He pulled at the shirt until she stood straight up. Still fucking her hard, he dragged her back into his chest and wrapped his bear paw-sized hands around her throat. I could see her face flush red from her neck to her head. He was choking her for dear life. He fucked her even harder, and she made more gasping sounds. Her face was utterly red while he pounded into her now dripping wet vagina.

I heard him make a sound like a growl from an animal. He gave one last thrust, and they both fell over onto the table, panting heavily. The bell from the elevator went off. The doors never closed from when I got off; they must be sticking again. *Damn! I'm going to have to call it in.* I panicked and ran back towards the elevator, just enough to make it look like I just got off, took out my cell phone, and pretended to have a conversation.

"Yes, sir. I'm checking on it right now!" I thundered. As I got closer to the door, I heard the latch click. I put away my phone and put it on my professional face. I approached the door and knocked hard. I wanted to be sure they heard me. The slim-built secretary answered the door fully clothed, and hair pulled back into a neat ponytail. *They had some practice with this!* I thought to myself as I sized her up. Her face was still flushed, and her neck was red from him choking her.

"Hello. My name is Ms. Humphreys. I just came to check on the guest and retrieve the dish cart from breakfast," I said with a smile. "Oh, yes!" she said with an odd excitement. "I don't think he knew what to do with them."

"No worries. I'll just take those right outta your hair. We were told to expect a lunch and dinner order."

"Ah! Yes, well... I will call down for that. His plans may have changed. But from what I hear, you are very notorious for making sure your guests are very well taken care of, and not DISTURBED in ANY way."

"Oh, well you know what they say, my reputation precedes me. But I do like to make sure every guest is comfortable and shown every ounce of courtesy I can extend. That includes discreet physicians that do full body and mental checks. Being up this high, the air can seem like it's *choking* you. Wouldn't want you getting dizzy!"

After hearing that, her smile went away, and it was replaced with a look of complete disgust. "Yes, well...thank you. If that's all, good day," she replied in a shaken voice while pushing the cart out the door. When the handcart was clear, she shut the door and the latch soundly clicked. I got behind the cart and walked away with a devious smile.

After getting the cart to the kitchen, I stopped by the kitchen to tell them lunch will be called in. I spent some time getting the lobby calm after rush times, called in the elevator for maintenance, and did a bit of some meet and greets. I made my way to my office to do paperwork. It's usually the only time I get peace and quiet. I did the supply orders, paid vendors for the pop, and snacks we sold, and was in the middle of looking over the liquor bill when my mind decided to interrupt me with flashbacks. I was already a bit irritated from what I walked into, and my thoughts were making me wet between the legs. I tried hard to focus on the work in front of me, but I knew I wanted to do something else.

I closed my laptop, unplugged the cord from it and the wall, packed it up, and grabbed my jacket. I picked up the phone and paged Ciera. While I was putting other important work in my laptop bag, my office phone rang. I called out for Ciera, and I told her to screen then hold all my calls, because I was leaving for a while. She said, "Very good, ma'am. Messages will be taken, and important ones will be forwarded to your phone." I thanked her, grabbed my things, and left.

I didn't know where I was going, so I just drove. My body apparently had a mind of its own. All I knew was that I needed somewhere to go for peace. But to end up here? What was happening to me?

IMPULSIVE ENCOUNTER

Him

I woke up the following day feeling like I got hit by a bus! *I haven't felt this bad since my college days.* There was an empty bottle of Remy VSOP falling out of one hand and my cell in the other. I got up, wondering what the hell I did. I sat up and checked my phone for new videos or pictures I might have taken embarrassingly. I didn't see any, so I checked text messages and calls. Then I saw it.

"I called Zora?" I said to myself in the most bewildered voice my brain could muster. *I don't remember what I said. I hope I didn't say anything stupid.* I wanted to call her and see, but my mind told me not to. If I did, then she won't answer anyway. If I didn't, then she'd call me. *Wait, she is an elusive creature. She won't call.* I got up and tried to gather myself. I inspected the room for extra garbage bags. I found them in a cabinet under the bathroom sink. I cleaned up the mess I made, threw the empty bottle of Remy away, picked up pieces of rolling paper, and cleared any other criminating evidence from the room. I don't want anyone to know or judge me or my company for anything I do in my personal life.

After returning from taking the trash out, I reached my room door, slipped my key card in the card slot, and pushed the door open. I let out a sigh of boredom, threw the key card on the coffee table as I walked past it and threw myself on the bed. I laid there for about fifteen minutes before I felt my phone vibrate against my leg. I dug in my pocket for my phone and saw it was Alex. I thought twice before I answered the phone.

"Whas up dude?" I answered.

"Nothing much bro. Just trying to see what' cha doing this evening. Might have some fun lined up for us later. Would you be interested?" he asked with a chuckle.

"What kind of fun are we talking about here?" I asked as I sat up, curious.

"The kind that makes you forget how much fun you actually had."

"Oh! *That* kind. Pennies carrying over?"

"I found dimes in the well. We already counted the change. It will be enough to get us all some ice cream and candy."

"There's bound to be a candy store around. My sweet tooth has been acting funky since we landed. Do you want me to Google one and we go on a hunt, or do you guys already have one in mind?"

"We actually found one. It's a bit of a walk, though. You up for some walking? Possible jaywalking, and/or speed walking."

"The jaywalking is possible," I said while eyeing my bag, "But not sure about speed walking. The chilly air might fuck with me. I wanna be functional if people call. I know you guys can handle whatever is being thrown at you."

Alex went silent for about a minute and a half, and then I heard his breathing again. "So will you be ready in a couple hours?" he asked.

Now I chuckled and replied, "Yea man. Couple hours."

"Cool!" he responded, and I heard the click of his phone. We used codes for going bar hopping, smoking joints, and picking up girls in college, and we never stopped using them.

I got up to my feet and looked around the room, trying to figure out what I need to do to get ready. *I could use a shower and some food before I go anywhere.* So, I walked over to the room phone, called the kitchen extension, and ordered some food. I figured if, by the time I got out of the shower, food should be here.

I hung up the phone after placing my order and headed to the bathroom while stripping. When I reached the bathroom, I started the water and waited for the steam to fill the room. While it ran, I went for my phone to play some tunes to drown out the quiet. I searched for a playlist on the way back to the bathroom and chose a random one. The first song to play was a rather provocative song about eating pussy and fucking it deep, but I didn't mind it. It kind of completed my mood.

I got out of the shower and was reaching for a towel when I heard knocking at my room door. Without thinking, I ran towards the door to open it. *Oh my God! How long have they been out here?* I got to the door out of breath, yanked it open, and died all in the exact same second. Standing there was Zora, with my food. My heart sank so fast and so deep, it felt like gravity pulled the floor from underneath me. Not only was it a shock to see her at my door, but I was butt-ass-naked dripping wet from the shower. On top of my astonishment, I was a tad impressed with this woman. I never told her where I was staying, but she found me all the same.

After about five awkward moments, I grabbed my jacket off the coat rack and covered myself. “Zora!” I said in an incredibly nervous voice, “What are you doing here? Is that my lunch?”

“Uhm.... I guess,” she replied, confused. “It was here when I showed up. I just knocked like three seconds before you opened the door.”

“Oh. I uh. I'm sorry. I was in the shower. And I ordered food, and I didn't want to miss the guy that was supposed to bring it. So, I jumped out of the shower without thinking.... I thought you were lunch.” That sounded as if my words were coming out at a million miles per minute. She stood there and smiled.

“Well lunch is already here. I brought dessert,” Zora replied with such sass. I forgot about being embarrassed and reverted to normal behavior when she said that.

“I suggest both get in here so it can be properly eaten,” I replied with a devilish grin. She grabbed the food cart and pushed it into the room. I moved to let her in as she sashayed past me. Today she smelled like shea and cocoa butter, but no raspberries. I was curious. I wanted this not to turn out like the other times. I didn't want her to “Batman” away. *I have never met a woman like this. She is so witty, intelligent, and such a mystery. Not a lot of women have that confidence, either. She is the entire package, and I got lucky to be sitting next to her on the plane, and I do not believe in coincidences.* I was thinking of ways that I could get her to stay. *Dicking her down the right way just seems to give this woman energy, so fucking her to sleep is out of the question*. I needed an idea quickly. She was giving me that look she gives when her appetite is surfacing. I could tell she came here to be satisfied. I wondered if she ate food like a dumbass because I had never seen her eat. In that same thought, I smacked my mental self and said, *Dummy.* Then it came to me.

"If I have my dessert first, can I have company for later with my reheated hotel lunch?" I asked. She roared with a laugh that was damn near hard not to find cute. She snorted but caught herself and put her hand over her face and continued to laugh. It seemed like she hadn't laughed all day. *Curiouser and curiouser,* I said in my head in my best Alice in Wonderland voice impersonation. "For that, I guess it wouldn't hurt if I didn't pull a "Barry Allen"," she said, sliding her jacket off her shoulders. She was ready, like a lioness stalking prey.

I, on the other hand, was in my head going crazy. I asked my mental self; *did she just make a comic book reference?* He had to confirm it because my shock and amazement took me to a whole new level. *The fact that there are so many levels to this woman turns me on.* I dropped my jacket and let my lower strong-arm show. She bit her lip and started towards me most sensually. She stripped as she approached, so by the time she reached me, she was only wearing a black bra and blue boy shorts, not cheekies. Something was weird.

She took her hands and let her fingertips gently slide up my arms to my stomach, tracing my muscles and over my chest. She went the opposite way but didn't go back to my arms. She traced my waistline with her fingertips slowly, and it gave me chills that made my dick jump. She saw my excitement and gave that well-placed ego-driven smile while biting her lip. *Damn! This woman is sexy.* I wanted to let her know what was on my mind. I picked her up by her waist on an animalistic urge. I kissed the part of her stomach that was in front of me and made my way to the bed. First, I gave her small taps of kisses that turned into me running my tongue across her waistline. Then, I rolled my tongue up and kissed and listened to her heart skip a beat. When we reached the bed, I let her fall hard, so that she bounced a bit off the bed. The moment she landed; I was on top of her. I wanted to go straight for the pussy and eat like I hadn't eaten in days, but something told me that that's not what she needed.

I was right on top of her, deadlocked in her eyes, and I softly pressed my lips to hers, waiting for her to let me in. I slid my tongue across her lips, and she opened her mouth and slowly sucked my tongue. I pulled away slowly from her face and slid down her body. Kissing random places as I went lower and lower, I finally reached her pleasure box. I kissed above her panty line and in unexpected places as I slid them down her thighs. She softly lifted for me to remove them entirely. Without thinking, I threw her panties in some direction and immediately focused my attention on her by biting her inner thigh. She jerked and made a noise that sounded like she was whining and moaning at the same time. I licked the spot I bit and dragged my tongue up to her throbbing pussy. It was like she was waiting for me all day.

I took my fingers and spread open her caramel glazed lower lips and licked from top to bottom. I took my lips and covered her clit and ran my tongue across as slow as I could. I felt her shudder in my arms, but I could tell she was still tense. I wanted to make her relax. I let go of her clit and licked her pussy slowly. I made her anticipate the lick, and she hung to the routine. I switched it, so she was waiting, needing to feel my tongue on her. I sped up to an average pace, grabbed her legs, and pulled her in close as if to say, “You're mine.” I locked my arms around her to say she belongs to me and showed her pussy the best care. I made sure every spot was licked, sucked, and catered to. I tried to dig into her soul the way I ate her. Her moans went from a frantic to relaxed pace, and the tension in her legs was gone.

The moment she let me know that her guard was down, I went from gentle to the predator. I sped up my licking pace. She grabbed the sheets and made a shrieking noise. I pushed her legs back so that her knees touched her ears and licked from front to back. She squealed like a little girl that was being tickled and couldn't handle it. She tried to squirm away some, but I held her down and pushed my tongue in her hole. I fucked her pussy with my tongue until she let go and came on my face. I didn't stop, though. I sucked up the juices and licked every inch. Her legs shook, and her body trembled as I sated my appetite on her dripping lips. I made a sudden stop and went back to going as slow as I could. She arched her back like I hit the spot I wasn't supposed to. I stayed on that spot and felt her entire body quake. She grabbed my head and ran her hands all over it. I could tell by the way her hands moved she was trying to restrain herself. I took my time in that spot, and she couldn't take it. She finally took my head and pushed it into her flowing box and moved her hips up and down. She fucked my tongue back, and it made my dick jump.

She rocked her pussy on my face until she had an orgasm that left her quivering. I dropped the part of her I was holding and crawled up towards her with my dick oozing precum. I went straight up to her face, and like the good girl I knew she was, she opened wide for me. Her mouth felt so good. I let my head fall back and moved my shaft in and out of her mouth. She moved her tongue and her neck in rhythm with my movements. I slowly made love to her mouth with slob dripping from the sides of her mouth and her moans echoing through the room.

I pulled out and eased back. I came face to face with her and wrapped one arm around her neck. On the other hand, I put myself in a position that gave me ease of entering her. I placed the head of my dick between the opening of her pussy, brought my other arm up, and wrapped it around her neck. As I pulled her close to me, it felt as if she was wrapping herself around me. She let out a sigh that almost, to me, sounded as if she was nervous. I pushed myself further inside her, and I felt her arch her back and her body folded into me. I could feel her heart trying to jump out of her chest. I looked her in her eyes and pulled out slowly, which seemed to give her chills. Then it came to me. I never was slow and gentle with her, and it's always been aggressive and fast.

I rolled my hips as I entered her again. She moaned a new sound I never heard her make before. I kept the slow but steady pace I was going as I moved in and out of her throbbing pussy. I could feel the pulse in her walls as it wrapped tighter around my dick. I tried hard not to show that it felt the best when she grabbed at me. The moans she made sounded like a virgin having sex for the first time, which intrigued me. I released an arm to unclasp her bra, used the other to grab a handful of her voluptuous "C" cups, all while still maintaining my pace. I slid my tongue across the nipple of the one I was holding back and forth. Her moans got a little louder, and I immediately sped up. She made that new sound again. I stopped sucking and switched to kissing up her chest and her neck. I licked her on the side of her neck, and she jerked from me. I guess I found a sensitive area, so I went for it again. She didn't flinch, but she jumped when I first put my tongue on that spot. I slowly licked there for about three minutes, still fucking her with a steady pace.

I was starting to get lost in the feeling of her juicy love box, the moans she was making, and the way she started rubbing on my back. I moaned and bit her on that spot. She dug her nails into my back and scratched it up. I released her and kissed where I bit. She calmed down, and I got up. I pulled out gently and laid down on the bed. I guided her to rise and to straddle me. She wasted no time and put my still hard, cock in her. She gave that smirk that I'm all too familiar with and adored. I thought she would do her usual thing and make me forget where I was for a moment, but I was wrong.

I grabbed her waist, guided her down to me, and she laid her chest on mine. She put her arms around my head, and I whispered to her, “Slow.” She moved up and stayed there for a minute before coming back down. She rocked this time, friendly and slow. I moaned in her ear, “Mhmm. Yea. Like that.” Her breathing was heavy and fast, panting. Her grip got tighter, and she moved her arms around my neck. I moved my hands down to her waist and started thrusting from the bottom, matching her speed. She let out a small moan and sat up at an angle. I grabbed firmly on her waist and pushed harder, still at her pace. Her moans got louder, and she moved her hands to my chest. She used me as leverage for a better bounce and just took over.

Still, she bounced and rode me at a slow pace like she was trying to tame a wild horse. I finally let go and let the feeling take me to that place where nirvana is not too far away. Instead of obscenities, she let out a slew of moans that sounded like angels singing me into heaven. The occasional “yes” came out, but this was different. I watched her movements flow as if she was an underwater attraction. I felt myself reaching that point of ecstasy, but I wasn't ready. I was enjoying her this way.

I rolled her over and got back on top. I moaned, and she scratched as I moved in and out, making wet noises between our legs. As I went deeper, harder, and slightly faster, her moans became screams. I put my arms around her again as I felt myself reaching the point where I might explode. I let it take me, and I bit her on her ear. She jerked again like I wasn't supposed to touch them, so I bit harder. She grabbed my arm and held on for dear life as if she were on a roller-coaster, just reached the top, and about to go straight down. I squeezed her in my arms as I came and felt her cum. I let go of her ear and kissed her from ear to cheek. She laid there panting heavily like an out-of-shape jogger. I stared at her for about a minute before I decided that I'd kiss her. I mean, *really* kiss her. I let my head fall, and my lips touched hers, and I felt a warm chill creep up my spine.

They started as taps then led to heavy tongue kissing. I let my eyes close as our lips intertwined and let myself feel this brand-new feeling. She rubbed her hands all over my back, and at some point, pulled me in close. As I was blissfully enjoying being in this new place, she suddenly pushed me off and got up. I sat up in utter confusion as I watched her scramble around the room, gathering her clothes. She threw her pants on and tried to put her shirt on while shoving her feet in her shoes. She grabbed all her belongings and rushed for the door. I jumped up and made it halfway to the door when she put her hand on the knob and stopped in her tracks. I heard a heavy sigh and she turned to me with sadness in her eyes and said, “I'm really sorry. I don't really get this....... I .... I have to go.” Like a plastic bag in the wind, she was gone. I felt worse that time than I did any other she pulled a “Barry Allen,” as she called it. I thought I did something wrong. *Did I read her body language wrong?* I asked myself. *Did I not satisfy her? Did I overstep my boundaries?*

Everything in me wanted to call her and ask what I did, but I didn't. I saw Alex called three times. I had missed my night out, and I didn't care. I couldn't get my mind off what just happened. I sighed heavily and let my phone just fall on the love seat. I walked over to my bed with a frown and fell back onto the sheets, still naked. I put one hand behind my head, and with the other, I rubbed from my chest to my stomach repeatedly. I stared at the ceiling and went over everything in my head. *We had a good time, we were enjoying ourselves, and we were on the same cloud. So, what the hell happened?* I tried to figure out what she was trying to say as she was leaving. *She usually does not what? Get where?* Then it hit me. She didn't tell me her name or number until after fucking a couple of times. She always ran away straight after and never got on a personal level to talk or tell me about herself. She doesn't want to get close. She said she doesn't get “this", and I think she wanted to say close. *Does that mean she feels something for me?*

I was more curious than ever now. Something in me told me that I was right about her feelings. It made me kind of proud. She is a woman who has been at this for a long time and knows how not to get close. It's part of her programming. So, what was it about me that made her switch programming? What was it about her that had me so intrigued? What was it about us together that makes the chemistry so great? I wanted answers to these questions. I wanted to know more about her, but not in the stalking kind of way. I just needed to figure out how.

I stared at my phone, still fighting with myself about calling. However, I risk the chance of her not answering, so she doesn't have to explain. I was stuck. I had no idea what to do. I tell myself all the time that there is always a way to do something. Nothing is impossible. I just have to think outside the box. I was serious about this. I jumped up from the bed and started pacing. I tried to think of what I already knew about her. *I know she is intelligent, independent, strong-willed, a sex goddess, and likes comics. She knows when it is time to get to business. She maintained her entire composure during that meeting.* I thought back to that and how she was strictly business mode and then a whole one-eighty to her aggressive side. I thought about how she took charge of setting up a room for us, knew I was there already, and the notes she left for me like she knew my every move.

I was digging way too deep. I started to wonder things like if she knew I would be in that meeting. Did she see me leave my hotel for her to leave those notes? What if I didn't come to the room? I gave myself a panic attack being so excited about this, and I moved back to the bed to sit down. *This woman is outside the box itself!* I can't tell myself to think like her; I don't know enough about her. I told myself, "Stop overthinking. Let's start over."

I never went after a woman with the intent of making something resembling a semi-serious or "Let's see where this goes" kind of relationship. I was always trying not to get caught up in something profound. But for Zora, I might take a leap of faith. I'm intrigued as I have never been before. Not like this, not the way she leaves me with more questions than answers. I wanted to get to know her. Maybe that is the door to what they call love. I may be surprised after all. I just got to get her to go out with me first! I am still clueless about how I go about that, but I won't get any of my questions answered if I don't try. *Planning this will take tremendous effort. Me and some frat brothers came up with a small business plan that we have been thriving off for over six years while we were drunk. I can think of something great for a date.*

After about what felt like forever but was only two hours, I crashed on the love seat in my hotel room. I stared at the ceiling some more, feeling so hopeless. I was starting to feel like maybe that one impossible thing. I heard my phone buzzing like crazy, so I got up to check it. Halfway to the love seat, I could see the screen and I saw that it was Alex calling. *He probably wants an explanation for bailing. I do owe him one.* I walked slouching to my phone and answered, “Sup Bro!”

“Nothing man,” he started, “Just making sure you're still alive, you know. We didn't see you and no answer to the earlier calls, you know.”

“Uh, yea man. I kinda got tied up here into something,” I said. I could tell by how many “you knows” he said that they had fun without me. “I wasn't like...*needed*, was I?”

“No....no... We found our way fine. I was just worried about'cha is all, you know. We had a great time, you know. Met some *really* nice new friends, you know, and they showed us the best time ever, you know. You missed out, buddy.”

“Naw, yea, that sounds like I missed a lot. But I just couldn't get away, man.”

“Well, tell me what the hell kept you from a night out with the bros, man. Like, it better be a woman, you know.” I sighed heavily. I knew whatever I told him then may be remembered, but I felt like I needed to say it out loud, so I don't lose my mind.

I gave him the cliff notes version on Zora, our meeting, and the last encounter we had. All the while, he let on that he thought she was a great girl. I was wondering what another man in my position would do. I guess I was looking for advice. So, I asked, "What do you do when you think about someone all the time and it eats you up inside that they aren't right there next to you? Could this be my curiosity making me want her this badly? I have to take all this into account before I start chasing a woman I barely know and start shouting about feelings. I wouldn't want to push her further away. I know she doesn't want to get close, but I think she is already feeling me. The kiss never lies. There was too much passion behind them for them not to mean anything."

"Awe man, I don't know bro," he answered. "Me, you know, I think we're too young and got our whole lives, you know, like why just have one grape, you know, man? You don't need no bitch to tell you what to do every day. We have fun, you know, the three amigos! Bahahaha. Yea man, you know, you just gotta ask yourself if you wanna really let someone in, ya know."

"Yea. I hear ya, man. It's just a date. Not like I'm trying to marry her. I just gotta ask her out."

"Dude, you are the best guy I know besides me, you know. You got this. Don't worry. So, you're good then? Brunch tomorrow? I may sleep in a bit," he replies, followed by a hearty laugh.

"Yea man, go. I'm good. Later, yo."

I heard the phone click, and I hung up on my end. No, he was right, though, and I am pretty awesome. I'm just missing something here. I don't have enough information to complete the mission ahead. I can't be wrong about the kiss. I felt it, and I know she did too. I needed to be sure. I wanted to talk to her. I can't do it like I'm some crazy, obsessed guy. guy. I thought long and hard about what I want to do. *The whole not knowing anything about her is throwing my focus off. My focus needs to change from what to do to how to find out more about her.*

I gave up thinking for a while. I could smell the smoke coming from my ears. I had leftover food in my little refrigerator from various places, so I took my pick of pizza and half of a club grilled cheese. I put the food on a plate and into the microwave and went to get my phone. I opened my Facebook app and scrolled through my timeline. I liked a few statuses, watched some crazy videos, and then I heard the microwave beep. I put my phone on the coffee table and went back to the tiny kitchen area to get my food. I grabbed the plate, popped it out of the microwave, and went to the little couch. As I ate, I continued to scroll through my timeline. Halfway through my plate, I noticed a post about comic con coming to Colorado Springs' town shortly. I thought, *this is perfect. I know she appreciates a good comic book. I caught almost all her references. I need to see if she will be available to go. I want to get tickets now, but I will not if she can't go. How the hell am I going to figure that out?*

I had the best idea. *Anyone at her high level of employment should have an assistant or two.* I made my way to the hotel phone to call the Weston Inn. I looked the number up on my phone and dialed it. The line rang twice before some young-sounding woman answered. Her greeting sounded like she was showing all teeth in her smile. I politely asked for Zora Humphreys. The young-sounding woman said that Zora has not been in today, and won't be in. She offered to direct my call to Zora's assistant, and I excitedly accepted.

"This is Ciera," a woman answered, "How may I help you?"

"Hello, Ciera," I said in the most suave voice I could muster. "How are you today?"

"I'm good, sir. Can I help you set up a reservation or alter an existing one?" she asked.

I chuckled before I answered, "Well, I'm not interested in a reservation, actually. But I would be super delighted if you could tell me if Miss Zora Humphreys has a personal assistant or a number one to go to?"

"Well Mr. ...???" she replied, holding on to the last syllable.

"Mr. Jefferies."

"Mr. Jefferies, I assist Miss Humphreys with anything and everything she needs. I am sorry, but currently we are only hiring for bellhops. Perhaps I can transfer you to our Human Resources department for more information on that position. Please hold."

"Wait!" I yelled. "No, I'm not looking for a job. I'm actually looking for you. I think maybe you would be able to help me plan a great surprise for her."

"I do apologize sir, but I don't believe I know you or ever heard Miss Humphreys mention you before. I don't think I can help you."

I had to think quickly. *She is right. I have not known Zora long enough to just ask about her schedule. I highly doubt she talks about her personal life at work. She is too professional for that.* Then it hit me.

"Ciera, was it?" I asked.

"Yes, sir."

"Ciera, you work closely with Zora and know her better than anyone there. You know she doesn't discuss her personal life. But if you must know, Miss Humphreys and I have been enjoying each other's company lately, and I would like to do something nice for her. My only problem is, I know how important her work is to her- so I want to make sure the dates I picked will be ok for her to be out of the office. Do you think you can help me with that?" There was a long pause, and I thought I lost this battle until I heard her sigh into the phone.

"Yes Mr. Jefferies, Miss Humphries does not discuss personal business," she started. "I really shouldn't be doing this. She helped me get this job and I'm so grateful. But I think she needs something good in her life other than this place. She gave this hotel life, and she deserves something for it. So, which dates are we looking at? Maybe I can help you figure out if she will accept."

I immediately got excited. I ran down the convention dates and mentioned that we would need some extra time for travel. Ciera looked up the future reservations to ensure there would not be presidential suites needing Zora's attention. Ciera said that Zora likes to make sure all the higher suites are taken care of personally, so she may refuse to accept if she feels the need to be there. I asked if there was any chance I had to get her to take some time off. She told me that the dates look good for now. "The presidential suites are booked months in advance, so the next couple of weeks should be ok," she said. I thanked Ciera with much gratitude and promised an Edible Arrangement when I got Zora to accept my offer. I could hear the smile in her voice as she bid me a friendly and cheerful farewell. I hung up, jumped off my bed, did a victory dance, and looked around to make sure no one saw me. I was so excited I didn't waste any time going back to the convention site and buying two tickets. I stared at the email confirmation for about five minutes before the smile on my face went away. *Damn! I forgot that I need to talk to her to ask her out!*

I was right back to where I started. The only thing I accomplished was making sure she was free. I wanted to call her or reach out, but I wasn't sure how. If I tried calling, she might ignore me. I needed a way to reach out that she would see without wanting to reject it. No phone calls, emails, and damn sure not calling her job again. *No, she likes to keep her life private, and out of respect for her, I will keep it that way. How do I go about getting this woman to respond to me, knowing that she is on reject mode right now? I guess I did not do my outside the box thinking yet.*

I thought about getting a new email, and the possibility of her ignoring it because it's from a stranger. I thought about sending her a text, but she could ignore that, too. I was racking my brain about how to get this woman's attention. It took a while, but I figured it out. I knew what I was going to do. I didn't have any new business to get to for a couple of months, so I knew I could spend some time in Chicago to understand Zora better. I had what I thought was an airtight plan. Did I know exactly how to execute this? I did my research and got every detail down. I had some leg work to do, but that could wait until tomorrow. I was tired, and anxious about this new excitement coming into my life.

Her

The lounge was buzzing with people as usual. I was making rounds and ensuring things were running smoothly, like I always do. But today, something had my attention. My focus was either all over the place or not there at all. I smiled at guests and other employees as they passed me, and the smile would fade just as they left my sight. I just couldn't get my mind off what happened and how I reacted. I don't know what I thought; I was embarrassed. My pace picked up the more I thought about it. I was making myself frustrated, and it was showing. I needed to get back to my office so I could breathe in peace.

When I closed the door to my office, I let out an enormous sigh of relief. I walked over to my desk and flopped down, then I put my fingers to my temples and tried to relax. I don't know why I was getting so worked up over this; it was just a kiss. I reacted so rudely, though. I can't even figure out why the hell I responded like that. "What the fuck were you thinking, bitch?" I kept asking myself. A lousy kiss set me off and rattled my day, and it made me curious. But I also know where my curiosity would lead.

My concern at this moment is how I even let myself get to that point. I am always careful and always make sure I do not slip up. So how the hell did I end up in this mess? I retraced what happened in my mind. I remember him asking if I could stay, and I agreed. I remember him leaning in to kiss me. My heart was beating so loud it sounded like I was front row at a Blue Man Group Concert. I remember him kissing me, and feeling like the room was spinning. Then, the room stopped spinning and went dark, so I panicked.

"UGGGGHHHHHHHH!" I groaned as I got up from my desk. I paced back and forth, trying to wrap my mind around why I let him get to me. *This is not good. I need to focus on work, and the guests, or anything else other than what I'm thinking.* I took a deep breath and tried to mentally adjust back to a professional mindset. I put a hand on the doorknob, put on the biggest smile I could muster, and pulled open the door. I saw what looked like a jungle of flowers, to my surprise and shock. The bellhop carrying it jumped as I opened the door.

"Oh!" he exclaimed. "Sorry, Miss Zora. I didn't know you were here... These came for you at the desk, and I thought I should put them in your office." He handed me the flowers. I was still confused. *Who in the world sent me flowers?*

"Uh... Thanks, Henry," I said as I turned around and tried to find a spot in my office to put them down.

The bouquet was beautiful, a vibrant mixture of tulips, lilacs, and some other flowers I recognized but didn't know the name of. I'm not a flower kind of girl. I put the bouquet down in a spot I found on a wooden cabinet. I brushed my hand over the flowers, just for a feel, and noticed something inside the giant bouquet. It wasn't a card, but a small brown envelope big enough for a CD, DVD, or a greeting card. I took it out and turned it over twice in my hands. It was plain, with just "For Zora" written on it. It felt like something hard was inside. I was curious as fuck now. *Who would send me something here? Could it be one of the clients from the presidential suites?* I wondered if it was from the previous guest I encountered in the suite. I had so many questions, and there was only one way to find out.

I opened it, and a DVD fell out with a note. I opened my laptop, put the DVD in, and pressed play. As the computer started the movie, I opened the letter. I glanced it over enough to know it was not a letter but was a confirmation page for tickets that someone bought. Before I could start over and pay more attention to what I was looking at, I heard a voice say, “Hello, Zora.” It was him! I couldn't believe it. I sat down to pay better attention to the laptop.

“Um, I understand if this may seem a bit out of the blue and the box, but I didn't know how else to approach. After our last visit, I thought you'd be more comfortable if I didn't blow your phone up with calls and text messages. I thought that I'd save you and myself the whole ‘should I ignore or not’ scenario. Listen, I want you to know that you don't owe me any explanation to your actions. I am not looking for one. I just want to spend some time with you. I do not know much about you, only the little things I pick up in our brief time together. During our witty banter, I noticed that you made a few comic books references. So, I am officially inviting you on a date to the Colorado Springs Comic Convention. Cosplay is encouraged; I know I will be participating. You don't have to call me and tell me what your decision is, and you don't even have the same travel plans as me. Inside the envelope with this message is your ticket to the convention. So, you can come when you are ready. I will be there for the full convention, and it runs over three days. I won't look for a text from you or a call. I won't put that pressure on you. I will send you updates on the convention like where I'll be staying and other details as it gets closer. I don't expect you to call. I will not ask you to. I just hope you take the time to realize that you can have a life. I hope I see you there. You have a good day at work."

The video ended, and I sat there with a half-cocked smile on my face. *Wow*, I thought. *This guy has some balls on him, sending flowers to my job with a video, asking me out, and on an out-of-state trip at that. He knows what I do and knows how I feel about my job. How? No one pays that much attention. Did I let some of me slip out while with him?* I looked at the confirmation page again and shook my head in disbelief. I couldn't believe what was happening. None of the men I have dealt with bothered going through this much trouble to get my attention. When I disappear, they don't come looking. Keith was different. There was an effort here and I liked hard workers.

Wait. Am I considering this? I don't do dates. I never wanted to date. I started to panic and looked at the dates from the confirmation page. I checked the dates against my future bookings. When I saw what was on my screen, I let out a stern chuckle. According to my schedule, we have two presidential suite reservations. I usually take care of all the 1600 reservations, but these were college kids' parties for the beginning of the year. I was highly confident that my assistant, Ciera, could handle these on her own. Not to mention, it could shine some light on her here and further her career here if she wanted. That would depend on how well she does on her own, which I fully supported. *I do have vacation time saved up. I could take the week. I could go up early and look around, work my nerves down before the date, and get familiar with the surroundings if I decide to leave.*

I had to stop myself. *Do I want to do this? Am I getting excited?* My dad, guy that acted like he was my dad, used to say, "Science can't explain feelings. They can trace the chemical reaction in a person's body based on feelings, but they cannot explain what feelings actually are. You have to figure out what to do with the feeling when it comes. When you make that decision, whether it turns out to be good or bad, it was that good feeling that led to that ending. And stories of the journeys are always good teachers." I took that to mean always to trust my feelings and learn from the experiences they lead me to. I sighed and admitted to myself that I was considering this date. By the time I actually walked out of the hotel, I was confused, curious, and excited all at the same time.

Struggling with my takeout and my keys, I forced my way into my apartment. I used the back of my foot to close the door, then walked to my kitchen island to drop the things in my hands. I made sure nothing would fall off and went back to the door to lock it. Kicking off my shoes, I hung my coat on the coat rack in my narrow hall and turned on some lights on my way to my bedroom. I took a shower and put on pajamas. I tested the food, trying to see if it was still warm. Satisfied, I made myself a plate, poured myself a drink, and went to my living room. I set the food down and turned on my tablet. As I ate, I investigated this comic convention. The schedule of events they had lined up looked great. I saw a lot of things I wanted to participate in. I could let my geek out amongst other geeks, pick up some fantastic collectors' items, and maybe go on my first actual date in forever.

By the time I was ready for bed, I had booked my flight, put in my vacation days, and got them approved. I even reserved my unlimited pass for the events. I didn't book the hotel yet, even though I did research them. I didn't know if I wanted to wait and see if he would give me his hotel info, or if I wanted to go off blind faith and just book a room. *It does not matter if we are in the same hotel. I think it would be better if we are in separate places if this is a bad idea. I do not know the guy all that well, but I like his vibe and our chemistry together.* I didn't know if I wanted to pursue this as something serious. I told myself to breathe and relax; I was thinking too far. The invite was just what he said it was. It was a date to get to know each other, and I could use it to answer the questions I was asking myself.

PLANNED ENCOUNTER

Him

Colorado Springs was swarming with nerds, geeks, and introverts of every size, shape, and color. It was supposed to be the area's busiest time, and I don't function in crowds. I needed my privacy. I was staying in Manitou Springs, about fifteen minutes away from Colorado Springs. The area was seventy-eight percent marijuana-friendly, including the hotels. I was going to need to smoke, so I'm not tripping over Zora. I knew there was a possibility that she wouldn’t come. This was a chance. I just needed to remember that, so I don’t lose it.

I arrived at my hotel sweating like a pig. It was still hot outside like it's the middle of July, and the cab I was in had no AC. I rolled my eyes as I paid the cabbie and closed the door. After checking in and inspecting the room, I wasted no time checking on my costume like it was porcelain and might have broken in transit. My outfit was like my baby, and man was I proud. I wanted a costume that spoke to my extended support of the nerd community and acceptance in the culture. I was positive that I'd find more dressed like me, but that's part of the fun in cosplay. People get a chance to see how others represent and view their favorite characters, shows, books, and video games.

The area I was in was supposed to have pot smoker events to support the legalization. I just think it's businesses that are smart and know what will bring in the money. After getting my things put away, I was bored. I walked around the room to really examine it. There were several event brochures for daily activities for the smoker community. Pot bingo looked fun. I started to wonder if you win more weed when you get bingo. The movie in the park is a bit different. Apparently, it's the only time people can publicly smoke because of the event. The various restaurants and vape clubs made me rethink coming alone. You never know what kind of people you'll run into. Most of the smoke community is good, but we do have those few. At that moment, I knew I was hungry and needed to smoke.

Pausing my exploration, I made my way to the lobby. It wasn't very crowded, which was perfect. I had eyed the person I was looking for. Working in this business, you learn that if you want quality, talk to the bellhops and busboys. They know the least expensive but damn near top quality of everything, from print shops to nightclubs that sell the best ecstasy. I eased my way to the slender, red-haired boy. He stood in a corner talking to another patron. I waited for him to complete his business, then I approached. I nodded to get his attention, and he stopped. "What's up dude?" I started. "I was wondering if you could help me?"

"Uh yea sure," he said nervously, "What can I do for you sir?"

"Oh, God. No sir. I'm not that old yet." We both chuckled. "I know you get a lot of questions about the best places to go, especially from the smokers, and I am also aware that most of the tourists are occasional smokers. They come here just so they can smoke. I am not one of them. I'm not a tourist. I don't want the 'everyone in the world' batch."

"I don't really know what you're asking. Everything around here is pretty good. It's medically grown. You get some of the popular br..."

"No. Yea, that sounds good," I interrupted, "But what I want is the same shit you smoke. When you go home to unwind from dealing with fake assholes like myself, you need that calming high. I want that." He stood there in all his late twenty's glory with a look on his face that said he was profoundly thinking. He sucked his teeth and sighed. "A'ight man. I'm actually getting off now. Give me ten minutes to clock out and change my clothes," he said. I chuckled and nodded as he ran off.

I walked over to a lounge chair and sat down. The longer I sat there, the more I felt like I was back in my frat house. There was a different fragrance of weed in every direction. I glanced around, scanning people to pass the time, like a bored child in a lady's shoe store. I was excited, too. Exploring new weed is always a good time for me. I pulled out my phone, scrolled social media, and checked text messages. About five minutes later, the bellhop came back in his street clothes. He wore a pair of whitewashed jeans with random tears that looked like they were ripped straight out of an eighty's movie. His short-sleeved tee-shirt rested on top of a long-sleeved black shirt. He reminded me of the skate punk era mixed with a little bit of emo. "Ready to go?" he asked. I stood up and nodded, and he led the way.

During the ride, we talked on and off. I found out the bellboy's name was Ronnie, and he was in college, working at the hotel to make his way. The place we were headed to was his brother's house. Ronnie told me that what they sell in the clubs and vendors is cool because it's medical, but the best stuff is still homegrown. We arrived at what looked to be an enclosed, gated community. Stopping at a giant bronze gate, he put a code in on a keypad He then turned to me while the entrance was opening, and said, "Don't be fooled by how perfect this place looks. Everyone here has a story."

"Oh dude, I'm not really trying to be nosey. I just want good bud. If we become friends after a while, that's cool. Perfectly fine keeping it business," I replied.

"Oh, so you're planning on coming back. I thought you were one of those just here for the con."

"I am here for the con," I laughed. "But in my line of work, I travel a lot. Having a connection where I travel saves me time."

"Oh, okay. I got it," he said as we pulled into a driveway that was attached to a ranch house. It looked dark and lonely, tucked away behind the bigger houses. We got out of the car, and I looked around. Other places were lit with porch lights and garden lights on the lawn, yet the only light from his brother's house was from the streetlight. Another light came on when his brother opened the door. He stood in the doorway and lit a cigarette. Ronnie motioned me to follow him, and I did. His brother moved aside so that we could enter, and he closed the door after us.

Inside was nice. It looked like the typical bachelor pad, with a big screen TV in the living room. As I came around the corner, I noticed he had three different game systems, a wall of DVDs, and a home theater system I only dreamed of. "Have a seat," his brother said. He was taller than Ronnie and me, with a firm build and buzz cut. He had that "I just got home from the army" look. Ronnie mentioned his brother's intense face was due to all the online gaming he does. He told me to call him Sunny as I moved to sit on the cream-colored sofa. It went great with the white tile flooring he had.

Ronnie went into the back of his house and came back after about five minutes with a shoebox. He placed it on the table and opened the top. My eyes lit up like I was a kid who just landed in front of Disneyland. There were so many different kinds. Some were dark, colorful, and frosted. I told him how much I wanted to buy, and he insisted I smoke before I go. Pretty sure it's to make sure I was cool. Sunny pulled a weird-looking bong from under the square table in front of us and packed the bowl. Ronnie took the first hit. Then me. Sunny stood there and watched till I choked. My lungs felt like they were on fire. My eyes watered as I tried to catch my breath. I stood up and walked away, still coughing, and put my face in a corner to finish dying. I could faintly hear Ronnie and his brother laughing behind me.

As the cough was leaving me, I walked back over to the couch. I sat down and wiped my eyes. "That shit's wild, my guy," I said, still catching my breath.

"Frosty is always good, my man. That one choke got you feelin' right tho', yea?" Sonny enthusiastically replied.

"Fuck yea. Is that what I'm getting?"

"Yup. And I throw in some fruit. Make sure you come back when you're in town."

"Oh, most definitely. Trust." I looked at Ronnie and got confused for a minute. "Ronnie?" I asked.

"Yea man, sup?" he said.

"How am I getting back?" I asked, then laughed. He and his brother laughed, and he said he'd take me. Sunny even came along for the ride. They dropped me off, and Ronnie said he'll be at work tomorrow, and that maybe he'd come to get me for his break to smoke. I said cool, and waved bye. I went up to my room, smoked, and passed out.

The next day, I was so excited! It was comic con time! My costume had to be perfect, down to the haircut. I enjoyed the many perks of visiting a marijuana legal state and had an edible breakfast made with cannabutter instead of actual butter. By the time I had finished my shower, I was feeling the effects. I got dressed in my costume and put on my accessories. I took one last look in the mirror before I left.

The Chapel Hills Mall was already packed with its regular patrons. The convention was being held in the mall's event center. Having to go around the mall to reach the ticket booth, I saw its regular wall crawlers, and extras were coming in from all over. As weird as it may be for someone outside the geek world, these are the most anticipated events of the year.

The line for the ticket booth was long. I sucked my teeth and frowned when I noticed how lengthy the line really was. I was early, though. There was still about thirty minutes before the doors opened. I needed to be here early. Knowing Zora, she won't come until the middle of the event when she thinks she won't be seen. *When I check-in, I will have Zora's left at the booth. I don't want to wait for her at the door. She might have decided not to come.* I let myself think that she did come. I told myself, *he might be watching me right now. She loves to keep her mysterious reputation.*

While deep in thought, I felt a shove from behind. Without thinking, I snapped out of my almost daydream and turned around, prepared to go off on someone without manners. When I turned around, there was this five -nine, two-hundred thirty-one-pound white guy with this searing look of disappointment. The creepy scar on his face made the look feel so real. I immediately credited it to his costume and bowed. "FN-2187, Report!" the guy said in a stern voice. "Sir, my apologies, I..." I began, but then, from behind him came a slender, caramel woman. She grabbed my hand and pulled me upright. She looked around as if to see if anyone was listening, and then said, "Don't worry, Finn. He won't get BB8, I promise."

The three of us roared with laughter. Our costumes were from the same movie, *Star Wars.* I chose to be Finn, one of the newest heroes in the current series. The man dressed as Kylo Ren, the newest Sith who also happens to be the previous heroes' offspring, and the woman was dressed as Rey, the newest Jedi. "I'm sorry about earlier," he started, "but when I turned around and saw who you're dressed as, I couldn't help it."

"No, it's fine. I forgot all about it when you used my stormtrooper number," I said in between laughs. "I wasn't even confused when Rey here grabbed me."

"Oh good," she said with relief. "I was kinda worried that I might've weirded you out."

"Not at all. I know exactly where I am," I said. "I'm Keith, but today you can call me Finn."

"Oh, I'm Elliot," the guy said, stretching out his hand to shake mine. He pointed at the woman and said, "This is De'Borah," and she reached out to shake my hand.

"Did you guys come together, or just meet here?" I asked.

"I just met this guy, but my children call him Dad for some reason," she replied. I laughed and said, "Married life is grand."

"It is when you marry someone as creepy as you," Elliot said. "Are you here alone?"

"I invited someone, but I won't be upset if they don't come. Busy life."

"Well, if you want you can hang with us. I don't see why we can't stick together. Our costumes practically make us a group."

"Yea, no... That'll be great! I brought my good camera too. If you want, we can take some really good, professional-looking photos."

"Are you a photographer?"

"Not really. It's just a hobby. But I take all the photos for my business if needed."

"As long as they don't come out super horrible, I'm not complaining. I want all the memories of this day."

"My thoughts exactly."

The line started moving, and I got excited. Standing in line, I learned that Elliot and De' Borah have been married for six years and have two children. This was Elliot's third comic con, but De' Borah has been to six, including this one. De' Borah's parents were from Montreal, and they lived in Niagara Falls. They attended at least two comic cons a year here in the states. They talked my ear off about the different cosplay ideas they went through. It helped pass the time. The next thing I knew, we were so close to the entrance. I could even see some of the different panels set up inside. I was getting so excited that my new friends' voices were drowned out by my inner child; doing cartwheels for excitement for the day I was about to have.

I snapped out of it when a voice asked about tickets. I turned to look, and I was at one of the ticket booths. I reached in my pocket for my email confirmation and handed it to the young lady sitting at the counter. "Thank you!" she said, with such chipper enthusiasm. "You have two three-day passes. Are you picking both up?"

"No. I'd like to leave the other up front, if possible," I replied.

"No problem!" the ticket lady said. She was somehow even more enthusiastic. "As long as they have the confirmation page. If I can have your wrist, I'll put it on for you."

"Will I get a new one for tomorrow, or do I have to bring my confirmation again?" I asked while she was putting my wristband on.

"No. It doesn't come off," the attendant said with a smile.

"Okay, so how will I take a shower or if I need to take it off?"

"It's fine. You can take a shower with this on. It's like clothes, but not really. It will get wet. But it won't take long to dry. You'll just have to cut it off when you get home after the comic con is over." I chuckled and just went with it. She gave me a perky, "Thank you for coming!" and I went inside. I stood on the other side and waited for my new friends. It only seemed fitting, considering our costumes complemented each other.

After Elliot got his band on, we all walked through the entrance with our barcodes showing. There were tall pillars throughout the hall. They were brightly decorated with comic con banners for this year, pictures of comic books, Sci-Fi, and flyers for the guest speakers. As we walked through, we saw other cosplayers and their groups. There was barely no one here without a costume, and that's what these things are for. We saw a group of differently dressed Spider-Man cosplayers. There was the original Spider, one dressed like Miles Morales. and one was dressed in a Black Symbiote-Spidey costume. There was even one with fake extra arms from the episode where he mutated into a spider monster.

There were so many dressed in Star Wars gear, like my new friends and me. We stopped to take pictures with them, and acted out a few of the scenes that the characters were in. The children's costumes were the most precious—we saw a mini–Super Mario and Luigi, tiny Captain America, and a pint-size Wolverine. The day was going great.

We managed to walk our way through one side and headed towards the middle exhibitions. We stopped at the smaller booths to buy whatever souvenirs we wanted. They had over two hundred comic book vendor stands. It's the only place to buy, sell, and/or trade comic books for a reasonable price—even the infrequent ones. As we approached a trinket-selling vendor, we saw a Chewbacca standing there, looking over the different Time-Tuner necklaces from *Harry Potter.*

We had seen some costumes before this one, but this was the only one that used stilts or high rises on its shoes to accentuate the height. He was tall, and his outfit didn't look half bad. But I knew for this to be perfect, I needed to talk to him. I looked back at Elliot, and he gave me a nod as if he knew I was going to test the Chewbacca. I walked up to the vendor booth and stood there, looking over some of the metallic pieces. They had old Celtic symbols, mini dragon figurines, and almost any tiny trinket from all the raving movies. We saw Arwen's necklace from *Lord of the Rings*, and *Harry Potter* keychains with the different houses. They even had some *Golden Compass* replicas of the actual compass, with spins and all. I got closer to him, so he'd notice me. He brushed me, looked down at me, and then turned to walk away. I thought I lost hope, so I turned back to Elliot when suddenly I was in what felt like a bear hug. All I could feel was fur and hear what sounded like Wookie coming from the Chewbacca. Not only could this guy speak excellent Wookie, the language of Chewbacca, but he even displayed overbearing affection, just like Chewbacca does in the movies. He passed the test.

After he let me go, we all howled with laughter, including the vendor. The guy stood back and took a look at our group. He moved his hand over his Chewbacca face and lifted the nose. Underneath was his natural face. When I first saw him, I mentally tried to guess his race. I was wrong. It was the face of a black man with pearly white teeth, staring at us with the broadest smile. “You guys look great,” he said. “Best ones I've seen yet.”

“Yea, we were thinking the same about you,” De’ Borah said. “That's why I came over to try and test you,” I added.

“I figured when I turned around and saw who you were dressed as,” he replied.

“I'm Elliot and this is my wife, De’ Borah,” said Elliot. He pointed to his wife.

“I'm Keith.”

“Cool. Nice to meet you. I'm Ralph. Ralph Conetti. I know the name doesn't match the face. I'm adopted. It's easier if I get that out the way,” he said as we all laughed. We started walking again and talking to Ralph. We told him what we did for a living, and he told us he was a warehouse supervisor. As we passed exhibitions, we talked about some of the things we saw, like anime, the TV shows, some of the pictures. We debated the most notable characters, and somehow, Ralph took pics with us and joined our group.

It was two hours into the con, and I hadn't had a word of Zora. I was starting to wonder if she even came. I even began to feel like a dumbass knowing what kind of woman she was. While the gang was looking over some comic books, I pulled my phone out of my pocket and checked it to see if she even tried to contact me. There was nothing. I could feel the disappointment and sadness creep up and fill my face. I could feel myself frowning, and I was trying not to let my friends see. I had to tell myself that I knew this would happen, and this was on a whim. As I was trying to pull myself together, I felt this presence near me. I almost felt like she was coming and getting closer. Boy, was I wrong!

I turned around and standing behind me was an excellent fucking replica of Captain Phasma, the person my character has to confront. The complete chrome Stormtrooper armor with a black cap trimmed in red was standing in front of me, intimidating and [some other word that isn't too cliche]. I froze in my shoes. I stared into the helmet and waited for something to happen. Nervous and a little uncomfortable, I tried to back up slowly. When I moved, the lights on the front of the helmet came on, and someone spoke. The helmet even had a built-in voice changer. "FN-2187, submit your blaster for inspection," said the ominous voice from the helmet. I wanted to laugh; it was a direct line between these two in the movie. I tried to stay in character and thought about which lines I should respond with. I pulled my pretend blaster from the holster on my hip and slowly raised it. In a blink of an eye, I switched stances and pointed it at Phasma.

"Not this time, Phasma!" I responded. "That's right, I'm the boss now!" I quoted lines from a part in the movie when he did confront her and took her hostage. When I was done, Ralph approached from behind me with his crossbow on Phasma, speaking Wookie. People were stopping to watch us act out a part of the movie. It was great! Phasma pulled this big-ass blaster out of her cap and presented to standoff with us. She walked up to Ralph and me with her finger on the trigger. We walked in a circle as if we were really about to duel. I took a second to turn around. I looked at Elliot and De' Borah to see if they would join in, but she was taking pictures and being amazed. I should have kept my eye on Phasma.

Out of nowhere, Phasma threw a rope at Ralph's Chewbacca feet, and it wrapped around his ankles, rendering him immobile. By the time I turned my attention back to Phasma, she was already in my face with her blaster. The lights on it whirled and flickered. I closed my eyes to accept the inevitable, for the crowd I was still acting. I heard the trigger click, and I opened my eyes to roaring laughter and cheers from everyone. It appeared as though Phasma pulled a page from the Joker's playbook and had bang flags shoot from her blaster. It was clever, I loved it, and I had a good time. I high-fived Phasma and had her take pictures with the group. We then continued to walk around and talked about what just happened. We didn't really give Phasma a chance to introduce herself. I wasn't really thinking about it; I was just having a good time.

When we left, I told everyone I was going to hit a vape bar, and whoever partakes could join. I also told them that I would develop the pictures I took and deliver them before leaving the city to exchange info. Everybody gave me their contact info and we said our goodbyes. Most of us were coming back for the next two days, so I knew I'd see some of them again. But two of them were tagging along with me to the bar. We met this guy named Josh, dressed as Vader while we were outside, and I invited him, too. Everyone but the married couple was coming, so I was feeling better about not having seen Zora. I was going to get high and enjoy this time I had.

Dressed like Vader, Finn, Captain Phasma, Chewbacca, my new friends, and I headed to a bar called Studio A64. It was a legal weed vape bar. They sell food and the best strains around. When we walked in, the lighting was dim, but you could still see. There was a live band playing music, but the place wasn't crowded. There was an actual bar area. They had tables where we could sit and order food, a lounge in the back, and the place still had room for the band's stage. It was my first time there, so I just took in everything. From the look of it, we seated ourselves. I nodded at everyone to follow me. I headed towards a booth towards the back that I spotted when we came in. When we got there, we saw there was an ashtray, a lighter, and wrapping paper with cones attached, right there at the table. There was a menu for the strains we could purchase to smoke, and a menu for their drinks and food. They even had an edible menu. I was impressed.

We took our seats and waited for service. When we were approached by the server, he brought 3 complimentary joints, pre-rolled. "Welcome to Studio A64. I can tell you guys are new here," said the semi-chubby server. He put his gift on the table. "My name is Jay. As soon as I check ID's I'd be more than happy to get you started on drinks or appetizers." We all pulled out our IDs, and he checked them, smiled, and handed everyone a paper menu. Apparently, they had a sale and some meal deals going for the day. We ordered drinks and smoke. Phasma was still using her voice changer, which I thought was pretty cool. The dedicated ones never break character. She did remove the helmet after a while, though. I was wondering how she would drink and smoke. After four joints, some yummy entrees, and icy alcoholic THC-infused drinks, I was not sober by a long shot. While we laughed and joked, I was actually starting to dig Phasma. But I felt guilty; I wanted to be here with Zora. However, I had to tell myself that I shot a shot at Zora and gave her a chance. Not really my fault if she didn't take the offer.

By the end of the night, we exchanged info with Josh and made plans to meet over the next couple of days for the con. Phasma was stuck to my side. I thought that she liked me, too. While bidding the rest an inebriated goodbye, I stopped Phasma and asked if she wanted to end her night with me. The thing about being intoxicated is you don't remember what you say or do—some things I could recall. I remember getting in an Uber with her. I remembered getting back to my hotel, and the acts that followed. We reached my room, and I offered her more to smoke. She declined. I tried to talk, but she wasn't really in a talking mood, I guess. I figured that she was there for just what I wanted her there for. So, I wasted no time. I approached her in the darkness of my room.

I removed her helmet and tried to kiss her. She moved away and pulled on my shirt like she was leading somewhere. She led me to my own couch. As guided me into my seat, I started to undo my shirt. She left me to my own costume and removed her own. Between the darkness and me being drunk and high, I could barely make out her face. At that point, I wasn't apprehensive. I could see she was taking off her costume. I saw her approach me, and when she was closer, my hands caressed her thighs. She felt soft and warm, which led me to kiss her thighs. As I moved in closer, she smelled like Zora to me. Not the raspberry smell or cocoa butter, just the natural smell. It drove me mad. I let out a heavy sigh, picked her up with force, and kissed her with passion. In my intoxicated state, I was ready to release every bit of warmth in me.

I got so lost in our kissing that I almost forgot to put her on the bed. I let her gracefully fall onto the bed without warning. I rubbed her head and approached her with my exposed member throbbing and already leaking with precum. Ready, she took me into her mouth, and I was shocked, and more turned on. She licked my dick like it was a popsicle. Making sure her tongue touched both sides, she would reach the tip and slurp the juices from me. I moaned, and that must have set her off. She moved to the edge of the bed and sat in front of me. Using no hands, this woman gave me the best head I had since Zora. She moved her head around as my dick went in and out of her mouth. Looking down, I could see saliva dripping onto the floor as she made my thick member wetter with every stroke. My moans got louder. I couldn't help myself.

I pushed her off and didn't even go to eat her pussy. I ripped the panties off and proceeded to enter her. I took my time. I slowly entered as if to tease her. She was already wet as I slid inside. I could feel her heartbeat speeding up against my chest. When I was all the way in, I just stayed there and let it throb inside her. The moment I moved seemed to be what put her over the edge. I moved, and I heard a gasp release from her. I moved again and again, slowly making my dick hit every wall she had. Her gasps started to turn into moans, as sweet as the first bite into a strawberry. I reached for her hands and put them above her head; I didn't want her to touch me. I tried to fill her and force her to feel only me. I wanted her restrained to just feel pleasure. Her scent and her moans made me think of Zora so much that in my mind, this was Zora. And all I wanted to do was make her feel good. I wanted her to feel safe with me, even when she was not in control. I wanted her to judge how much passion she made me create.

While my mind was on the feeling, my body was speaking it into existence. As I thought about the massive fire between Zora and me, I had Phasma squirt slowly down my penis. I kept a slow, steady pace, moving in and out of her vagina. I would hold still every now and then, let her catch her breath, and then I thrust hard, back into her pussy, to feel her shiver beneath me. I picked up the pace and fucked her harder. Her sounds turned into a mixture of cries and moans. I could feel trickles of her sweet nectar being released, and I slowly pulled out. I kissed her from her neck to her navel and lifted her leg to get a better look at the juices she was leaking. The smell of me on her took me to a place that I hadn't been before, yet somehow it was familiar. I took my lips and wrapped them around hers and sucked the juices from her. I wanted a clean plate, I wanted to make fresh juices. I sucked and flicked at her clit as she moaned and trembled in my arms.

With her hands running over my head, I could feel her muscles tightening on my tongue. I knew she was close to climax. I went crazy. I moved my tongue faster and sucked a little harder, until her hands were forcing my head more into her. Her sounds got rough, like she was fighting the feeling. I smiled a bit and let my tongue taste the inside of her. Her thighs closed in around me, and I pushed my face through to make sure I could still lick. She let a cry of pure ecstasy as she leaked juices, grabbed at my head, and quivered. I gave her no warning when I came up and slipped my dick into her still pulsing walls. The sound she made was like a cry, but softer. She grabbed my arms and tried to restrain me from scratching. It felt so familiar and good I lost myself. My thrusts got more demanding, and I sped up. Her breathing was so erratic that her moans in my ear felt like wind singing to me. The feeling of her breath on my skin and the sensual hugging from her pussy sent shaking chills down my neck all the way to my toes.

I put my hands around her neck and pulled her closer. Moving my hips in a circle, harder and faster, I could feel my eruption building. I moaned and cursed through it. Trying to hold onto this feeling, I moved faster and harder to the point where I was beating her pussy up good. I felt her finally let go and gush an entire waterfall onto my dick. That was what got me. Feeling that rush of sticky nectar flow from her glorious box made me cum so hard that I couldn't move. I stayed in her, throbbed, trembled, and caught my breath. I rolled off to the side and curled up, bringing her with me. I whispered, "My Zora," and fell into a blissful sleep.

The morning after was like the morning after prom... I was dazed and confused yet, satisfied. I remembered going to the pot bar and someone coming home with me. At that moment, it was as if I was wide awake after a shower. I immediately looked to my side and noticed the empty spot where someone had been lying. I laid there thinking. *There is only one person I know that can get away from me.* I started to wonder if Phasma was, in fact, Zora. I never told her what my costume was. I wondered if I announced it on my social page. *She can't be that good, can she? I could be giving her too much credit. Either way, I want to know, and there are two more days of play to figure it out.*

In the shower, memories of last night came to me. I was trying to force it. If I could remember her face, I'd know. Almost as if I were drugged, my mind grew more cloudy when trying to remember specific details. I took pictures, but knowing her, she probably didn't allow a good image of herself, if it was her. By the time I was out and moving to the bed where my clothes lay, I had convinced myself the pictures would be useless. I was starting to get a headache from thinking too hard. *Today is a new day. I was caught off guard yesterday, and she got me. She always does, but I will be ready for her this time.*

After tipping the doorman for bringing up my breakfast, I rolled a joint. I turned the TV on just for ambient sound. When I started to feel a buzz, my mind started floating to different areas. I started remembering that I did tell Zora that I'd play her game. *I did say that I was interested. So now it is about strategy and knowing when it is my move. If I know her patterns, she made her move last night. I just haven't found my clue yet. The next move is mine to make. Figuring out if this is the move to make that throws her off or plays into her hand will be hard.* I finished my joint and ate. I decided to go to the second day in street clothes and just be a part of the crowd. *I know she will still find me, but she has no choice but to face me this way.* I figured it was time to turn the tide. *She might be a dominant woman in her waking days, but she wants to be submissive to me.*

I got dressed and pulled out my bags. Rummaging through my luggage and pulling out various things, I finally found my portable digital photo printer. After putting everything back, I looked around the room for my camera. Not remembering the night before, I haven't a clue where I left it. Surprisingly, I found it next to the bed on the side where Phasma slept. Curious, I picked it up to turn it on. The screen flashed twice, and the low battery notification blinked across the screen. “Damn!” I sighed. As Iplugged up the camera, my phone went off. It was an alert that my Uber would be here in five minutes. I decided to leave the camera and let it charge for the day while I was out. *I can take pictures on my phone. Fitting, actually. Zora will have to get close to get in the picture.*

Patting my pockets down with my foot in the door, I made sure I had the key card for my room. I looked up and yelled for the guy standing at the elevator to hold it and added a pretty please for the yelling. After feeling my key card, I took off for the elevator, arriving just in time. I thanked the man for holding the door and let out a heavy sigh of relief. The guy was taller than me by a foot or more, at least. He seemingly looked down on me and, with a deep voice, replied, “Oui, monsieur, most welcome!” His musky voice and his French sounded scary, not clean like in the movies. I felt a chill up my spine that made me want out of the same space as him. I played off my eerie feeling by holding my smile and pulling out my phone to check on the Uber. Out of the corner of my eye, I saw him staring at me. I pretended not to notice. “Oh shit!” I said. “Sorry,” I added, and looked up at the man, “It's just...my Uber is outside. I think I'm late.” I waited an awkward silent two minutes before I responded with, “They charge you if you make them wait.” The man seemingly was just excited to be in the same elevator as me. He nodded in mutual understanding.

The situation couldn’t have gotten any more uncomfortable as the doors slowly opened. I waited to see if the threatening shadow would exit first, but he just stood there. Finally, I left, saying, “Have a nice day!” I didn’t dare turn around. That man was creepy in a serial killer kind of way. Seeing the sun outside brightened my mood. I was getting excited to see if I was right about Phasma being Zora. *She has to be. The vibe is too real. I’m almost positive it is her, but I don't want to jump to conclusions. For now, I'll enjoy my vacation and mystery until it's time to make my move.*

I was set to meet with Elliot and friends inside during a Q&A panel set for various anime creators. This way, people could stick to their regular schedules with openings for extra shenanigans. I thanked my driver while getting out. I then headed for the long line for the entrance to the convention center. When I got to the door, I just flashed my wrist band, and security nodded me through the crowd. Even though I was there the day before, I still felt like a kid in a candy store. I didn't know where to start. And so many costumes again!

There were the common ones, but every now and then, you run into a unique ensemble. For example, Phasma's costume was uniquely tailored. I ran into a *Hellboy*, complete with tail and horns. I thought I would see more, but I only saw one Pennywise the Clown from the remade *IT*. There were tons of anime cosplayers from classics such as *Dragon Ball*, *Pokémon, Sailor Moon*, and *Naruto*. There were about a hundred *Deadpool, Spider-Man, Wonder Woman, Catwoman, Superman, and Batman* costumes, all with different tweaks and personal additions to set them apart. The most interesting, I think, was running into someone dressed like Ciri from the *Witcher 3*, an underrated video game that wasn't widely known then. I didn't expect to see anyone dressed as her; I was expecting more *Witcher* cosplay following the release of the show. It was amazing seeing how many people could be so creative.

After walking around, taking pics with random awesome cosplayers, buying souvenirs and comic books, a few posters, and characterized calendars, I made my way to the hall where the Anime Q&A panel was held. Josh, Darth

Vader from the day before, was already standing there waiting. I waited for the crowd to pile in before approaching the door. I greeted Josh with a head nod due to the noise of passing inquisitors. I pointed to my ear and shook my head. He understood and shook his head to agree. At the back of the crowd, I spotted Ralph, Chewbacca; he was the tallest guy. As he got closer, I noticed Elliot and De'Borah were at his side. The gang's all here. But Phasma was missing. I let everyone talk in front of the door about how wild the night was and catch up on proper introductions. I stood looking around, waiting to see if she'd show. I was interrupted by Josh saying, "Come on, before we have to sit in separate spots." I smiled and nodded. With one more look behind me and a bit of sadness in my heart, I proceeded into the hall.

After an hour and a half, the panel was over. We got to hear from creators from anime and manga such as *Hunter x Hunter*, *Black Butler*, *Fairy Tale*, and *Naruto*. I asked a few questions, got a few autographs, and forced my way through some laughs. However, I was wondering what could have happened to Zora the Phasma, or if I had gotten it wrong altogether. Zora didn't come. Elliot broke my thoughts by asking about the photos. "Oh yea," I replied, "I forgot to put the camera on the charger, so I left it at the hotel. I'll have photos for everyone by tomorrow. If you guys want, I'm going to come back out tonight. If you wanna text me where you're staying. I'll just drop them off. No big."

"That is actually perfect! My girlfriend made dinner plans for us tonight, so I can just pick them up at the desk when we get back. Thanks, man," Josh said as he pulled out his phone to text me his hotel information.

"Yea, I guess that could be better, El," De'Borah said to Elliot, nudging him to pull out his phone too.

We walked around for another hour, laughing, and taking pictures until I couldn't fake my disappointment anymore. I said goodbye to my friends and promised to have the photos for everyone before the morning. I caught a cab sitting outside the convention center. I asked the taxi to stop at McDonald's, offered to buy him dinner, and got dropped off at the hotel. After dragging myself through the lobby, up to my room and through my door, I flopped on the little loveseat in my room and just stared at the ceiling for about five minutes. Letting out a heavy sigh, I ate my food. I rolled a nice blunt for the night. I needed a heavy high to get through the night of darkness. I didn't want to keep guessing as to what happened to either Phasma or Zora. *Jumping to conclusions and crazy stories is the first sign of trust going away. There is one more day, so I haven't completely lost. There is still hope.*

The words marching across my brain gave me new strength. Like I was never sad, I took the last bite of my sandwich and made my way to the table where the camera was. I turned on the device and synced it to my printer. I started going through the photos but noticed that there were more than I expected. I just let the pictures print, and I rolled another blunt. Halfway through the blunt, I got up to check the progress. It was coming up on the last ten pictures. I picked some up, looked at them and smiled, remembering the laughs when the photo was taken. Then I saw it. The previous image taken was her move, and she made sure I'd see it and know the next move is mine. *Damn, this woman is crafty!* The last picture was of Zora and me in the bed the night before. In the photo, she was holding up her phone on a text message page. I brought the picture closer to my face to read the message. It said,

"Same hotel. 3 floors up. 925."

I was right! She is Phasma! Now I know where to find her! Everything in me was ready to bolt for the door, but I didn't move. The thoughts of what could have happened to her today kept me from moving. I took another puff of the blunt as I walked back to the loveseat. I sat down and tried to think of an excellent move to make. *If I rush up there, I might seem too eager. At the same time, what if she was waiting on me all day? What if I was supposed to show up this morning? What if I missed my chance to make a move? I do not know what rejection looks like from her. I did not even know she liked me until now, really. So how would I know if I missed it? I think I know what to do.*

I put my blunt out and went back to the pictures. I separated the copies for everyone and put them in envelopes. With most of the area set up just for tourists, everyone else's hotels were within excellent walking distance. I planned my walk to start with the farthest and seeing Zora last. I had three different conversations in my head, and they all led to her leaving with me. Whether it be for dinner or a walk, I just wanted to be out with her. The whole time I was getting the pictures ready, I was dreading the worst-case scenario. I didn't want this to be the end. I was enjoying the chase, the mystery, and God, the sex was fucking amazing. *Zora is like no woman I've ever met. People can say pussy is pussy all they want, but there is a difference. Zora just sex either, and she makes that quite clear in business and how she carries herself. Her character demands respect even if you do not know her. It is just what happens in her presence.*

I had until I came back to the hotel to think things all the way through. I even calculated for extra time in case some were in their rooms and wanted to hang out. First up were Elliot and De'Borah. They were the farthest, and I didn't know what they were up to that night. As I approached the front entrance of their hotel, I saw them coming out. De'Borah was dressed like she was going dancing. She wore a black dress with spaghetti straps that fell to knee-length, with sequins that looked like crystals. They sparkled in the light when she moved. Elliot was in jeans with a salmon-colored dress shirt and a white suit jacket without a tie. With De'Borah in his arms laughing, I called out Elliot's name. They were on their way out on a date and almost passed me by. I handed off the photos and bid them a fond farewell, reminding them my info is inside and we should keep in touch. They agreed and happily went on their way. Pulling out my phone as I turned around, I mapped Josh and Ralph next. *On to the next stop to continue on my mission!*

Josh wasn't there; I remembered he said he wouldn't be. I asked the front desk to put his photos in the room mailbox and left. Ralph was right next door, so no journeying needed for him. Ralph was out too when I got to his hotel. Again, I asked if the photos could be left in the mailbox for his room and left. This was actually perfect. I got time to spare and think to myself, and really wanted to see Zora. When she didn't show, I started to worry. *I hope she is alright.* She has been putting on this solid front, but she is a human being, and life can kick us at any minute. *I mean, I know she is a very elusive woman and doesn't give you a chance to get to know anything about her, but if she were here for me, what could have happened to her?*

By the time I got back, excitement had replaced the worry. I nodded to the red-headed bellboy who hooked me up before and smiled at the front desk attendant as I went towards the elevators. I got on and was about to hit my floor out of muscle memory, but I drew back and struck nine. My palms were sweaty, and I really was nervous, but I couldn't wait. *I want to make it like that time she showed up at my hotel in Chicago out of nowhere. I have seen her purest form so far, and it was like her as a vulnerable woman for the first time.* The memories of that day came to me, making me lick my lips in anticipation of her accepting me after waiting all day. The doors opened, and I forced myself to calm down and walk slowly and smoothly.

Approaching her door, my smile started to fade. The side of the hall near her room was dark, like the lights had been broken or blown. I got an eerie feeling with every step I took towards it. The hallway felt cold and empty, as if no one but Zora was on this floor. When I finally got to her room, the door was not closed, but opened. I found it to be severely strange since most hotels have heavy doors that close independently. I stood outside, wondering if I should go in. This didn't feel right. Something was off, and it felt like danger signs were flashing all around me.

Despite the red flags, I slowly pushed the door open enough for me to walk in. The room was dark, yet I saw a flicker of light as if a candle were lit. Out of all the scenarios I played out in my head, I did not think this is what I would see. It wasn't supposed to be like that. It was my chance to have her all to myself. Anger, confusion, and disappointment swelled in my throat. And with tears forming in my eyes, without waiting for an explanation, I turned and left.

Her

D*amn! It got hot in this car.* I was happy when I finally pulled into the hotel. A thin, red-headed boy in a hotel uniform approached me while I was getting out of the car. "Would you like valet service, or would you like to self-park?" he asked. I handed him the keys for the valet and said, "Thank you!" with a sigh of relief.

"No problem, ma'am. Just give this ticket to the front desk, and I'll make sure your things get to your room when you check in," he responded as he handed me a ticket stub. He took the top part and wrapped it around my key ring, then he gave me an enthused smile and jumped into the driver's seat before taking off. I stood back and looked at the hotel entrance, asking myself for the hundredth time if I really wanted to do this. That inner voice was telling me, *Once I check in there, is no turning back. I have to see this all the way through.* I took the deepest breath I could and forced my legs to move.

By the time I reached the front desk, my nerves had calmed enough to properly sign the agreement and receive my keycard. Attempting to quiet the loud butterflies in my stomach, I took a hard swallow when I reached for the keycard. My tension started to calm down as I got off the elevator on my room floor. Wasting no time, I dropped everything and flopped on the bed when I got in my room.

Once I was spread out over the comfy bed, I felt completely cured. I laid there for about fifteen minutes, just not thinking. I needed my mind clear. There was a lot to take in. *Is this going to mean something that I came? Am I showing interest in commitment?* I was working my nerves up again, which was rare for me because I'm usually more in control. I was between severe fear and extreme excitement. *I want to be here because I have never been to a comic con before. Nobody really asks or pays attention to the fact I am indeed a great patron of the nerd order. That is one of the reasons I do not like getting close to people. Besides, my costume is the shit.*

My extreme excitement took over when I heard a knock at the door. I knew it was the bellhop. *No one really knows I am here except my assistant, but I want to check on my costume. The color could have gotten scuffed in transit, and it needs to be flawless.* The same red-headed valet was at the door with my bags, and he brought them along with his smile. I tried hard not to roll my eyes as I retrieved my bags. He was too perky, and it made me feel weird, like he was on drugs. Then I had to remember where I was, and I didn't feel strange anymore.

I gave a ten-dollar tip, and as I was closing the door, I said, "It's the weed," and laughed to myself. I went looking for the more minor square case. My costume was in pieces; it had to be assembled. I took every part out and inspected them. They seemed to be intact, so I put them away and finished unpacking. I was a day early and ready to explore. I wanted to get the "lay of the land", as they say. I called downstairs to ask that my rental be prepared in ten minutes. I grabbed my sunglasses and the chocolate off the bed, knowing what could be in it, and headed down.

I was driving around for about thirty minutes before I started to feel the effects of my chocolate. I knew I was near downtown, so I looked for a place to park and walk it off. Feeling the gratuitous treat from earlier, the weather, and myself a little bit, I decided to indulge a bit more. There were vendors in the square next to the grand park selling treats that I was sure were laced with marijuana. As I approached the crowds of people, I saw a sign that read, "Smoking in the Park." I laughed out loud and turned around in a slow circle to examine my surroundings.

There was more than just treat vendors. Local smoke shops had tables set up like a swap market with different kinds of strains they sell at their store. I saw temporary tattoo stations, face painters, tie dye artists, and even a flower child making flower halos. The atmosphere was intoxicating, and not just from the fumes being emitted into the air. The vibe was chill, and the people were congregating like the troubles of the world didn't exist. There were so many blends of nationalities and colors of people laughing, dancing, and singing to music. It was simply carefree, and I wanted a piece.

Realizing I would bump into people if I kept spinning, I stopped in the face paint direction. So I took it as a sign and started there. After being painted like a kitten, having a few drinks, downing four small brownies, and dancing like a nutcase, I thought it best to call it a day. I had officially worked off my nerves and I was ready to face the man of my emotional fears.

I needed to stop by a store before calling it a night. I don't like trying to pack the little stuff I can buy anywhere, like soap and toothpaste. I'll forget something and have to go buy it anyway. To save me the panic, I just get them when I get into whatever town I'm going to. I walked past a little corner store on my way to my car, so I ducked in to see what they had. I was pretty buzzed and didn't really feel like shopping, and it was pretty late. I found some simple items. I wasn't sweating the fact that they didn't have my scent or brand; I was ready to crash. This festival made me all the more excited for the comic con. I was starting to think that I made a good decision in coming.

My mind wandered to Keith while I got ready for bed. I wondered if he thought about me or if he was here already. I had serious chills from flashbacks of our encounters. I felt his hands rub on my skin and smelled his scent in the air. I laid on my bed for all of three minutes before I noticed I was obsessing. I told myself, *it's the weed. It has to be. I do not obsess, but I am the one who gets away.*

I jumped off the bed and tried to shake away the thoughts. But my mind had other plans, and I couldn't rid myself of the flashbacks. They sent the warmest chills up my spine. The more I had, the further they reached through my body. It ran through my toes, up the back of my leg, until it came to my womanly nature. I felt the pulse like a heartbeat in my pants, and I couldn't stop it. *I need a shower and sleep!* I forced myself into a short shower, then flopped back in the bed. I closed my eyes tight and tried to empty my mind until the quiet took over.

In the morning, as part of festivities to support the smoking community, a complimentary tray is left at every guest's door. There was the choice of a rolled joint or a packed bowl. I partook in a couple puffs before getting in the shower. Forcing myself to sleep was not like me. *I always find what I need no matter where I am. That's my specialty, in and out, and nothing to keep me. This guy, Keith, he is persistent, though.* I half-smiled and chuckled to myself. Still, I was intrigued. *After all the men, all the people I met and made forget me, this one guy has the time to pursue me. I kind of like the chase. This is the most excitement I have had since Montreal.* Before I could allow myself to start bringing up the past, I stopped the shower and remembered what I was doing. It was almost time to start the games.

I was careful about putting on my costume, making sure it didn't get scuffed in the process. I had my assistant dig up everything she could find on this Keith character. If he was going to be around, I needed to know something about him. At least I'd know which games to play. I stopped moving as if frozen with fear. I realized that I've had more interactions with this one man by sheer fate than I ever have when I'm purposefully looking for a new toy.

"A new toy?" the voice in my head spoke.

"Huh?" I responded. "Why not? It is fitting, isn't it? People use each other and throw them away, like last year's toys at Christmas. Why can't a woman do the same?" I was getting off track. I mustn't argue with myself.

After getting my costume on and bravely making my way to the lobby, I waved down a valet and requested my car. I didn't know how hard this was going to be with the costume on! I tried to get in the car, but the outfit was too big. It felt like if I adjusted my car where I was comfortable, I wouldn't fit. The valet tried to help me get in at every weird angle, but it was no use. I paid the boy a twenty for his effort and asked him to put my car away. I scheduled an Uber, but it would take 45 minutes to reach me. With the convention being in town, it was busy.

I waited in the lounge and ordered a drink or two while I waited. I was already excited, but now I was impatient. I get that way when I make plans, and they don't go according to how I plan them. I spent time looking into Keith and what he likes. His company is doing business with my hotel, so they practically gave me everything I needed. Being a small company, they mainly advertise themselves. Social platforms gave intricate details of their friends' backgrounds, like where they were from, what school they went to, and what degrees they each had. It wasn't hard to find out other things about him after I knew those things. *It seems we have a bit more in common than I thought.*

We both have an infinite love of all things comic book and nerd related. I'm pretty sure I let my nerd slip once or twice during our banters. He did show favoritism for the Star Wars movies. *He is on a higher intellectual level than most men I deal with. He could not have picked a better place for a nerd convention and a pot head's candy store.* I was way overdue for some sessions that didn't start because I was stressed. I read somewhere that couples that smoke together are much happier. While we smoked, we could play video games. We could spend a whole weekend playing *Dungeons & Dragons* and enjoy solitude, arguing about which version of Greek mythology is the correct version. Knowing that he could very well be my equal made things interesting for me.

Drifting too far into the daydream, I overlooked the petite, red-haired bellhop from before, as he was approaching me. I jumped a bit when I saw his hand reaching for me out the corner of my eye. He pulled back, apologized, and told me my Uber was waiting. I, too, apologized as I grabbed my helmet and made my way out of the lobby. I thanked the boy again for helping, apologized for earlier, and climbed into the van in front of me.

“Julia, right?” I asked as I got situated. “Yes!” she said, with a super awesome perky kind of attitude. “You must be Zee. Nice to meet cha! OH! I love your costume! I know where you're headed.” We both chuckled, and although mine was fake that sealed the bond, and we drove off. There is a moment when meeting someone new where you feel like you can let your guard down. The chuckle was our moment. This moment is usually followed by small talk to further ease the tension. However, I don't do small talk. I like to be forgotten as if never seen. But Julia, a pink-white lady with curls to match her charismatic nature, blue eyes, and roughly around 320lbs, was a sharer. She talked about her husband, kids, how she got into Uber, and what she thinks of the city. I just let her talk. I wasn’t really paying attention, but I did just enough to respond when needed. I picked my job at the hotel to be only friendly when I'm paid to be. I'm not really a people person. But I'm good at my job, and people skills are required.

I knew I was late when we arrived. Well, maybe not late, but it was well after it started. With the event being held next to a busy shopping area, you could tell who was here for the event and who was just regular mall shopping. Onlooker patrons were staring at the wandering cosplay dressers. The cosplay dressers were going about life as this was normal to them every day, not noticing the stares. I took in the diverse scenery as I approached the ticket booth.

The woman at the booth (who seemed younger than me) gave me a more extensive, perkier smile than Julia did. I smiled back and handed her the confirmation page Keith sent me. She looked at the paper and said “Wooo, a plus two! Your companion is already inside, just waiting for YOU!” I tried not to cringe at her over excitement. Nerds are introverts, so we have to try very hard to be friendly and interact correctly. I can't stress the "correctly" part enough that we overdo it sometimes. Hence, perky Julia and extra enthusiastic attendant. *But did it really need to rhyme?*

Good to know he was already here. I wasn't trying to be late. I actually wanted to be here before him to keep an eye on him. To see what he is like being himself and not trying to impress anyone. After getting my wrist band, I put on my helmet and went in. The moment the doors opened; it was crawling with so many different people. I didn't know where to start. I immediately was getting praise for my costume. I wanted to really show out, but I was saving it for a special moment. I put a lot of effort into this costume, and I was starting to enjoy the praise.

My first time here, and I am a hit! I saw so many other ensembles. It was terrific! I saw a couple customarily dressed, but their kids, who all looked under 8, dressed as the original characters from the first *Mortal Kombat* game. There was Sonya Blade, Scorpion, Sub Zero, and Raiden. I was amazed at the detail in the costumes. I saw an entire group dressed like the Scouts from the *Attack on Titan* anime. There were about a hundred different Spider-Man outfits. I was caught between my own excitement and my mission. But something was about to tell me that my having fun was the mission.

I almost forgot about finding Keith; I was having so much fun. I had already purchased two comic books that I had been looking for since childhood, and a few souvenirs. About an hour passed, and no sign of Keith. *This place is enormous, and I have two more days, I will find him.* Right when I decided to not worry about seeing him, someone brushed by me, looking down at their phone. He immediately stopped in his tracks. It was like a scene from a horrible 80's chick flick, where the light came in from out of nowhere. The moment turned cheesy when it seemed to slow down as he turned around. He looked at me with shock in his eyes, which made me nervous. I couldn't tell if it was from the costume or if he knew it was me. He stared at me, and I froze. My mind began to race. I totally didn't think about how to start this game. I was having fun! I forgot to.

I snapped out of it and noticed who he was dressed as. Seemingly frightened, he tried to back away as I hit the button for the lights on my helmet. “FN-2187,” I spoke through the voice changer in the helmet, “Submit your blaster for inspection!” I stood still, hoping he would get it and respond appropriately, but I started to fear that I spooked him or he knew it was me. He looked confused, looking in all directions as if he were awaiting help from someone. He slowly reached for his blaster and started to present it to me. However, at the last minute, his stance changed.

In the blink of an eye, I was staring down the barrel of a pretend blaster. Simultaneously, I recited a famous line from a scene in which that character finds his strength. Like his character in the film, he gloats and gets cocky with his rebel companions, cosplayers dressed as Chewbacca, and what appeared to be Rey. I pulled out a self-made, giant blaster that was attached to my back behind my cape. We circled around as if in an old Western, squaring off for a standoff. I noticed we started to draw a crowd, so I knew it was the moment for something spectacular. It is a vast scene that will leave everyone in awe, so much that I fade away into the background. *I found him, now I can watch him.*

Quickly surveying the area, I saw Rey was busy taking photos, and the other two heroes were enjoying their premature celebration. I went for my rope in my utility bag and threw it at Chewbacca's feet. If he moved, he would trip. By the time Keith, dressed as Finn, noticed something had happened, my blaster was in his face, and my finger was on the trigger. He stood still, and before he could take his next breath, I pulled the trigger. The lights flickered, and the self-proclaimed "BANG!" flag was projected from the end of the barrel. The crowd roared with laughter and applause. I couldn't hold back my laughter and I joined my stage mates and the public in the joyous sounds. Keith walked towards me with his hand up, so I obliged, and we high-fived. Rey ran up and demanded we all take group pictures. Others passing by were taking pictures of and with us. The moment was incredible. *I enjoyed that, and now I can say I have a memory that I made with someone.* It was feeling like one of the best days of my life.

During the crowd-splitting commotion, I heard people exchanging names and numbers where Keith and his friends were. I slipped back into the group just as he confirmed that he would develop the pictures and get them all to us before the weekend was over. Some said goodbye and went their separate ways, but Keith invited the rest out for food and drinks. I was actually having fun, and I wanted to observe him more, so I followed.

Still in cosplay, we arrived at a vape bar. It reminded me of a rave with the color and the lights. They sold THC-infused food and drinks, and they also sold legalized marijuana. We got a table, and I removed my helmet. I wasn't worried about him noticing me; my voice changer was a partial mask that covered part of my face. It almost resembled half a VR headset. It didn't have the bulging earpieces, though. I wired it instead with some store-bought earbuds. I wanted to see and talk without my forehead sweating and suffocating. It also helped that it was like a rave. There was darkness in the corners with the strobe lights flickering. We drank, ate, smoked, and laughed. I didn't say a word. I sat there and listened to the outrageous childhood stories of strangers. I watched Keith interact with them like they were old friends whom they haven't seen in a very long time. *This is a nice change of pace. This is what it is like to go out and be normal.*

When it was time to go, I followed Keith's lead. I knew where this was heading, and I wasn't going to deny him. I wanted it, too. When we got back to the hotel, I could tell he was pretty fucked up. *I am pretty sure he still has no idea that I am the one he has been waiting for.* This kind of made me question if he just goes home with random girls. My thoughts were interrupted by him offering me a joint to smoke. I declined and sat quietly for a minute. He put the joint down and approached me, and I lost that thought completely. There was more care and give this time around. It might have been the fun he had or the fact that he was intoxicated, but something told me he really felt this moment. We climaxed together, and I collapsed, breathing hard. I usually look for an opportunity to detach and get away. Before I could even think about leaving, he pulled me into him as he laid down and whispered, "My Zora," and fell fast asleep. I couldn't believe what I just heard. I didn't know if he knew it was me or if he was thinking of me. Either way, it left a slight smirk on my face. I wrapped my arms around him, s and gave into the feeling of being wanted.

I woke up, and Keith had rolled over to the other side of his bed. As much as I would have loved to stay, I just wasn't ready to get close. No matter what I felt, this was the only way. I got dressed quickly but quietly. I left my mysterious calling card like always, tiptoed towards the door with shoes in hand, and put my hand on the knob. I stood, with my heart pounding so nervously. I turned around and looked at him, peacefully sleeping. I sighed and turned the knob. *It is a good thing we are in the same hotel. I can leave and not really leave him.*

As I got on the elevator to go to my floor, I started smiling. I think I was starting to like Mr. Jefferies, and I could definitely tell he liked me, too. I was thinking about how much fun we had doing our little show for the crowd, how he would flip when he found out it was me the whole time, and how excited I was to see him again the next day. I got off the elevator and smiled all the way to my room. Like a dazed teenager with puppy love, I was moving and operating on sheer muscle memory when I opened my room door. I was so out of it, I didn't notice the object swinging towards my face. Something hit my head so hard, my ears started ringing. I felt a warm liquid on the side of my face. As I reached to touch it, I blinked my eyes and couldn't find the strength to open them. I let the darkness take me.

Still dark, I could feel the inside of my brain pulsing, and the ringing in my ears were louder than anything I had ever encountered. I tried to move but felt restrained. I struggled to open my eyes. I could see I was still in my hotel room, and the sun was setting, so it was into the next day. I glanced around the room, and next to the drawn curtains was a small end table. The clock on it read, "7:27". *Okay, it is the end of the next day, and I missed the con's second day.*

I closed my eyes tight and kept them closed. I opened them after a moment and looked down to see the tiny blood pool below me that must have come from my head. I realized what I was restrained in, and that meant only one person could be here. I was secured in a twisted homemade version of a sex swing. This swing had all the standard attachments, with hand and ankle cuffs added to devices to make for an ultimate torture weapon. With my hands suspended, I tried to see if I could feel for a buckle or lock. Breathing heavy, panicking, and frantically moving my hands around for any sign of hope, I desperately looked for an out. It all went away when I heard his voice.

A deep, ominous laugh came from the shadows. *I know that laugh. I have heard it before, but not from this side.* I only heard this laugh when my job was over. I didn't stick around for what happened after. My legs started to shake as a figure began to form from the shadows and came into the light. "Tisk tisk tisk tisk," went the voice with a heavy French accent. "Long time, cher. Long time. See I almost gave up looking. But no. The boss wanted you found by any means necessary. I guess having lookouts everywhere was a good idea after all. Did you really think you could just get away, mon amie?" Standing in front of me was Ali, a heavy, top-built, six-foot-nine, 385lbs black man.

A face from my past that I thought I'd never see again was plaguing my existence. I didn't speak. I stared him down with no fear. It was a good while before he broke eye contact and started laughing hysterically. "Woo girl, you shol' still got spunk, cher!" Ali exclaimed. He paced around me, and I eyeballed him as much as I could in my position. He slowed down as he got behind me, and I got a bit nervous when he stopped. He stood there, just breathing. My silence was vital. As long as I was silent, I was going to be okay.

He stood behind me for a while before I heard the slinging sound of metal, a pocketknife maybe, and felt a sharp point of a blade in the small of my back. He slid the blade across my back in circles to tease where he would stab me. I quivered, but I didn't make a sound. I closed my eyes tight to get ready for the impact of the blade. Seconds later, I heard the sound of tearing fabric and felt tugs on the clothes I was wearing. As he cut away the fabrics, I could see pieces of cloth hitting the floor and felt the opening of my skin from the random scratches from his knife.

Hanging naked in his contraption, his cold hands clamped on my skin, I felt disgusted as he touched me everywhere. But I made sure I didn't make a sound, flinch, or cry. His hands came from under my arms and around to my chest. Grabbing and squeezing my breasts, he got closer to me, and I could feel him brush against me. “S'posed to leave no marks if you gave a fight bringin’ you in, but you know, cher, I always liked you,” he said as he inched closer to me. His breathing got closer, and I could feel his pelvis bump against me. He pulled me in close by the back of my neck, with one hand on my hip as well. He licked the side of my neck, dragging his tongue to my ear. Not being gentle, he chewed on my ear as if it was bubble gum. The pain was annoying yet centered me at the same time. His hand moved from my hip to the bulge now in his pants. One hand rubbing my titties and rolling down my stomach to my clit, with the other hand stroking his cock. As he unzipped his pants, I bit my lip and waited for what was to come.

I never experienced Ali's malice; I had only heard stories. Girls begging to be with someone other than him. I've even seen girls marked by him, leaving scars of his work. I closed my eyes tight when I felt his plump finger touch the surface of my pussy. I tried hard not to react to him. I tried to lock my body to give him no indication that I liked anything he was doing. I should have known better. Science is science, and nothing can change that. When he put his stubby finger inside me, it didn't go straight in. He went in at an angle as if he were privy to my secret. I was right. The moment he pressed on that spot, I could feel my body trembling, and warm liquid started leaking out of me onto the floor. I whimpered but didn't cry as he fingered my leaking vagina. His breathing got heavier as he stroked himself and laughed. He took his fingers out of me and sucked on them like fruit juice just spilled on his hands. He made a sigh-like moan as he aimed his stone-hard dick at my pussy.

There was no easing. He shoved his dick right in my aching pussy and showed me no mercy. With every forcefully hard thrust, he grunted. I stayed quiet. I didn't want to give him the satisfaction. I could tell he was getting annoyed by my silence when I felt his dick get a little soft inside me. “No sounds for me, cher?” he asked, still pounding me from behind. He reached a hand forward and around my throat, and this wasn't the usual gentle squeeze. I was suffocating. I started gasping, and I felt his dick get hard instantly.

He started fucking me faster and harder. When I thought I would pass out, he let go. I coughed hard, trying to take in every bit of air I could. As I gagged on fresh air, he laughed amusingly hard as he thrust harder than ever and held his position inside of me. I let my body relax and just mentally escaped to a place where he could never touch me. I wouldn't cry or moan or scream. *I will not give him what he wants.* I heard a creak from the front of the room, and I opened my eyes. I felt an overwhelming surge of embarrassment, fear, and sadness. I wanted something good in my life, and I wanted him to lead me to it. But that dream went out the window when I saw Keith standing there with disgust and tears in his eyes. He ran off before Ali saw him. "Good," I thought to myself. Ali's laughter led me to believe he thought my tears were from him, but he just didn't realize that Keith got away.

DANGEROUS ENCOUNTER

Her

My body jerked around as if we were on the roughest road in the world. I don't think I was supposed to wake up during transit. It was my head hitting the window that made me wake up. I've been trained for these situations. *Do* not *let them know I am awake...stay calm and analyze the scene, and check for any exits you can see.* As far as I could tell, we were in an SUV with tinted windows. Ali was sitting next to me, and there were three other people, including the driver. The other three looked serious, business type, and I don't think I know them. However, Ali came to get me, so there was only one place we were going. I hoped Mom thought I was dead. At least, that's how I left things. *I never thought anyone would find me. I got away so clean.* I stopped paying attention to my surroundings and started going over my life to see where I made a slip. Flashes of things long since forgotten came flooding into my head, like I was watching it in fast forward. My heart sank with the thought of not seeing him anymore.

As I was allowing my heart to die, we were slowly coming to a halt. I quickly went back to being unconscious. I heard the car shut off, a heavy sigh from one of the other passengers, and the driver exited the vehicle. After making a two-minute phone call, Ali told the others to leave the car. "You can stop actin' now, cher," he said. "I hate phony fish.

Let’s not pretend that I don' know who you are, Neveah. Mata Hari herself. Bullshit you’re still out. HA!” I sat up and gave him the ugliest, meanest look. “Mom wants me back that bad, huh?” I asked.

“You kno betta’ dan anyone, Mom loses nothing. You like escargot here, Mata. No one has your skills, and no one ever got close like you. You may not believe it, but Mom cares. Too much if ya ask me.”

“If Mom cares that much, why not just let me stay where I was when it was known I was alive?”

“That you can ask Mom. I follow orders, mon ami. You remember my job. You want an explanation, go ask the boss,” he replied, while showing me the door like a gentleman as if he didn’t just drug and drag me all the way back home to Montreal.

Getting out of the car, the Canadian fall air hit me and took me back to the yesteryears of my troubled childhood. I had to tell myself to snap out of it. *This is not the time to be reminiscing*. I looked up and down Saint Laurent Street and immediately noticed the change in times. There were fancy new streetlights, shops and stores that were not here fifteen years ago. New bars and casinos, like a miniature Canadian Las Vegas, had set up shop where neighborhood stores used to be. I stood in front of Club Cleopatra; Mom's club handed down through generations. It was opened in the 1900s and is still standing until this day. I thought this place would fall. At least, I had hoped. The club had upgraded to a new neon sign with bright colored lights. Back then, it was home to cabaret drag shows with strippers in the back for unique clients. After all this time, who knows what kind of shit Mom incorporated here. To think that this run-down of a front for gays and prostitution would still be standing today made me chuckle a bit.

Anyone else in my position would be nervous, scared, and anxious. I lived the last fifteen years as a regular civilian, yet here I was, acting as if I just took an assignment last week. I was escorted to the door by one of Ali's lackeys while he stayed a couple feet behind me as if expecting blowback. The five-foot-six lackey opened one of the red double doors with the gold-painted handles, and the smell of weed and ass hit my nose like a fresh fart in the wind. The club was busy with patrons watching strippers on the stage, topless women of all colors walking around serving drinks and entertaining clients, and towards the back, you could see the restricted area where men stood guard. To my left, I got a glimpse of a guy in a business suit getting a lap dance and clinging to his entertainer like a little boy who hasn't seen his mother in years. To my right, all types of couples were making out at the bar. Some lesbian couples took it to the next level. The butch one was kissing the other's neck and caressing her exposed tits while men gawked and cheered. This was nothing compared to other scenes I've witnessed.

We kept walking until we reached the guards. Ali told the tallest of them to tell Mom we were there in his broken French. He looked back at me with a look that said I was in deep trouble, like an older sibling reveling in a younger sibling's demise. After a minute that felt like an eternity, we were led into the back of the club. Through the black curtains there was a long corridor with various rooms to the left and right. These rooms were for those who paid to have the services of the entertainer of their choice. Depending on how much they paid, they would be allowed to select from a list, not on the house menu. Mom had everything from straights that liked gays to sixteen-year-olds. Mom would not go younger than sixteen. Mom believed at that age, a person has some capacity to try to make whatever decisions and deal with them.

Walking through the hall, I heard noises coming from the rooms. Screaming seemed to follow spanking sounds, men moaning, and women crying out in pleasure and pain. The immature muscle, Ali, decided to laugh. The goons made childish comments about how to really "fix a bitch", using the same broken French as their idiot leader. At the end of the hallway, we followed the winding stairs up to Mom's office. Mom's office was big and secure enough to kill ten people, have their bodies carried out of the club, and get away with it. The Group has been getting away with everything for over a century, changing to make business more efficient. Mom dealt in drugs, prostitution, gambling, extortion, and even killing- and not just to set examples. Ali was one of Mom's favorite assassins. Once, a long time ago, I was number one.

Mom's office changed since the last time I was here. The floor sparkled and shone like we were walking on a giant mirror. Hesitant to walk into my death, I slowed a bit. The shortest of the lackeys pushed me along. I went for about a minute before putting up more resistance. He pushed back with more force. It started to look like we were wrestling for the first spot in line after a while. As we approached the most oversized desk that anyone could ever not need, a voice from the shadows said, "Enough now. Be nice to my Mata Hari. She hasn't killed you because she wants to know what I want. Isn't that right, Neveah?"

"Mom," I started, with malice in my voice. "Love what you did with the office. The giant windows, the shiny-ass reflective floor… I knew you were digging my comics. Got ya'self an evil lair. I love it."

"Just as smart assed as ever, I see. Age hasn't changed you, not one bit. Still fetching, too," Mom responded.

"Well," I said with a fake chuckle, "Now you wouldn't love me if I wasn't me anymore, would you, Milton?"

A heavy sigh came from the shadows, where seconds later, a six-foot-five, medium built, gray-haired man stepped out. As he walked towards where we stood, he patted his hands with a rolled-up magazine and started speaking in a tone that echoed through the office. "Imagine my disappointment, knowing you were still alive and didn't come home. You hurt my heart, child. I spent all this time mourning. Then, I see my precious daughter, grown, and on the cover of *G.Q.* magazine. Thank God Walter gets the U.S. subscriptions to the club now. Otherwise, I wouldn't have found you." He slammed the magazine on the smooth desk surface, and it slid. As he stepped closer to me, he began again. "What? Nothing to say? No smart retort? No wise-ass comeback?"

With all the boldness that I had I responded, "We both know I'm the smartest, no need to put the rest of your underlings down. As far as a comeback, I'll revel in that victory after I'm the one that kills you." The smile he gave was so warm and inviting, like seeing your dad after being away for years. The smack across my face was therefore unseen.

I expected as much. There is no way I will get away with anything at this point. But if I am going to die, I am going out as me and no one else! My face stung so sharply; it almost brought a tear to my eyes. To ease my lip from the sting, I licked it. I tasted the tiny speck of blood on my lip. This enraged me, and he knew better! *He knows I hate being hit. He knows I hate being hit in the face, no less!* I touched my lip and let out a low laugh. I pushed away from the smallest lackey I was wrestling with, and he landed in the hall. When we came into the office, I football sidestepped him so that we stood face to face. Too fast for him to see, my fist broke across his face, making him stumble and fall flat on his ass.

After the clatter subsided, Milton and Ali let out hearty laughs of enjoyment. Milton even clapped for me. “Yes!” he exclaimed. “There is my Mata Hari! Tomas, she broke your nose, guy. I suggest you let it go. I don't want to explain to your family you got fucked up by a five-foot-four bitch who could pass for a high schooler. Please, she is way more dangerous than you think.” He finished off his laugh. The tallest lackey walked over to Tomas, who was now holding his badly bleeding face, and helped him up. Shaking his head, he told him, “Let's go fix this,” in sloppy, broken French.

Breathing heavily from anger, I turned my sights on Milton. I took one step before hearing the many clicks of guns being taken off their safety. “Tsk tsk tsk tsk,” came from Ali as he sucked his teeth in disappointment. He was aiming his custom-made Desert Eagle at my head. “Come on, cher, you know betta,” he said.

“Do I? Or is it you that’s ignorant. I was fucking number one for seven years and found a reason to leave! Is that not registering for you?” I asked.

“See, I always chalked it up to you being a sensitive-ass woman, who can’ handle the job anymore. Honestly, ah don’ even know why he chose you as number one in the first place.”

"WOOOOOOO sounds like a challenge," I said maliciously. "Do you wanna fight for it? There's a reason I'm Mata Hari. Don't forget that shit!"

"This li'al' bitch thinks after all this time, she can beat me?" Ali laughed. "Enough!" bellowed Milton. "Fact, you took a life from the Group. Fact, you set to repay the life for a life debt. Fact, you can only leave with your death. Fact, here you still stand for all to see," he preached. He started pacing around. This wasn't good. Pacing meant he was in the process of accepting something he would never do. There aren't many people he would hesitate to kill. I was banking on the fact that I was one of them. However, if pushed, I could lose that spot. The nervous breakdown I was witnessing was telling me I was losing big.

Most of the goons in the room had put their guns down. Ali was the only moron trying to show he had something to prove. His arms had a slight shake from holding them up for such a long time. I smiled and flipped him off as I approached the desk. "Permission to speak?" I asked. Milton looked as if he was shocked to hear my voice. I was wondering where his head was when I interrupted his thoughts. After a sigh of discontentment, he waved his hand in approval. "I have my reasons for leaving," I started, "And I wouldn't change it if I had the chance. So, if you're going to punish me, hand out the sentence already, Judge Judy. This intimidation shit into begging for my life ain't gon' work. You know that. So, let's get this show on the fucking road already."

Staring me down with a hard-to-read expression, he adjusted his stance. He faced me fully, straightened his shoulders, and fixed the cuffs on his sleeves. "Fine," he responded, still adjusting his clothes. "You're right, I do know you're not going to beg. I also know you refuse to bow to anyone. So, what's the fuckin' point. You broke my heart though, kid. I'm still curious as to why you left. You know me, I need to know. Ali, if you wanna have some fun and see if you can get that out of her before you put one between her eyes, be my guest." He approached me until he was nose to nose with me, and he said, "Make sure no one knows she ever existed. Both identities. Make it believable. Something to bring a tear to her old man's eye, but still be proud. That's how I want to remember you. My sweet daughter," he finished, with a crack in his voice.

Two new lackeys from behind me grabbed my arms and proceeded to take me away. I resisted and pulled. I was able to yank one of my arms free, and I yelled back, "Fathers don't destroy a daughter's innocence! The same innocence she killed to protect. And they definitely wouldn't dare ask them to live with a reminder of that betrayal for the rest of their lives." His face looked like he just had his soul sucked from his body. That was enough for me. That told me that he knew exactly why I left. "Get out," Milton said, with a tone so low and broken that it took a while before anyone started to move. I was then dragged away wearing half a smirk.

Back down the winding stairs and through the hallway, I was escorted through the club. We weren't going far. *I already know how this is going to go. The question now is how many? If Ali really is going to be involved, I can expect some brutality. He likes to rough his girls up first.* The power over them turns him on, but not more than killing. He's known to choke a bitch out and not care if they die. Even if they died, he'd still have a raging boner. He was definitely a sadist.

As we were walking through the club, I tried to put together some plan. Ali would want last, and I would be cleaned up for him. He won't take sloppy seconds. However, I was betting that he would think these weasels would be able to wear me out some. I was a tough bitch to take down. If I was right, this could work. There was the hope of me getting out.

I was led past the bathrooms, to the basement door, and then downstairs to where the real action happens. Underneath the club, Milton hosted many illegal and secret attractions, like fights with men and women, and illegally drugged hosted orgies. There were parties hosted to promote the unwilling women that were newly employed by Milton and the Group. I was trying to relax and keep my anxiety in check. *If things do not go my way, I am a goner.*

They took me to the open room where the entertainment happens. At first glance, I noticed a few things. There was a sex table, designed to restrain a woman in a permanent doggie-style position. I saw Ali's real torture swing: a bigger, more stable version of what I had the pleasure of being in before. There were a few beds. Some were made, and some looked used. I was taken to a bed that wasn't touched yet and tossed with malice intent. I rolled over the bed to the other side, stood up, and fixed my hair. After wiping my mouth, I said, “Okay, boys. Who’s first?”

The three muscle heads that escorted me down laughed as they took off some clothing piece and threw it on the floor. “Boys, boys,” I started as one approached me from behind. “Was there anything you heard about me up there that said this would be easy?” When I felt myself bump into the guy behind me, I stepped on his foot as hard as possible. This forced him to lower his head to my elbow's reach. The thud of my elbow into his head was blunt enough to cause a ripple of pain through my arm. Thanks to adrenaline pumping through me, I was already aiming for his testicles with my foot when he hit the floor. Instead of removing my foot, I left it there. When he went to grab his swelling nuts, he grabbed my foot, allowing me to gain leverage to raise my other knee to his face. Rolling over that dead weight, I got up and faced the next lackey. "One down. Two to go," I stated as I squared up like we were in a ring at MGM Grand.

After processing the scene, muscle man number two got serious. He balled his fists and got into a boxing stance. That was stupid because he just told me his fighting style. We circled around each other, feeling out the scene and trying to predict the next move. I got tired of waiting and decided to throw a fake. He did, as expected, and dodged backward. Instantly, I put my foot forward to trip him. Again, as expected, he caught on and stepped backward. I gave a nod of approval, more so impressed. He gave a half of a smirk and then adjusted back to being serious. Boxing really isn't a position for one as small as me. I could counter with different martial arts, but all he would need is one time to get his hands on me, and it would be lights out for me.

After throwing some jabs, he got an uppercut in that made me stumble backward. Had I lost my footing, this fight would be over. I caught myself and bent over a little. Waiting until he was just about standing near me, I came up, hitting him in his stomach. I then stood straight up and landed a lower jab to his face as he doubled over. I started to smile as the hope of me getting out of here was getting better and better. I could knock him out, sneak out of here, and find a safe house. *Milton underestimated me, yet I am not surprised. I stayed away for more than ten years. I was good at my job. I made it work, and I do not regret anything.*

I needed to get back in this fight. *I cannot lose the upper hand now.* He got up, and we circled each other again. As bad assed as I was, some things you just don't see coming. With no warning, he lunged at me at full sprint, screaming. In a blink, he had both his arms around me, pushing all his weight on me towards the floor. Unfortunately, by physics laws, a spear from someone twice my size put me on my ass. My head bounced on the concrete flooring, and darkness was instant. *NO. NO. I lost….*

My arms felt stiff, and my head was spinning. My body was jerking from being moved. I didn't know where I was, what was happening, or who I was for a minute. I hit my head hard. I felt weighed down as if I had a weight on my chest. *What happened? Where am I right now? Wait. Was there something I was supposed to be doing?* I couldn't remember. I just hoped it was Saturday, and I could sleep in more. *I think I studied too hard for that one final.* I felt a tugging, and I tried to adjust my eyes to figure out what was going on. I blinked hard three times and saw the light. I could feel someone breathing on me. My eyes were partially adjusted, and I caught what looked to be the ceiling. There were cheap lawn lights hung around the top. *Am I in a basement?* At that moment, everything came flooding back. *Shit! I remember.*

By the time I fully came to, the last lackey already had his dirty penis inside me. He was on top of me, huffing and moaning while slowly thrusting in and out of my pussy. He rose up to look me in the eye and moaned louder as he gave me a hard thrust; the proverbial sticking it to me. My hands were tied to the bed, and he had only managed to get me out of my pants and panties. I was still wearing my bra, shirt, and socks. Noticing that I wasn't paying him any attention, he grabbed my face and forced me to look at him while he fucked me, smiling. I went to move my legs and found my ankles were bound. He let out a devious chuckle and let my face go. He stopped and pulled himself out of me. I felt a lot of my liquid leave me, which seemed to please him. He moved backward until his face was above my waist. Caressing my thighs, then moving his hands to my dripping wetness, he played with my clit for a bit before lowering his face to my now quivering lips. *Fuck! I'm in trouble.* Being a nymphomaniac, I'm not going to be able to hide or keep from reacting. It's like my fucking kryptonite.

He toyed with me; started licking at a breakneck pace on my clit and stopping, starting again for a bit longer and stopping. After a while, I found myself fighting to not shake my legs. I bit my lip and let out a heavy sigh. He adjusted himself and placed his whole mouth over my clit and started to lick and suck. Shit! I was trying so hard not to give in. I began to move my hips as if I was itching around in a seat. I was close to an orgasm. My pulsating pussy was a dead giveaway as he moaned in excitement. He put a hand on my left thigh to hold it down; he was aware of what was coming. He released his suction for a moment to breathe, and like a suckerfish stuck to the side of a fishbowl, he was back on my clit. I jerked from the shock of the sensitivity. Moving his hand under his face, he inserted two of his fingers into my pussy. Slowly moving them in and out, he played with muscle contractions my body was having.

I tried to hold my composure, but it was no good. I lost all my morals and let out a moan. Slipping his other hand under my other thigh, he pulled me more onto him while slowing down. That's what most don't get. That speeding up during the official climax is not what gets us. It just drags the feeling out until we can't take it anymore. Those of us only clit stimulated will lose an orgasm and will have to start over. The trick is knowing what kind of woman you were dealing with. Word must have gotten out that I was a leaker, or this idiot was very perceptive.

I felt the last bit of my dignity leave my body; I could feel the onslaught of my orgasm. Through the brute's fingers, the lackey felt it too. As my orgasm progressed, he hummed on my pussy as he licked the juices up flowing between my legs. I kept my moans to myself. I breathed heavily and closed my eyes as he mounted me again. His now throbbing dick slipped a few times before he grabbed himself to reenter my wet pussy. He stuck the same two fingers inside, and finger-fucked me fast. He was forcing me to have another orgasm. I couldn't help myself. The sensitivity from the first one was still fresh. I started to pant and wince as I approached the start of another orgasm—*my God.* The flood gates to my golden nectar opened wide as I began to feel my juices leak down my ass. Satisfied with the pulsing he felt on his fingers, he thrust his solid, concrete-hard dick inside me. It swelled to fit and fill my walls almost perfectly. But he was a bit shorter than average. He was good at the head for a reason. Shorties know how to make up for their shortcomings.

He grunted and moaned as he aggressively fucked me. He rotated his hips in a constant motion trying to dig, but he didn't have the right dick size. This is where he tried to create friction between his body and my clit to heighten chances of me cumming without hitting my G-spot. I could feel his dick moving against my walls, which told me he was getting his pumps in. He started to slow down, and I could feel him throb inside me. He was close to cumming. I couldn't tell if this ass hat was wearing a condom or not. *It wouldn't matter I can't get pregnant, but the fucking diseases these idiots could have.* He stopped rotating and started rabbit humping at my pussy, drawing out as far as he could without actually pulling out, then harshly thrusting back in. I let out an automated shriek from my body being hit hard with every jab.

He moaned, cursed, and pulled on my hair as he started to move faster. He was cumming, and I could feel liquid shooting out of him into me. He wasn't done, though. He kept pounding faster and faster, and his dick became rock hard all over again. He grunted louder as if he was struggling. I grabbed my restraints and pinched my eyes tighter. He held both my shoulders and fucked me so hard I couldn't help but make sounds. After about five minutes, he bellowed louder than ever. He held me tight and stayed in me as he came. Feeling relieved that he might untie me and I could gain an advantage again, I opened my eyes, and for the first time ever, I was scared.

When I opened my eyes, lackey numbers one and two were standing there, naked and stroking their exposed dicks. Their faces were bruised and knotted from our fight earlier, which somehow didn't keep them from smiling in delight. Analyzing the scene, it became clear to me that I did indeed lose. A tear formed in my right eye, and I tried hard to keep it from fully surfacing. Much to my surprise, I was pulled up and yanked to a new destination. I was thrown against the sex table and bent over. My hands were tied to the poles in front of me and my ankles to the table legs behind me. Lackey number two adjusted himself promptly behind me and shoved his dick in. He wasted no time getting his nut off. He fast fucked me, and in five minutes, he was cumming. He slowly banged at my vagina, trying to rouse his penis again. I could slowly feel him come to life as he sped up. He played with my clit as he continued to get himself hard inside my pussy. Lackey number one approached me with the intent of sticking his dick in my mouth. I closed my eyes and clenched my teeth. I prepared for the worst.

As I started to accept my fate, the party was miraculously interrupted. It sounded like the club was falling in on itself. Glass shattering, not just from broken bottles, but busting windows were most of the sounds we heard. I thought I heard something heavily solid hit something else, and the club rattled a bit. Everybody stopped what they were doing. Hell, even I was curious enough to wriggle my hand free of one restraint. I put my free hand on the ground and closed my eyes. The ground was definitely responding to an outside force. I opened my eyes to find the three lackeys staring at me as if they were waiting for an order. "Something big hit the club," I said. They looked at each other in shock.

"Who would be stupid enough to hit this club?" Lackey number one asked.

"Not sure, but if this club was hit it was on purpose" I said, "It's bad for Mom, idiots!" Forgetting about me, they all rushed to scatter. Putting pants on and grabbing shoes as they ran upstairs, I tried to free myself from the table. I looked around as I worked at the rope, spotted my pants and a crack that opened from whatever hit the club took. It looked like it led outside. It was a trim fit. Perfect for someone my size.

I thought I was dead. I felt such relief. I didn't know what happened, but I was thankful. I had the best guardian angel looking after me. Removing the last restraint around my ankle, I darted for my pants and didn't even bother with my shoes. I didn't want to chance someone coming back early. Dashing for the crack, I saw the foundation's whole side was damaged. Years of wear and tear, coupled with the impact, caused the side of the building to crack. I started to think that maybe this wasn't a coincidence.

I tried to squeeze my way through the opening and had trouble. It was really a slim fit. I tried to put my top half through first but failed horribly. I backed out and put my leg through first, and this time there was progress. I tried putting my other leg through, but that wasn't going to work. I tried to pull the rest of my body, though, and made some progress but got a little stuck. I was struggling to get through. This was the only way. I started to panic when I felt someone's hand grab my waist. At first, I fought to go back into the club. After a bit of struggling, I realized they were trying to pull me out. I stopped fighting and allowed them to help me.

After some maneuvering, wriggling left to right, I finally got free. I coughed from inhaling some of the dust, stood up, and shook off the debris. I am a person known to go about everything alone, but not so stubborn that I refuse help in the face of danger. However, I would've never guessed I would be saved by him. I wanted to keep innocent people away from my hidden world. As shocked as I was, happiness and reassurance began to take over the emotional part of my body. I thought that I would never see him again. Worst, I figured they had already killed him. I wasn't sure how much of an eye they had on me. They found me on vacation, so there was no telling what they knew.

"You look okay. You can tell me what the hell is going on when we get somewhere safe," he said, sounding out of breath and excited at the same time. "Let's get the fuck outta here!". Keith grabbed my hand and pulled me into a sprint. The tear I was holding back all this time finally fell and rolled down my cheek.

Him

Smoke filled the air as I breathed out heavy clouds of weed. I was on blunt number three; I was self-healing. Trying to process what I had seen; I took the most prolonged pulls I could muster. I stared away into the ceiling of my hotel room as I held my breath for as long as I could before letting out heavy sighs of heartache in the marijuana smoke streams. Approaching the end of the blunt, I sat up and felt the tears I was trying to hide fall on my cheek. I wiped them away and ashed my blunt. My mind was swirling, and I had way too many questions. Something just wasn't right, and I could feel it. My anguish was trying to figure out if I really wanted to know or not.

Seeing Zora with that man from earlier brought up a lot of worries. *Was he coming from Zora's room earlier? Was she really here for him?* I was starting to wonder if she was moonlighting as an escort or something. I shook my head at that thought. *That guy looked rough! He reminds me of one of those old war vets that can't let go of the past. I don't see how Zora could fall in with his sort.* I poured myself another shot of the hotel's cheap whiskey and downed it. It stung on the way down. I couldn't wrap my mind around what the fuck I walked into. *Was it the shock of the entire scene or the fact that I saw Zora being fucked by someone else that is eating at me at the moment*? I seemed to have worked myself up trying to figure it out. I didn't know what could be said to me at this moment that could make me feel better or adequately explain things so that I don't have this hole in my heart.

After sitting around for about forty-five minutes, I started to pack my things. I left out clean clothes and the picture of Zora. I avoided it until everything else was packed. I wasn't sure what I was going to do with it. *If I keep it, will it hurt? Can I throw this away and not feel bad or sad that I didn't mark it?* I was tormenting myself again. Apparently, I was a glutton for punishment as I walked over, picked up the picture and just stared. Putting it back in the same spot, I grabbed my clean clothes and headed for the shower. After picking up my clothes, my pocket started to vibrate. I pulled the mobile device out of my pocket with disdain. It showed as unknown, and I didn't care. I sent it to voicemail and threw the phone on the bed. Walking into the bathroom, I could hear the phone resume vibrating, but again, I didn't care. I just wanted to wash the smell of depression off me before I started to become it.

Lacing up my sneakers, my phone started to go off yet again. I picked it up and saw the screen flashing unknown again and got confused. I stared at it until it stopped and went to voicemail. *I will listen to whatever it was on the plane. I am in no mood for anything right now.* Again, my phone started going off from the same unknown caller. I got pissed and answered. Before I was able to speak, a distorted voice came through and said, "Do you have a computer, or a tablet? Over the phone is unsecure. Set yourself up and go to the site I just texted you. The text will automatically delete five minutes after I hang up. You don't have time to try to analyze this right now. It's do or don't. If you care about her and want to help. Go to the site!"

The line clicked, and the screen blinked to the lock screen. The call was over. Still frozen, I watched a text come in from an unknown sender. I didn't hesitate. My body moved on its own. I grabbed my laptop from my other bag and tapped impatiently as I waited for it to connect to the hotel's Wi-Fi. Opening the text, I put the link in my browser with shaking hands. The first time it told me it was an error. I started to sweat as I pulled the phone closer to my face as I reentered the site. The screen went black. It stayed that way for five minutes. The text had disappeared, and I didn't know if I put the right place address in. I felt like a failure. Something was going on, though. Whatever it was, it had something to do with Zora.

Fear had me frozen in one spot for another ten minutes. I was worried. I didn't know what to do, expect, or think. I was about to give up, when visual snow came over my screen and then readjusted to a widescreen. The image was blurred, but it looked to be a silhouette of a person. They adjusted the screen, but the image was still a blur. “Keith? Mr. Keith Jefferies, yes?” the voice asked.

“Y-Yes?” I answered and waited. I didn't want to ask questions, and I didn't know what to ask anyway.

“Good. You're not panicking. At least not on the surface. I need you to sit and listen. I know you got questions. Rather, needing answers to questions you don't know to ask yet, is that about, right?” he asked.

“Well, yea. Right now, I need information before I can ask questions,” I said, wiping the sweat off my forehead.

The figure on the screen let out a heavy sigh before he started talking again. *I know this feeling. I better not interrupt until he finishes.* “I'm sorry that you had to see what you saw. I'm sorry that you have to find out these things about someone you deeply care about. This is a secure chat room. We can't be traced or recorded here. However, there are still things that can infiltrate it. Hence, the blur on my face and my voice being distorted. I will tell you my name, but when we meet. All I can say to you now is Zora is precisely who you think she is. All business, hard-working, and a force to be reckoned with. But those particular skills came from being molded from a different profession. Not an ideal one for a young lady, but she managed to get out. And then they found her. I love her like my own daughter. I did everything I could to keep them off her radar. But the fault of old age, human error, and letting the job become me has put her in danger. I can't save her myself. Just know if I tried, more than she and I would perish. I'm sorry to put this burden on you. I don't even know if you have the skills necessary to pull this off. But she needs help and needs you."

"As we speak, she is being transported home to our boss," he continued. "This will be dangerous. Very dangerous and probably won't make it home. We work for bad people. I just wanted her to be free. If you care about her and want to help, there will be a ticket to Montreal waiting for you at the airport. I couldn't put you on the same plane. That would be reckless of me, throwing an unknown into the mix. They will have a head start of about five and half hours. So be prepared to see her with bruises, something like what you saw already, or if my speculations are wrong, worse. Saving her from any torment cannot be your thought process right now. You can't do anything to prevent it. Deal with it so that you can focus more on saving her life. If you don't let yourself, get wrapped up in the battles, we can win the war, okay, son? I won't wait around for your answer. They'll call me if the ticket isn't picked up. I will tell you as much as I can when we meet. The rest is up to you. The plane leaves in two hours and fifty-seven minutes. Good luck."

Damn. Damn, damn, damn, damn, damn! That's all that came to mind. Never mind that I didn't get any of my questions answered, let alone asked, but I was left with another decision. *What the fuck did I fall into? Who am I to say that I can save her from something unknown? I have no idea what I'm walking into. Necessary skills? What kind of skills are we talking about? I put Zora in every profession, from secret agent to ninja. I took a judo class at the rec center, but that's about all I know. Oh, man!* I was starting to think I was over my head. I stood up and began to pace around. Is *this worth my life? Do I care about this woman that much?* I stopped walking when I caught a glimpse of the picture of Zora. My heart sank where I stood. I would feel like complete shit if I did nothing and then hearing of something tragic. *I* ***do*** *care that much. I don't know what I'm doing, but it looks as though I have to try and help.*

I arrived at the airport an hour and a half after hanging up from the unknown helper. I got out of the cab and stood there looking at the people on the tarmac. *Montreal, huh? Okay. I can say I had an adventure, at least.* I walked straight up to the customer service desk. I saw a manila envelope with the initials "K.J." on it in the basket behind the desk. I rang the service bell, and a small white girl with seemingly yellow bleached hair emerged from the back. She walked up smiling, showing all her pearly whites. I think I even saw wisdom teeth. "Hi! What can I do for you, sir?" she happily asked as she approached the desk.

"Uh, yes. I was supposed to pick up my…"

"Oh, yes!" she interrupted. "You look just like your picture, Mr. Johnson. I can't imagine what it's like losing your things in a new country. But your uncle let us know you were coming. And he was able to provide everything for us to help you." I wore the most confused look as she walked around behind the desk area and gathered more than just the envelope. She pulled out a case from under the desk, a white envelope from a safe, and then she grabbed the manila envelope. "I hope you had a nice time here. I mean apart from the "losing your things" bit. Lucky to have an uncle in politics, though, right?" she asked jokingly as she placed everything on the counter. "Here is your ticket, your plane leaves from gate H8, and your personal effects are in the envelopes and case. Is there anything else I can do for you today?" she asked, clapping her hands together.

"No," I said, satisfied. "I can't think of a thing. You've been great!" I grabbed the items and walked off. Putting the case on top of my other bag on a cart, I pulled over to a sitting area. I opened the manila envelope and poured out the contents. I was surprised and creeped out that there was a new I.D. with a fake identity, and my real face. They kept my initials, but now I was Kevin Johnson. I put the passport and I.D. in my backpack. I opened the white envelope and found it packed with Canadian currency. I even found a Visa and MasterCard with my fake name on them. I looked around to see if I was being watched, and to survey my surroundings. I took out the two cards and grabbed a handful of bills. I then put the envelope in my bag. I went to look at the case, but it had a lock on it. I wasn't sure about that. I started to think that I was crazy for going through this. I was nobody. I was heavily doubting myself.

After checking my bags, I wandered around the terminal until they announced loading for my plane. I kept the locked case and my backpack. *I hope to watch some Netflix or listen to some music until I drift off. I do not want to think about anything until I land. I do not have enough information to try to think any of this through. The person that is helping me knows what they were doing and is obviously sticking their neck out for Zora- and has been.* I was starting to eat my words about there not being an explanation that I would understand. Being kidnapped by your old Kingpin of a boss is definitely understandable. I laughed a bit at this part, knowing Zora would get my goofy comic book reference. The more I thought about it, she was reminding me of Black Widow. I felt a surge of bravery come over me when I realized this was like Nick Fury just called in Hawk-Eye to save Black Widow, his number one spy, from danger.

I took my bags off the conveyor belt and turned around with a hopeful smile. I pushed through the crowds of people, following the exit signs. I got outside and looked around. People were being picked up, cab drivers advertising for tourists. I just stood there, taking in the scene. After a while, my smile started to fade. I had no clue what to look for. The whole flight over here, I was telling myself I was some kind of hero, and I don't even know what my first move is. I took out my phone to see if I missed any calls or texts, but it was dry. I hadn't missed anything. I rummaged through my bag for the envelopes to see if I overlooked anything, and sure enough, I had.

In the manila envelope was a stack of folded papers. It was confirmation for a rental from one of the airport rental places. I quickly turned the luggage cart around and ventured back through the airport. With newfound enthusiasm, I found my way to the car rentals and checked in without problems. They brought me a Trailblazer and helped me load my things into it. I took the keys and thanked them for their assistance.

Sitting in the rental, I got comfortable. I adjusted everything to my liking. I was ready to go now. I just didn't know where.

Again, I was left with the feeling of failure. I didn't have time for this. At the same time, I understood why everything couldn't be so cut and dry. *Come on, Keith, think. I have seen enough movies, T.V. shows, and comics to know how to figure these things out. He could not come to get me yet left me a way to get to somewhere on my own- but with help. He left me the car, so I could move on my own.* I started looking around the car and noticed the navigation system in it. I took a second look at the reservation. Reading through it, I found that this particular rental was requested. Also, most Trailblazers have their GPS systems built-in, not installed. I turned the navigation system on and waited. It looked normal, and there were no places starred. I pushed the home button, and the system automatically set a course. I hit the wheel in excitement and started the car. All I had to do was drive. Hopefully, there were answers wherever this road was taking me.

I made sure I followed the navigation system step by step. When it told me, I arrived at my destination, I felt like maybe I made a wrong turn. I got out and stared down at what looked like an abandoned amusement park. I hoped I was in the right spot and wished I weren't, at the same time. The place was giving off a severely creepy vibe. It felt like I was waiting on the Joker to pop out from the shadows with his maniacal laugh. I walked over to what looked like a chained gate. As I tried to move the gate, the chain crumbled into rusty dust. Starting to feel unbothered this far, I said out loud, “Shit, how long has that been there?”

I drove further into the park and didn't see any sign of life. No one could be here; it was too desolate. I came too far for this to be a dead-end. After passing what seemed to be the Ferris wheel, I saw the light. I stopped abruptly and saw the light was accompanied by a shadow. I got out and just observed. I didn't want to go, “Hey, are you the creepy guy that called me?” I walked around the car to keep sight of the light and shadow. Before I could notice, I felt the barrel of a gun against my head. My heart was pounding so loud, I couldn't make out what the guy holding the gun was saying. I was too scared to ask him to repeat or say “Huh,” so I remained quiet and still. “Who are you and what are you doing here?” he repeated.

“Oh,” I started, “Okay see, I'm not sure. I think the guys fooled around with my GPS and sent me to the wrong place. I just think I'm lost, honestly.”

The gun-toting man patted me down and took my fake I.D. out of my pocket. He walked around me, which brought his gun right between my eyes. I held my breath and tried not to look scared, but at this moment, the fear had left me. I was trying to figure out the best way to survive to get back to saving Zora. After staring at me for about a minute, he lowered his gun and motioned for me to follow him. I exhaled with relief and followed him. As dark as it was, I could still make out the path we were taking. From my rental, we passed many stands that looked to be where carnival games were played. As we passed what used to be fairgrounds, I saw small buildings. The letters “KAE” with a space in front of *“k”* and between *“a”* and “e” was out front. It was probably a skating rink way back when. Passing the picnic area and some run-down bumper cars, we came to a shutdown carousel. We walked past the different ponies and through the middle, then stopped in front of the maintenance door. I was expecting him to flip a switch and see lights come on, and then the puppeteer behind the scenes would pop out. I put too much into that thought.

There were no switches or wires, but it was hollowed out and revealed a staircase that led under the carousel. I tried to hide my geek-out moment at the sight of the most astounding secret entrance I had ever seen. I kept my smile and nerd noises to myself as we walked down the manmade stairway to the dank yet dusty basement. I imagined us descending deep underground and walking until we uncomfortably started sweating. Again, I was putting too much thought into it. As soon as the ceiling cleared his head, we were on the ground level. It looked like a homeschool had been set up down here. Old portable chalkboards were turned in the corners, school desks and chairs were scattered around and collecting dust, and a few actual desks were positioned throughout the mess.

"In 1923, Montreal saw Belmont Park open its gates and put smiles on thousands of residents," came a voice from the shadows. A man wearing a brown jacket and what looked like an old striped baseball cap stepped out. He was heavily built, clean-shaven, and bushy browed. "But by the end of the 1970's, the city saw that the park was pulling in more than the city-owned park. For three years, small things started happening. It took a robbery, vandalism, and even a sex scandal to keep the gates from opening to the Montreal patrons. But it was an unnecessary police raid in 1983 that brought the owners to close. No charges against the park were ever brought up. 'Til this day we don't know who called it in or why. But the embarrassment of the raid was enough to give the park a bad name and close its doors for good. It was then that we knew that someone had the entire police force in their pockets."

I approached the mysterious man and waited for the silence to be broken. The elderly gentleman walked to an old desk, took his hat off, and placed it down. "You must be Keith," he said.

"Yes, sir," I responded.

"No sir needed," he chuckled in his strong French accent. "You are a brave man! Coming all this way. I can't tell you how 'appy I was to see she had someone in her life that cares. Attachments are hard to come by in her line of work."

"I'm sorry but, can you tell me what the fuck I stumbled into?"

"I'll let Miss Zora tell you her story if she feels you're worthy. What I can tell you without her blessing is that she used to live a different life. To the Group she was young Mata Hari. To me, she was just Neveah. I watched them train her and take her emotions like they were stripping her soul. The best at her job and it earned her a number one spot with Mom. Our boss was proud of his creation. Mom, aka Milton McWilliams. Irish descent. Family came here in the early 1900's. Milton is the fourth generation to run the Group. Neveah found a way out. And I helped. She led them to believe that she was dead. I did everything I could to keep them away."

"I tend the club for Mom. Have been for forty-five years," he continued. "The magazine subscriptions, we get some from the U.S. We never really get those, so I signed up for it. You know, keeping up my job. I didn't know she'd be in one. Mom noticed and recognized her right away. They tracked her to her job and found her assistant. The girl, Ciera, was one of mine. I placed her there to keep tabs and keep a contact if needed. Neveah didn't know. CiCi was tortured into giving up where you guys were on the weekend. Left you out to them. But she told me. If not for CiCi keeping you a secret, there'd be no hope."

"So, being an unknown, as you put it, we have the element of surprise...right?"

"Not so much. No offense to you, but our surprise would be more efficient if you were a black belt or something. But we'll be able to cause a distraction big enough to make a move to save her."

"With all the time that has passed already, is it possible for her to still be alive?" I moved more into the light so he could see the look on my face. He looked back as if he didn't want to answer the question. He looked behind me to the guy that brought me in and nodded. He replied in French. Even if I did know a few phrases, it was way too fast for me to catch. The elderly man replied back and gave me a concerned look. "Tell me," I said. "Please! I need to know," I begged.

"You don't need these things on your head if you're going to save her," he replied with a sigh. Turning away, he went on, "Just know she is alive."

"Well, how do we know we have time to properly pull off your idea? What makes you think we can get there in time if she is still alive?" I became aggressive during the questioning. However, these were bits of information I needed to know. I wasn't at ease. *I am ready to do anything to save her, but I do not want to risk my life and then find out she was killed before I got there.*

"Look," the older man started, "Mom approved 'fun time'. He really wants to know why she left. She's being tortured for it. Until she gives him that reason, she won't die. She's been highly trained to withstand almost every torture tactic known to man. She is a deadly killing machine. She knows that if she doesn't tell him, the longer she'll have to stay alive and figure something out. Have some faith in her, please. Right now, I need you to focus on the task at hand. Let's get to her first. And we can argue semantics later."

He picked up his hat and walked towards a door in the middle of the basement. After disappearing behind the door, he re-emerged, carrying an armful of things. Under his arms were rolled-up papers. He placed them down on the same table he picked his hat up from and went back into the room. I noticed the papers looked to be floor plans and city-drawn maps. Knowing I could not read French, I was still trying to figure out what the plans were. I snapped out of it when he placed a heavy case on the table. The case looked like my small case with the lock on it, still in my rental. I found out moments later why it probably had a lock on it.

The more significant case he opened was full of guns and ammunition. I stood gawking with my mouth open in amazement. I stood back and let them work while they loaded the few small firearms. They caught my eye, and the older guy asked, "Have you ever fired a gun before, Keith?"

"I went to the range a few times, but I never shot at anyone."

"Okay, that's good. Just know it's you or them, okay. There is no trying to save them. Being an unknown has its disadvantages as well. They won't hesitate to kill you dead. Got it?"

"Got it," I said nervously. "So, this plan of yours, what do I do?"

He swept all the papers off the desk, picked up the city map, and pointed at a building. "This is Cleopatra," he said. "The building is over a hundred years old. Mom may have remodeled the inside and outside, but he never got the foundation resealed. There is a crack in the foundation here, where the basement party floor is," he stated, pointing to a corner of the drawing.

"If we hit the crack the wrong way or too powerfully, won't we bring the whole building down?" I asked, being serious.

"Now I know why she likes him," he said to his companion. "Yeah, which is why we won't be blowing shit up, ya junkie," he said, giving me the "whoa there" look. "We're going to set off a suspension bomb under their SUV on the other side of the building. The explosion will create a shockwave that will rattle it like a small earthquake."

"Ohhhh! And the crack doesn't provide that side with proper support so it will crumble under the building, making a bigger crack and possibly an opening from the outside!" I said excitedly. They laughed and went on explaining the plan. He talked as if he were confident that I understood every detail. I asked questions where I needed to, and he explained without judging. It seemed nuts and crazy, but what I did understand was I was saving Zora. After a while, I was going over the plan.

Wrapping up all the details, the older man nodded to his associate. The silent man took the case up the stairs. He came down, and the other man approached me. "The case?" he inquired. "You still have it?" I responded light-heartedly, "Yeah, in the car."

"Leave it there," he said. "When we get Neveah out, you give it to her."

"I don't know if I can get used to that name," I said in a sad voice.

"Don't worry," he replied, patting me on the back. "She likes Zora better. Neveah is a reminder of her past. I'm just used to using it. So, are we ready?" he asked.

I stood up and gathered whatever emotions I had and answered, "As I'll ever be." He patted me on the back and gave me a look like a proud uncle. He motioned to his companion to move out, and I grabbed the small case in front of me. We headed through a back entrance that led to another side of the park. What I can only guess to be his and his companions' vehicles were sitting outside. As we loaded the cars, preparing to meet a war, he spoke. "By the way, they know me around the club as Walter, but my friends on the force call me Billy."

I watched Billy's associate plant the device in the SUV sitting outside club Cleopatra. The plan was to plant the device and drive the car into a specific part of the building. The cue for me to act would come once I saw him get clear. Nervous, I kept a watchful eye on him. Seeing the momentum pick up, I left the van we were in. Billy was to go so no one would see him. Walter was still a valuable member of the Group. Billy's companion ran from the car, and I followed parallel to watch for impact. The moment I heard metal scrap concrete; I pushed the button on the device Billy gave me. It wasn't a loud crash or explosion. It was more like a hard bang. I saw the building rock left to right and heard a commotion from inside the club. I stood frozen for a minute, not knowing when to take my chance. I ran around to the spot where the crack was supposed to get bigger. I saw it there, a clear line of sight into the basement.

I couldn't see a thing, being across the street. I heard people screaming as they ran from the club. I glanced back to see if anyone was coming my way, and then back to the gap in the building. I felt so useless. I felt like I should have run into the club, guns blazing, like some modernized version of Clint Eastwood. I was sweating from anticipation. "Come on... Come on!" I found myself saying out loud. Keeping an eye for anyone coming this way and looking back to the gap, I started to get impatient. I felt as if I should be doing more. I closed my eyes tight, trying to pray she would make it to the gap. While my eyes were closed, I heard shuffling coming towards me. I ducked behind the car that was in front of me and waited. I was so nervous, and I had no idea what I was going to do. As the sound got closer, I looked around on the ground to see if there was a weapon I could make or use. My foot hit a sizable rock that I quickly picked up. I stood at the ready for whomever to come.

The footsteps got closer, and I clutched my rock as if it were an extension of me. I inched closer to the front, ready to pounce out. As the shadow came closer, I didn't hesitate. I lunged out and hard clocked the figure in front of me. To my surprise, it was a woman! Before people start losing their minds, this woman was taller than me, head clean-shaven and carrying a gun that would have shot up the entire club. She looked like she just abandoned the Dora Milaje from Wakanda to join the Irish Mob. I didn't feel bad about knocking her ass out. It was probably a good thing, anyway. I was looking at everyone as an enemy. Immersed in my victory, the sound of a brick hitting the ground startled me. It came from where the gap was. I circled back around to get a better look. I saw a tiny figure that I was all too familiar with trying to get out of the gap. At that moment, my heart took over, and nothing I did was of sound mind.

I sprinted off into the direction of the gap. I kept my eyes locked on that area. At the same time, I saw everything in my peripherals. People were still running and screaming from the club, cars were now trying to fly down the streets, and shirtless men were examining the vehicle that hit the building.

I almost got hit running out without looking. The clarity of my goal made it possible for me to dodge in time. I wasn't losing her again. I was determined to leave this place with her. I was even prepared to take her home if she was dead.

When I finally made it to the gap, I was so out of breath, my chest sent pain through my body every time I inhaled. I told myself that it was the panic just now registering to my body from earlier. I approached, and no sound came out of my mouth. I didn't know what to say. All I knew was that you do not sneak up and startle a master killer. I saw the struggles she was having. I felt stupid just watching, and then something like an invisible slap to the back of the head pushed me forward. I ran closer, climbed down to where she was, and grabbed her waist. She tried to fight me off at first, but then she came out with ease. I figured she would fight, not knowing who was here. *Would she be happy I came?* I wondered, tugging to pull her through the gap.

I started to doubt my position in her life and felt my grip slip. I shook my head, saw how far I came, and my grip tightened. After a few minutes, I pulled her all the way out. By that time, you could hear gunfire from around the corner. I looked up in shock. When I looked back at her, I felt a warmth come over me. Whatever had my words frozen a while ago was gone. The first thing that came out of my mouth was, "You look okay."

PAST ENCOUNTER

Them

Zora and I ran for what felt like eighty miles. I needed to catch my breath. I looked behind us to make sure we were clear. Turning back around, I spotted an alley, and I dashed for it. I got to the middle of the alley before I came to a stop. I let go of Zora's hand and put it on my own chest. My heart was pounding so hard it felt like it would rip out of me like a xenomorph from *Aliens*. I leaned back on the brick building behind me and just stared at her. Zora walked around with her arms across the top of her head. She was breathing just as heavy as I was. She seemed to be looking at both ends of the alley. I pushed off the wall and walked over to where she was pacing. I grabbed one of her arms, and she turned with a surprised look. As I stared deeply into her brown eyes, which shone even at night I forgot where we were and what was going on. I pulled her in close and put my other hand under her chin to lift it.

No words were needed. I kissed her, and she welcomed me. I felt the tension melt off of her body and respond to the warmth I was putting off. She wrapped her arms around my head and kissed me back with so much passion, the alley could have caught fire. I closed my eyes as my tongue explored hers. I welcomed her back, washing away reality in our kiss. She felt so good in my arms. For the two minutes it lasted, nothing else mattered, and all with the world was right. As Zora slowly pulled away from me, I let out a sigh of exhilaration. I felt like life had been breathed back into me. It was at that moment that I declared to never leave Zora's side.

"Are you okay?" I asked as reality came back to us. She stepped back and stared at the ground. Whatever happened to her there was flooding back to her, and it showed on her face.

"I..." she mumbled. She played with her hands and turned away from me. "I really don't know what to say. I've seen and been through a lot. And nothing really shocks me anymore. But when I saw your face, I... I just didn't know how to feel. I never thought anyone, let alone you, would come for me. I never wanted you involved in my life. I'm sor..."

I approached her with such haste as if she cursed at me and said, "Don't you dare say you're sorry. If you regret meeting me on the airplane, say it. If you regret spending time with me that first night in Chicago, say it. If you regret showing up at my room, seemingly having no one else to turn to, having me there for you for whatever you needed at that moment, say it. If you regret coming out to Colorado with me, meeting new friends, expressing a side of you not everyone has understood, and having some fucking fun, fucking say it. But don't you fucking say you're sorry for coming into my life. You apologize for almost getting me shot!" I expressed as I pointed towards where we ran from. I lowered my tone and approached her closely again. In the softest voice I could muster, I replied with, "I'm not sorry I know who they are. I'm not sorry you made me chase you. And I'm not sorry that I love you."

As the words left my mouth, I was expecting to be shocked at myself. All I felt was anticipation and fear. *This was real fear. I do not think I have ever been so afraid in my life. What am I thinking? She is an assassin and a master at manipulating emotions.* I was losing my mind in those thirty seconds. I was ready to accept whatever harsh rejection she was about to hand out. When she turned around, the anger, the doubt, and the fear had all disappeared. Her eyes were swollen with tears, and her face screamed humbleness. I don't think I've ever seen her look so genuine. She rushed back to me with arms wide and jumped into my arms. She started crying into my jacket, borderline sobbing. I was shocked and relieved at the same time. "Has no one ever told you they love you and meant it?" I asked in her ear. She slid down from me slowly and looked up at me as if she were ashamed to answer.

Before she could go into it, we heard a car screech toward us. It came too fast, and we didn't have time to get away. Frightened, we stood still until I heard a familiar voice shout, "LET'S GO!" from the car window. It was Billy's friend! He found us, thank God, and I was so happy. I said nothing to Zora as I grabbed her hand and ran towards the car. "I'll explain later," I said to Zora as I opened the back door and helped her in. I joined her in the back seat, and he took off before I could close the door all the way. We turned the corner and I leaned with the car's weight. The door hit me in the hip as it forced itself shut. "Man, how'd you find us?" I asked.

"You are still new to this. It was most obvious how long you would run before you needed to catch your breath, and only an idiot would think to be safe in an alley," he replied in a stern and severe tone. My pride was hurt a little, so I fake chuckled, and patted him on the back.

I sat back and leaned on Zora. She gave me a warm smile as we went along for the ride. I could only figure we were going to the abandoned park. I sat up, and she put a hand on my knee. “First,” she started, “Let me say thank you for coming for me. I fought hard as hell back there and just when I thought it was lights out, there was that explosion. I wouldn't be here without you.” I smiled back, and before I could explain, she reached ahead and patted our driver on the shoulder and said, “Both of you!”

“I had help,” I replied.

“About that help,” she said in a curious tone.

I laughed a bit and said, “I was given a choice I couldn't refuse.”

“You'll have to tell me that story when we are laying down. But what's the plan now?”

“Honestly, I've been letting my body move on its own. The crash wasn't my idea. I went along because I was worried about you. I needed to know you were safe and okay.”

“Okay so now we figure out what they'll be doing now. If Walter was still in the club, we'd have a line of sight.”

“About Walter...”

“Please don't tell me he's dead!”

“No! No. No. Don't worry. It's okay. We're almost there and things will be explained for us both, I hope.”

When we finally arrived at the abandoned park, Zora's reaction was that of familiarity. She wore an excited smile as if the park were still open and couldn't wait to try a ride. She didn't need an escort like I did. She ran through the maze-like park, straight to the secret carousel door. She opened the door like a child entering their grandparent's house. I followed her down the dank stairwell, and I was enchanted watching her. It didn't matter that we were still in danger. I think I was just so relieved she was safe. The panic I had in my chest, wondering about her, was no joke. I never wanted to feel that again. Even if she didn't want to be with me, I'd still be by her side.

Billy was waiting for us in the room. Zora saw him and shrieked with happiness. "Walter!" She ran to him and hugged him tightly. I watched what looked like a daughter reunited with her father after fifteen years.

"I'm here, love! I'm right here," he replied, hugging her back. "I didn't see you at the club and then Milton said you ordered the magazines, so I figured you'd think I was mad and I'm really not. I was so worried!" Zora went off on a hysterical rant. Walter/Billy laughed heartily and let her go. He snapped his fingers, and his associate came forward with the case I brought to Montreal. Zora turned, and I swear I saw stars in her eyes. Now, I was seriously interested in what was in the case. I was starting to feel like Brad Pitt in *Seven*, wanting to ask what's in the box.

I watched with anticipation as Walter/Billy turned the numeric lock towards her. She tapped on the case before putting in the combination. So, the case was Zora's. I expected some really high-tech spy gear, but I let my imagination take over processing this whole ordeal. Inside the case were two especially custom-made sawed-off shotguns. They looked smaller than normal ones, but I think they were made to fit her.

The metal looked as if it was painted black, with shimmering, white lines. The design looked like it was dancing around the guns. The handles were silver with shiny gold triggers. They looked cool as shit, and she was excited to have them back. However, as happy as I was for her to have her toys back, worry washed over me. “Uh, Billy,” I said in a nervous voice. “Why did you say Zora, I mean… Neveah would need those when we got back?” At the sound of her real name, she looked at me with such embarrassment. I hated that I even used that name. She also looked confused at the name Billy. She turned to Billy and waited for an answer.

Billy stepped back, letting out a heavy sigh. Before he started talking, he pulled out a little black box from his pocket. When he put it on the table between him and Zora, it became clear it was a digital recorder. Billy took a dusty chair from the other side of the room and pulled it up to Zora’s side. He sat down and took off that old baseball hat. “This is Frederico Summé. He is my Lieutenant. We are the only ones left of this outfit,” he said, motioning towards his associate. He put his hands on Zora’s arms and guided her to sit on the desk. “Ughhh, kiddo. I’m sorry I couldn’t tell you everything. I did what I could to get you out. I even placed a really good second generation undercover with you to make sure you were okay. I set it up, so she didn't know who I was, just needed to know her job. There was no direct contact. But there were protocols in the event of something going bonkers. Ciera, your assistant, was one of mine. They got to her because of your job, not because of a connection to me. They haven’t figured out that I have a badge yet. But after tonight, it won’t take them long to figure out who helped you and where we are. We have about two hours tops. You know Mom has other badges in his pocket. So, someone will dig up the old files.”

“Wait. So, you’re the fuzz!” Zora spoke with a nervous crack in her voice. “You’ve been working for Mom for over thirty-five years?! How did you pull that off?” she asked.

"When the park here closed up because of that raid, my captain then was convinced that Mom or his then boss had some politicians and Mounties in their pockets. My unit was handpicked by my captain. We were the known line walkers, the good guys who never took a bribe and upheld the law with pride. Started with seven of us. Now... Just me and Fred. We infiltrated The Group from the ground up. I started running errands and numbers and just made sure to keep up pretenses to move up. One of us moved up fast and, well, life can take a hold of you. He turned on us and outted my captain and the others. Me and Fred came in late, so we weren't known to those already under. No one else knew about this outfit. So, we got stuck playing parts. I foiled some things and tried for so long to throw a monkey wrench in their whole program. But for every shipment I stopped, three more were coming in as backups. I couldn't do it with just me and Fred. And it took years before I could try to figure out who on the job I could reach out to. By then, I was Walter everywhere and no one even remembered who Billy Browne was," Billy told us.

"Life was good to you, Walter... eh... Billy," Zora responded. "Why not just leave? Take an early retirement? You had already been there too long by the time I came along."

"Yea, I guess I was. I'm not sure. Maybe the officer in me just couldn't leave knowing how many people were being hurt in my presence."

"You didn't owe anyone anything. Especially not some snot-nosed kid who bugged you every day."

"I was ready to leave once. But there was something about this one person...I couldn't just leave her behind." I could see the tears welling up in Zora's eyes again. Even though I knew he meant her. “And when you left, I had to be sure he’d never find you. I’m so sorry that you’re here right now, kiddo.”

“No! No... No, you saved me. I have a really good life over there.”

“But still being antisocial and hard to read, I see. This young man here surprised me. He’s got balls. I like him. Try to keep this one for a while, please. I’d feel better if I knew you were taken care of properly.”

“Yea, see. I’m looking at it like I’ll be doing all the protecting,” she said jokingly, turning around and winking at me. I felt warm. That solidified my vow to stay by her side. There was nothing and no one to make me leave it. “Now, you said we have about two hours. What’s the plan?” Zora asked.

“Me and Fred called in some favors to some old timers whose families have been plagued by The Group since the sixties. Some former Royal Navy friends set up some militia groups on the border. Word is Milton knows I’m missing and someone helped you. He wants you dead. He is leading the army that will destroy you and whoever is with you. It will take him a while to find us. There are some dots he still has to connect. My unit’s paperwork was still filed like any other undercover unit. He will find us. I'm too old and tired to run. I know you're tired of running,” he said, nodding towards her guns.

“A fight is coming. I don’t want people to die for me. How do we keep the casualties down? Do I give myself up?” she asked, and my body moved on its own. I blinked and was about a foot away from her now. She read my body language perfectly, and she turned to look at me in my eyes. Without saying a word, she smiled and gave me a look of submission. That told me she gave up the idea of going quietly.

Billy stood up from his chair and said, “Looks like you mean too much around here to just be handing you over. No. We fight. And on our own terms. Not just because or for you. But with you.”

“Okay, so how do we end him and the Group?” Zora inquired.

“In the time we have left, that is up to you, kiddo.”

“Me? Why me?”

“Because we never had anyone to turn on Mom and the Group until you. People tried to run and turn before, but they never lived long enough to give us anything. You were inside. You were close to him. When I helped you leave, I filed you away as a confidential informant. The report says you went into the Domestic Violence relocation program, so no one will ever know your name unless you want them to. I just need your story. Doesn’t even have to be the whole story, just bits to fill in what I’ve already reported. With this, we could open so many doors to so many investigations. I won’t force you, though. I know how you are about not wanting to share. But I think also, Keith earned his right to know the loveliest woman I have ever had the pleasure of knowing.”

Zora hesitated. She looked scared and nervous. She looked at me, covered in dust, debris, scratches, and dirt, and after a while, she nodded. “Okay. I'll do it. I can’t run from my past forever, right? I'd rather face it head-on with people I know care about me.” Picking up the recorder, Zora took a deep breath before turning it on. She put her hands together in her lap and turned to look at me as if she were speaking directly to me. “Every good story doesn’t start at the beginning. It starts where it matters. So that’s where I’ll start.”

Neveah

My life was never a warm one. I have always had it rough. I never knew either of my parents. I was a fire station baby, which ultimately meant ward of the state. Sure, they put me in foster homes and group homes, but I didn't stay. I was rebellious at a young age. I felt out of place everywhere I went. It didn't help that there was something wrong with every home they sent me. I was either used in some low-level con, or almost raped. I couldn't trust anyone, so I kept running, and they kept sending me to places. One day, after I turned sixteen, I stayed away.

In 2004, after my sixteenth birthday, I decided I could take care of myself. I fought off all vermin types, and the streets felt like home to me more than any place. I picked pockets, snuck in warm areas when it was cold, and stole things I needed. They didn't come looking for runaways in a particular part of town. I learned from earlier attempts. Mounties that were in the Saint Laurent Boulevard area were not there to catch criminals, nor were they focused on any crimes. Where the hoes and thugs hung was the same place where the cops hung out. I made my home in abandoned project buildings off Le Plateau, or Mile End. I traveled to the Vegas Strip of Canada to pick my marks. Drunks not noticing a small girl in their pockets, thugs with hearts of gold willing to hand me food, and transsexual males wishing they were women and looked at me like the daughter they could never have. I spent my money on necessities as needed and grabbed things I wanted. I kept a rich collection of American and Japanese comic (manga) books and video games. I stayed content.

I became friendly with some bouncers and head henchmen for some of the Group's leading men. They would pay me to go get them lunch or deliver a message. I did anything for a dollar except give my body away. I was feisty, and I fought off creeps like that. Some took the hint, but some still needed me to remind them. For the most part, I felt like I made a name for myself with the people that ran Saint Laurent. I smoked a little weed with the younger goons of their gang. They helped me get adult things I couldn't get on my own. I even started to trust a few of them. However, I learned that knowledge of the Group was not knowing the Group the hard way.

After getting a tip on a small delivery job from one of the club's dishwashers, I decided to stay out later than usual to see about it. It was paying more than my routine, and I was curious by nature. The only reason they'd pay so much is that it was necessary, too important for just anyone. I was looking out for number one, so I thought I could finally get away with whatever I was getting. I was to show up at the back door of the Cleopatra. Not knowing then that it was the big boss's hideout, I went with a plan to run off with whatever it was and leave the land for good! I heard about the programs in America for kids like me, and it sounded a lot better. I could even get emancipated at my age with no parents. As brilliant as I was, I should have known it was a trap.

I arrived at the back door five minutes earlier than expected. I said bye to some of the drag queens leaving for the night and told them I was waiting for Shaemus Malone. A few chuckled and told me good luck and went home. Confused by their remarks, I shrugged it off and kept waiting. I picked an excellent cell phone last week from a tourist. I pulled it out to play the games while I waited. The bartender, Walter, came to fetch me after I had been waiting thirty minutes. As he left the club for the night, he pointed me inside and told me to follow the black curtain to the back and take the stairs up. I did as I was told, with no thought about what kind of person I was dealing with. I walked into the entertainment area and looked around. It looked like I thought a strip club would look at my age. There were stages with poles, an extensive set with multiple poles and a bar covered with everything from confetti to unfinished food. I was disgusted already, and just wanted to collect whatever and get my money.

I finally made it up to the big office. It was decorated like an ancient opera house. Greek statues in the corners, the curtains on the windows were thick and red like stage curtains, and potted plants gave it a definite old man vibe. “Hello?” I sang in the seemingly empty office. I heard what sounded like someone with a severely runny nose, and I jumped as I turned around. In the shadowy part of the office was a table that could only seat two in the corner. It was next to a window that did not have curtains. I guess it was to let the moonlight in. I saw a thin, round-headed man bent over the table. He looked like he was sniffing the table. “I'm supposed to deliver something for Mr. Malone?” I said as I moved closer to the man. As I got closer, I saw he was playing in some powdery substance on the table. When he turned around with the powder on his nose, I knew now that the sound I heard earlier was him snorting cocaine.

I took a step back when he howled with a cackling laugh like the Joker. After more sniffles and snorts, he finally said, “Thank you for coming!” like he was a circus ringleader. He laughed more and came out of the shadows. I grabbed hold of my bag's shoulder strap, and he wobbly walked over to the lighted area. He stood a few feet from the desk where I stood. “You're uh, Doll, right?” he asked. “It's Rag Doll,” I said, annoyed. “Right! Right, right, right...... rag, rag, dolly dolly,” he sang, waltzing around the room now. He went to the wall behind the desk and disappeared. I backed up towards the door slowly, ready to run at a moment's notice.

“POP!” he exclaimed as he reappeared. He was tweaking hard off that shit, and I was getting uncomfortable. He held a thick brown envelope in his hand. I was thinking it was whatever I was delivering and put my hand out for the package. “Aht, aht,” he began, “You can't get paid without doing the job first.”

“Okay?” I asked, confused. “So that's my payment, and not the package?” He grabbed my shoulders and walked me back to the desk. “Tsk, tsk, tsk, this IS THEE payment,” he said, laughing hysterically after.

“Alright!” I exclaimed.

“Yes! That's the spirit!”

“What am I delivering?”

“Um... um. Um...um, um, ummmmmm?” he sang while tapping a finger on his head like he was thinking of something good to say. I guess the cocaine kept him from proceeding with his standard hook line and sinkers. He then told the absolute truth. “YOU!”

I tried to turn and take off running, but he was too fast. I felt the tug from my bag and turned to him, holding tight to the strap. He laughed out manically and yanked at the strap.

The fucking coke in his system made him about ten times stronger! I was flung backwards into the desk. I fell to the floor, face first. The stinging made me think about that time I ran away in the dead of winter, and the cold, icy, mountain Canadian air hit smacked me in the face for days. "Hmm," he expressed. I felt his hands on my jacket, pulling me to my feet. He stood me up and straightened me out. I was already pissing myself shitless from fear, but at that moment, I almost had hoped I could get away. Like a plastic bag in the wind, that hope was gone.

As he pulled his arm all the way back, my eyes grew big, and everything slowed down. I stood frozen, helpless to stop the incoming punch. I saw his fist come forward with all its might and contact my stomach as if I were watching frame by frame. The impact from the punch made me double over in agony. He caught me and stood me up and hit me again. This time was more vital, and I almost threw up on the floor. Instead, saliva ran from my mouth uncontrollably. I coughed hard, and he laughed and stumbled backward. I thought that I could get up and run since he stepped back. When I tried to move, the pain ran through my body faster than my own blood in my veins. I coughed again, starting to feel really grim about my survival.

I had come to hate his laugh. It pissed me off something terrible every time I heard it. He walked away, laughing, back to the table with his cocaine on it. He took another hit and exhaled loudly as he returned to where he left me drooling on the floor. He squatted down and moved the hair away from the front of my face. "You're pretty," he said. "I wonder- if we add colors to your face, will you look prettier?"

"Da... fuck does that mean, dickhead!?" I forced the words out through labored breathing.

"Hmmm... Melvin, tell the lady what she's won!"

"Just fucking kill me already. This game is lame."

"Oh no, no, no, no, no, Doll! No killing... I'm not done yet." Shaemus pulled me back to my feet. He tore the bag off my shoulders, my jacket off my back, and threw them to the floor. I was in so much pain; all I could do was gasp. He held my face in his hands, admiring it like he was going to paint my picture or something. Before I knew it, I felt the back of his hand across my face. He repeatedly slapped me until my lip was bleeding, and I uttered a cry. "Yes! That's the music I want," he said, licking my face where the blood dripped. He threw me onto the desk, face down. I had little strength left. I tried to struggle as much as I could, crying like a big baby. I was scared for my life, and for the first time ever, I wished I belonged somewhere.

While I was struggling, he laughed- that stupid, fucking high-pitched laugh. I was making it hard for him to use his other hand to undo his pants. I took that as a victory. It was short-lived when I heard his pants hit the floor. The fear in me increased so much I froze and forgot to struggle as he slid down my pants. Something instinctual snapped in me, and I immediately came to my senses when I felt his skin pressed against mine. My arms were flailing all over the desk. As I was trying to grab hold of the edge of the desk to pull myself away, I felt something. It was long and had a tip. I didn't care if it wasn't sharp; the point was good enough for me.

I swung my arms backward. With all my strength, I pushed the object in his flesh until he backed away from me. I turned around to see what I did. Looking down, I saw my hands were covered in blood. Also, I saw that I was holding a letter opener. I glanced up at him as he was holding his arm. *I stabbed him in the arm?* He was pushing himself backward with his pants around his ankles, still smiling. He pulled his hand away from the wound in his arm and licked the blood. He laughed again, and it drove me insane. If he had not laughed, I probably would have just run, but he laughed that stupid laugh!

The look on my face went from frightened to angry. I scowled and even growled a bit as I approached him, clutching the letter opener. Either he was whacked for real, or the coke was frying his brain, because he laughed more menacingly as I got closer. I stood over him and lifted the letter opener in both hands, like it was a heavy sword. I held it there, hesitating, thinking if I could actually take a life. This dumb fuck raised his bloodied hand and slowly wiped it across my still-exposed twat. In a red light of rage, I plunged the letter opener in his chest several times until I was out of breath. When I realized he was dead, I backed up in shock. Still clutching the letter opener, I backed into something hard. I slid down it and just sat there staring at his body. Tears ran down my face, but no sound came out; my eyes didn't react or blink. I wasn't sure how long I was sitting there. With my face still stinging, stomach in a knot, I stayed where I was and eventually passed out from exhaustion.

In my sleep, I heard echoes of several things. Coming to, I could hear various footsteps, distorted voices, and a slight ringing in my ears. I tried to blink to bring things into focus, but the sound in my ears kept me from keeping my eyes open. I shuffled a bit and hit the potted plant next to me. The noise ceased, and I froze. I heard heavy footsteps approach me, and I tried to open my eyes. I could make out a silhouette of what looked to be a man. There were other figures in the background; however, my blurry eyesight stayed on the one coming closer.

I clung to the letter opener in my hand while inching backward, still covered in blood. My pants were still down. I blinked a few more times so I could see better. The man approaching me was wearing a fancy suit and I couldn't tell what color it was. When he stood above me, I let out a small cry and trembled. He stooped down. I closed my eyes and tried my hardest to swing the letter opener. I barely had the strength to pick up my arm. It must have looked pretty pathetic; the room erupted with a thunderous roar of laughter. I didn't know what to do. I opened my eyes, and the man's face started to come into focus. He had a square face, strong jawline, and bushy brown hair. His mustache made him look like an average uncle, at least to me. His smile was genuine and endearing. After a moment, he stood up and stuck a hand out to help me up. Hesitant, I jerked back and stared at it. "Aye, lassie, no one will hurt ye' now. You've proven that you are not to be trifled with, girl," he said, and the room exploded in laughter again.

Still holding the letter opener in my left hand, I put out my right to grab his outstretched hand. He pulled me up, and I immediately pulled my pants up, then backed further into the corner. I looked around the room frantically, trying to see if I could run to freedom. There were four guys in suits standing over Shaemus's body, speaking a language I had never heard.

The bartender that let me in was standing at the door, and a slender, dark-haired woman in a fur coat stood next to the man that helped me up. The man that helped me up turned and disappeared behind a piece of the wall. He returned shortly with a chair from the little table in the corner. He didn't get too close when he put the chair down between him and me. I looked down at the chair and then back at the crowd of people in the room. I did this repeatedly, wearing a new phase of anxiety on my face until the man turned and said, “Okay. Everyone out. Liz, you stay Hun, will ya. Walter, bring my friend here some water and uh, order her some real food.”

My breathing was getting heavier and heavier with the confusion surrounding me. What the hell is going on now? I thought. I just stood frozen, watching everyone leave. The lady, called Liz, moved to the desk and took off her coat. She was wearing a sparkling, gold dress that went all the way to her ankles. She threw her jacket on the desk and sat on top of it. I turned my attention back to the man, who was motioning to me to sit in the chair. I was very skeptical. I didn't move. After about five minutes of huffing and staring, he threw his hands in the air and said, “Al'ight. I won't force ya.” He walked towards Liz and put his hands in his pockets. “Now,” he began, “What are we going to do here?” I raised the letter opener and backed further into the corner. He looked back in confusion. My actions compelled him to move towards me with the most endearing face. “No, love. No. I meant it when I said no one would hurt you,” he assured me. I slowly lowered the weapon and calmed my breathing. He smiled as if he had won and turned to pace.

With his back turned to me, I slowly inched over to the chair and sat down. I was tired. I was reasonably confident that this guy wasn't going to hurt me. After about twenty-five minutes, the man’s four different phone calls, watching Liz “powder” her nose three times, there was a knock at the door. It was Walter, and he had food.

After clearing its previous contents, the man brought over the table and set it in front of me. Walter, put down a glass plate, started taking the food out of the bag and putting it on the plate. Out of his pocket, he pulled out a bottle of water and some aspirin, put it next to the plate, and took his leave. I stared at everything on the table. The man stood next to me with a smile. He looked like he wanted to see me eat. His phone rang, and he stepped away.

While he wasn't looking, I took the water and gulped it down. I was so thirsty. It burned on the way down but felt so cool on my throat. With just a drop left, I placed the bottle down. I picked up the plastic fork and dug it into the single-serve lasagna Walter gave me. It was so good, like home cooked. I forgot where I was and let my guard down. I was hungrier than I thought. I noticed my food smile had formed across my face.

The sound of Liz's laughter made the man turn around from his phone call. Laughing at me, she pointed and called out, "Milton look!" I didn't think she was supposed to do that. Instead of the smile I'd seen, he looked furious. I didn't move anymore, and the smile went away. He approached Liz so fast she didn't see it coming. He pulled his arm back and slapped her with the backside of his hand. "My name, you whore!" he expressed angrily. Frightened, I reacted automatically and kicked over the table, trying to run out the door. As I ran past the man, now known as Milton, he grabbed me. I kicked and screamed. "CALM DOWN! STAY CALM KID!" he yelled as I yelled. Just having eaten, I couldn't put up much more of a fight without making myself feel sick. After a while, I stopped struggling, and he set me down on my feet. Breathing heavily, the man asked, "What's your name, girl?"

"Rag Doll," I said in a huff, and crossed my arms as I slowly backed away.

"No, your real name."

"Neveah."

"Neveah. That's pretty. Got a last name?"

"Dubblen," I replied, and he let out a hearty laugh.

"Well, whaddya' know!" he exclaimed. "That's where me pa is from!"

"You're Irish living in Canada? What's wrong with you?"

"Oh Yea... quick on ya feet I see. It's a family choice."

"Was he family?" I asked, nodding to the piece of shit by the door.

"He.... Is complicated. I tried everything to protect him from the outside world."

"By helping, you mean letting innocent little girls waltz right into their own doom?"

"I never wanted anyone to get hurt! Let alone kids, for God's sake!" he yelled. He swiped his forehead to wipe away the sweat. He paced in a circle, then walked over to Shaemus. "My own nephew. Into little girls. He was smart to keep it hidden. If you hadn't fought back, I would've never known. Apparently on his orders. The two goons he had working for him were keeping me in the dark and getting rid of the evidence."

"Why don't you just let me go to the cops and get them all out of the picture? The girls before me can get justice and your hands are clean."

"Oh no. I'm sorry. I can't let this be associated with the club, or me."

"So, what now?" I asked, trying to be complicated. I was preparing to make a clean dash for the exit if he said something about killing me.

"Now. We go for a ride. I'd like you to come with me."

"To where?"

"To get justice," he said, with a devious smile. He turned back and motioned to Liz to follow him. Liz jumped off the table and picked up her fur coat. She clicked and clacked across the room in her black high heels and sashayed out the door. Milton put an arm out for me to follow Liz. I let my guard down a little and went along with it. I figured that running would definitely solidify my death. I didn't see a way out, and there was no one looking for me.

I had to force myself to stop thinking of all the bad things that could happen while driving. I stared out the window of the car with my head pressed against it. Listening to them talk, I heard Milton say I was too valuable to let go. I was still trying to process the shit that just happened. I still wasn't sure what exactly was going on. One moment I was nobody. Now it seems I can't leave this guy's side. All I knew was I killed this guy, Milton's nephew, in self-defense. *He has to be someone important on the underground circuit, and it sounds like we were on our way to meet some guys.*

I started to doze off due to the ride's smoothness when suddenly, it was no more. When the car jerked hard to the right, I sat up and looked out the window. We were driving on dirt. I turned around and looked out the back window, and it looked as if we were in a landfill; nothing but dirt and construction trucks were scattered about in the space. Milton patted my knee, and I turned to sit down. I anxiously looked forward to seeing where the hell we were going. All I could see were shadows of odd figures out in the distance. As we got closer, the clouds came into focus. Three other cars were waiting in the space with men in a circle surrounding two more men.

All the cars had their lights on dim. However, when we pulled in, our lights were bright. We pulled up to the crowd, and everyone turned around. I saw men with guns standing around the two men in the middle. The short, stubby one was bald and had a scar across the top of his head so big, I was wondering how he was alive. The spot ran from above his left eyebrow to what looked like the middle of the back of his head. The taller one was skinny and wore a long black ponytail. Milton patted my knee again, this time with a smile. Liz, the driver, and another man I didn't know got out of the car. The doors closed before I could muster up the courage to ask if I could get out too.

I stayed where I was. I didn't want to imply anything, nor give Milton ideas. He approached the crowd and began to speak. I could barely hear what he was saying. I sat there just watching as different men took turns talking and pointing at the two in the middle. I squinted my eyes as if it would improve my hearing, and it didn't. I heard Milton say the words "disgrace" and "girls." I figured he was addressing his nephew's actions. Putting some things together, I was betting that the two in the middle were in charge of Shaemus. Milton's voice got louder, and he turned around and pointed back at the car. I could only assume he brought me up in the conversation. Some of the guys turned around to look. The guy to Milton's right reached out and touched his arm and spoke. Milton looked as if he said a very enthused "yes." There was a familiar roar of laughter throughout the crowd. I relaxed and rolled my eyes.

Milton put his hands up to quiet the crowd. He walked into the middle of the public, where the two outcast members stood with their backs to me. He stood there for a while, so I could only assume they were talking. The stubby bald guy reacted fast and hugged Milton. I thought something good would happen. The short man let Milton go, and Milton made a move too quickly to see. In the next second, I heard a loud pop in the air, and the short man fell to the ground with blood coming out of his ears. I shrieked at the sight and covered my mouth. Hyperventilating, I heard the tall man cry out with pleas. His words had now turned into deep sobs, and he was slowly getting low to his knees. I saw the tall man look up at Milton. With the same fast movement, another pop went off in the air, and the tall man fell backward on the ground. Milton turned around to what I thought was to walk away. As he walked past Liz, who seemed to wear a pleasing smile, he grabbed her arm and threw her into the middle with the dead outcasts. Before she could beg for her life, Milton had shot her right between the eyes.

I continued to panic. I didn't know what to do. There was nowhere to run. Even if I did, I didn't know where I was. As Milton walked back to the car with his driver and another associate, I started to tremble. By the time he opened the door, I had tears in my eyes and had moved all the way to the other side of the car. He got in the car and looked at me, confused. That scared me even more. He sighed and put his hands in his lap. The driver got in the car and asked, "Where to, Mom?" Milton hesitated before answering, "Let's get ice cream. I feel like ice cream is the perfect comfort food right now."

"You got it," the driver responded. He started the car and pulled off. I stayed as far away from Milton as I could. I made sure fear was written all over my face so he would keep his distance. The driver slowed as he put earbuds in his ears. I could hear music coming from them, and it was loud. It made me suspicious. *What is it exactly he isn't supposed to hear?*

Milton kept his hands crossed on his lap within my sight. I just sat there and stared at him. His confused look was replaced with a look of contentment. When the car hit the normal road, and I could see streetlights, I turned towards the window. I heard Milton shuffle in his seat, so I turned to see, and he had inched to the middle of the back seat. I grew nervous and angry at the same time. We sat like that for about fifteen minutes before I grew impatient. “Look. Like I told your nephew before he got shanked, kill me now cuz this game is lame!” I shouted. Milton let out a quiet chuckle.

“I told you already, no one is going to hurt you. Not even me.”

“I’ve seen what you do to people that trust you.”

“No. You’ve seen what I do to people I couldn’t trust.”

“Is that supposed to be a threat?”

“No. It’s a clue. Me telling you that no one will hurt you, and what I do to people I cannot trust should be very big clues.”

“Dude. I’m fucking sixteen. How am I supposed to deal with all this?”

“With my help, I trust you could land properly on your feet. If you’re willing, that is.”

“Willing? For what?”

“To work for me. To let me help you get on your feet. Maybe get back in school. And I’ll get you some interesting classes if you prove you can keep your grades up. I know you’re a smart girl. I just need to make sure that the beautiful brain of yours doesn’t go to waste. I wanna help you. See, you killed my nephew. Law of the Group dictates a life for a life. But I refuse to take the life of a child. No matter how close to an adult they are. Don’t get me wrong. I think at sixteen you’re fully capable of making decisions and understanding that there are consequences that come with those decisions. So, if you decide to turn me down and go back to the streets and, say, end up a hooker, I would not judge you- because somewhere along the line you made the decision to do that for whatever reason."

"I can turn this offer down?"

"No. But I was using it as an example."

"Bad example."

"Maybe so. Point is, you come to work for me. Let me help you. And we call it even in life. You can live and be something more than you are right now. Or you can think you can run and die for your troubles. Your choice. And I don't need an answer now. How 'bout you think about it over ice cream?" he asked as the tires made a screeching sound and the car came to a halt.

We pulled up in front of a diner. It looked like it was shipped right from the sixties. On the outside, it looked like two old streetcars that had been welded together. It sat right on the curb, with no steps. Milton got out and walked around the car. He stopped in front of my door and opened it. He didn't force me out; he just stood there and held it open. I hesitated for about 10 minutes, trying to see what all my boundaries were. I had to think about this the smart way. I finally got out of the car, letting out a two-year-old huff. He left the door for his driver to close and ran ahead to open the door to the diner for me. He was acting like such the gentleman. It was honestly the nicest anyone had ever been to me.

I walked into the diner and saw that it wasn't that crowded. A few people were sitting in the booths against the massive window on the sidewall. Only one person was sitting at the counter. I walked to the end of the counter and took a seat. I folded my arms and put my head down on the counter, facing away from Milton. My options needed to be weighed. *I killed someone from the Group, so it demands my head. If I decide to live in servitude, I live. And maybe become some underground gang queen in my later years.* I mentally chuckled at that idea. *On the other hand, I could take my chances and run. I just saw him kill three people. Why not? The Mounties probably need info on the Group. I know his real name and where they operate.*

I started to gain hope and tried to figure out how to play everything out. I was inside my head when I heard the sound of Milton's voice. As I tried to drown him out more, a grey cloud started to move in over my plan. In my head, another me came from out of the shadows and said, "You idiot! Because we know those things, it's more dangerous. He won't stop till we are dead. And who knows how far his reach touches? He already said no cops for his OWN nephew. Big time mobster boss, you bet he got badges in his pocket." I was right too. *Damn! What am I going to do? What's the worst he could do to me? Adopt me?* As silly as that idea was, the reality of that made me shudder in terror.

My thoughts were interrupted by a light clang in front of me. I totally dismissed the medium height, fair-skinned, middle-aged, red-headed server walking around. She placed a bowl in front of me, and it grazed my arm. The cold coming off the bowl made me snap out of it. When I lifted my head from the counter, there was a hot fudge sundae topped with whipped cream and cherries. Not only did it have fudge sauce on the top, but caramel sauce too. I started to feel weird. I looked at Milton, and he was wearing that caring uncle smile. Somehow, he was also giving off the endearing grandfather vibe. He appeared to have the same sundae as me. Looking at the spoon, I was trying to decide if it was poisoned or not. Something wasn't right here.

In my head, I said, “Fuck it!” picking up the spoon and taking a spoonful of the delicious cold treat in front of me. It was so good and didn't taste funny, but something was definitely off. This sundae didn’t use traditional vanilla ice cream. This sundae had been altered using chocolate chip cookie dough ice cream. The way I ALWAYS modify my sundaes in the Mile End. I dropped the spoon out of pure terror and jumped out of the seat. The few people in the diner turned to look. “WHAT THE FUCK IS GOING ON HERE, MAN?!” I yelled angrily...

“Calm down, kiddo!” Milton cried.

“No! No one just does that! How do you know about my ice cream?! To the very fucking detail? EXPLAIN!”

“Listen! Listen! Just sit down and I’ll explain, I swear! Just give me a chance. I gave you one,” he pleaded. *He has a point. Shit! He has a good point.*

I tried to calm my breathing as I reapproached the counter slowly. I looked around, and everyone was still staring. Milton apologized to everyone and offered dessert on his tab. I grabbed the bowl as fast as I could and moved over so that there was a seat between Milton and me. I sat with the bowl in my lap, took a big scoop of the sundae, and shoved it in my mouth. I wore a testy look as I enjoyed my treat. Milton sighed and tried to move to the seat in between us. I took the spoon and pointed it like a weapon, and he stopped moving. I motioned with the spoon for him to go back. He slowly sat back in his chair. I took another spoonful of ice cream and waited for him to start speaking. After about a minute, he was ready.

“It would seem,” he started as he too started to eat his ice cream, “That my nephew has a specific taste in girls. He was keeping tabs on you. He tried to catch you two months ago but you eluded him. He was angry and had his men find out everything about you. The plan was not to kill you but to make you surrender to him for years. But, well, we all know how that turned out." I rolled my eyes and continued to eat my ice cream. There was silence for about six minutes before he started up again. "Look. You don't have to live with me or anything. I'll set it up so you're not sleeping in abandoned buildings anymore. Your own space. You go to school. Even if it's one of those online thingies. I'll make sure you have what you need. You'll work. And I'll arrange for some extra activities, like fighting and shooting. Learning things for a particular trade. I honestly think you have great potential for it. And in return, you work for me once your training is complete. Become one of my lieutenants. I see a bright future with you by my side. Protecting me. At the same time, you'd earn respect from everyone on Saint Laurent Boulevard. Wha'da ya say?"

He let his spoon drop, and it made a clanging noise as it hit the counter. When he looked up at me, I was sitting there, stuck in my own thoughts. The scoop was in my mouth backward. I was looking past Milton, dreaming about what I thought my future could be. It was almost as if a fire was lit under me, and I was instantly hooked by the curiosity of it all. How would my life change? Traveling to different places and seeing other people. I sat there daydreaming and said nothing to Milton. His laughter broke my daydream and the silence. I jumped, and the spoon fell out of my mouth. I caught it before it could hit the floor. "Quick reflexes. Good! You'll need them," he said, standing up and reaching into his pockets. He pulled out a wad of bills and paid the friendly red-headed server. I sat there for half of a second after watching him walk towards the door. I quickly put the bowl and spoon down, thanked the lady for the treat, and ran to catch up. I made the conscious decision to change my life that night. I went with Milton and became the Mata Hari of Canada.

After being sent away for four different types of combat training, superior shooting instructions, training with monks, spending a year getting my GED, and another year and a half earning an associate degree in business administration, I got my first official assassination assignment. It was low level, but I took pride in it. I wanted to prove that all the hard work I had put in had paid off. I was told that I needed to do a couple things to finalize with Milton and the Group. In my head, all I could think was getting jumped in like any other gang you heard about in America. I was far from nervous, or at least I thought.

I was back on the land for about five months before I was contacted. Milton wanted me to come to a different location from the usual club Cleopatra. All I received was a text with an address. I stared at the address for what seemed like forever, trying to figure out what this place was. I was going to find out anyway, so I snapped out of my daydream and gathered my things. I was ready but not nervous. I wasn't sure if it was appropriate to be excited about someone else's death. I guess I still had compassion in my heart and that thought was enough to change my excitement.

Driving through the streets brought back memories. I fast-forwarded through the unpleasant parts but slowed down to enjoy the good features. I lingered on that night that got me on this path in the first place. I started wondering if I would still be alive if I hadn't taken Milton's deal. I felt grateful, yet at that exact moment, I was wondering if I should be. I almost missed the place, being in my thoughts and just driving. Being thankful that Milton taught me to drive made me realize he was so much like a dad.

I pulled up and leaned over the passenger seat to double-check the address. *Nittolo's Restaurant* was lit up on a stand-alone neon board in white letters. I pulled around the corner to an open parking lot. There were two other cars and the front part of a truck rig nesting in the parking lot. I figured it was empty because it was still kind of early. I turned off the engine and got out. As I looked around, the street was bare, almost like people didn't come here. I could tell that it used to be a busy street from the many dilapidated buildings, which also looked familiar. The building stretched wide, but short, almost shaped like a train or really long bus. This place seemed normal, and I could place it until I walked in.

I walked up to the entrance and peeked in. There were booths along the big glass window covering the entire wall, and a counter where people seemed to be sitting. I opened the door, and the bell on the top shook and rang. Some of the men at the counter turned around, and out walked a familiar red-headed waitress, who greeted me very cheerfully. I replied with a greeting of my own, though I was shocked. This was the place Milton brought me to! The same lady, slightly aged, was bustling around the counter with plates in her hand. The business changed a lot, but she made it the same old diner. I felt warm knowing that she was still around, and still able to work here when no other business survived. Then, the lightbulb above my head went off.

Nittolo's had to be one of Milton's places. He upgraded to a brick building and added? more land for a parking lot, so this place must have meant everything. The restaurant was a front, but a good one. It was still making enough money to stick around this desert of a neighborhood. I walked towards the back and sat down. Still in thought, I didn't see one of the men get off his stool and walk over to my table. When he leaned down, I jumped, and my initial reaction was defense. I just barely stopped myself from hitting the guy in the face. The commotion caused everyone to turn and look. When I apologized, the restaurant's windows rattled from the epic roars of laughter.

"I should have known you were home. The only person that can make a room full of killers and thieves cry out in joyous laughter," a dominant voice said from behind the counter. Milton had emerged from the back of the restaurant just in time, it seems. I inched around the still-startled man and apologized again as I slid out of the booth. I approached the counter like a daughter who had been away at college, anxious to see her father. The man sitting on the end in full biker gear lifted the counter for me as I passed. I didn't make it all the way behind the counter before Milton pulled me in for a tight endearing hug. I was confused at first, but after a while, I succumbed to it. Clearly, he had missed me.

Before it got awkward, we let go of each other and shared a laugh. He motioned for me to go to the back, and I went. I followed the long hall until I came to a small office. It looked like a bomb went off in there. It made me really wonder how the restaurant made it this far. I stood at the doorway, afraid to go in. I felt Milton brush past me, and I moved aside. He walked in and sat in the chair behind the desk, which was covered in papers of all different sizes. "So!" he said enthusiastically. "I know you are wondering why we're here and not at the club, right?"

"Well," I started, "I wasn't gonna ask if you weren't gonna tell me."

"That's a good rule to have. Right. So, business. We can catch up when we leave here. Separately, I might add."

"Sounds good to me," I replied and entered the room entirely, then closed the door.

"We have an issue on the inside. One of our own is drawing too much attention to himself. He happens to have a brother whose actions have put their coupled activities to light. The clear-headed one is an asset to the Group. However, we know he will do whatever to vouch for his brother. If they both have to go, then make it so." He turned around in his chair to the safe behind him. I tapped my foot and rolled my eyes. I was anxious, and ready to prove myself. The whole meeting thing was boring to me. When he turned around, in his hand he had one of those extra thick brown folders that looked like internal office mail. He tossed it over to me and said, "Everything you need to know is in there."

"Cool. So why here?" I asked. His story didn't really explain that.

"Ears, Doll. Speaking of… You get to pick a name for yourself after the job's finished. Can't express how much we don't need this info out. If the wrong person is still around, it could cause trouble for us. Fuair sé?" he said, asking if I got that last part in Irish. I had to learn the tongue of the trade.

"Tuigim," I replied, meaning I understood. Too many people on the inside were connected. If word got out to my targets, they could cause a civil war among the factions. "I don't like half the idiots you employ in the first place," I added as I flung open the door to leave.

"GOOD! MEANS I DON'T HAVE TO KILL ANY OF THEM!" he shouted after me like a concerned dad. I waved my hand and kept going. As I walked back through the diner,

I reached in my pocket, pulled out a couple of queen sheets, a Canadian twenty-dollar bill. Or sawbuck, as Americans say, and put them on the counter. When the red-headed waitress came by and saw it, I read her name tag and said, "Thanks for EVERYTHING, Nancy," and left.

Within the next twenty-four hours, I went back to town, hung out with people, had dinner with Milton and a few people from the club, and learned everything I needed to about my targets. Brothers Patrick "Patty" and Brian O'Riley were in charge of the import/export shipments for the Group. They had a headquarters set up in the docks. These two were either really fucking smart or really fucking dumb. Patty was being watched for having a hand in some museum heist in Montreal. Brian was arrested, charged, and out on bail for a fire that seemed to enlighten the said heist. Before this, they were highly respected among us, and some really wanted to keep Patty. Seems his IQ was too high to let him go on his own. Seems they also had a knack for coveting highly skilled people for personal gain. I was starting to feel sorry for Patty.

I had a plan. I had my info double checked and verified. I was ready to go. The night before I was set to make a move, I wanted to drink. My choices were the Cleopatra, or a shit hole that wouldn't dare card me knowing who I was. Milton would kill anyone who served his almost twenty-year-old ward, so, hole in the wall was where I ended up. People knew who I was and wouldn't want me to tell Uncle Milton, or Mom as he was called everywhere, which would upset him. As I was trying to drown my hyperactive brain in alcohol, my phone kept going off. I tried to ignore it. But it was starting to piss me off. *I could use a good fight before I set out tomorrow.*

I answered the phone and said, “Listen, whoever and whatever you want, it’s after eleven. Do I need to tell my Mom?” That was code for telling the boss. I waited to hear either a click or cursing, but it was just heavy breathing. I immediately lost the buzz I had and moved to the exit. I threw money on the bar as I left. “Who the fuck is this!?” I stood in the middle of the street, waiting for someone to answer me. I took the phone away from my face to see the caller ID and it said, “Unknown.” I started to hear talking, so I put the phone back to my ear. I guessed I missed the introduction and caught it mid-sentence. All I heard next was, “Not safe for you. I know everything. Even where you’re sleeping. You won’t be able to sleep not knowing when I’m going to knock down your door!”

“I'm bored of this game, dude. Let's make this interesting. You win and I won't tell my Mom about any of this,” I said, walking to my car. It sounded like the guy didn’t know what to say. There was some stumbling in his voice when he said, “This is for your own good. This mission is not safe for you. I know everything. Even where you’re sleeping. You...”

“Hey, why don’t we kill the *Manchurian Candidate* act?” I interrupted. “Tell me who this is and what you want.”

“I... You won’t ....”

“Right, right. Kill me in my sleep. Got it. Tell me something at least. How about how you found out about my mission and how you got my number.”

“Listen!” he growled. He was getting angry. *Good. I might be able to get info from him.* I started my car and took off towards my apartment. It would take me about six minutes to get there. I needed to trace the call if I couldn’t get what I needed. “I'm listening,” I said as I raced down the street.

"You don't know what you've gotten into. He gets angry and I can't stop him!"

"Sounds scary. And what do we call him?"

"You don't understand! People weren't supposed to die! They were supposed to be scared and run. Fear isn't enough anymore. The dreaded look of their lives being stolen is the only thing that calms him! He fears no one. I'm the older brother and I can't even control him." He sounded as if he was crying. I didn't know what to say. I didn't want to say anything that let him know that he slipped and told me who this was. After a real sob, I heard a click. He hung up. *Damnit! That was Patty, and he knew I was the one coming for him. This wasn't good. Milton was right about this one causing problems.*

When I got to my apartment, I noticed two cars I had never seen, and one idiot had the inside light on. I stopped at the corner and left my car running. I snuck up the back staircase to the door that led to my kitchen. I peeped inside the small window on the bottom of the door to see if someone was inside. I couldn't see anyone. I slowly opened the door, trying hard not to cast a light reflection from the glass. No doubt they were watching for the front. I crawled inside and stayed low. I knew my apartment like the back of my hand. It was the first thing I did when I got it. Milton owned the place, and I was the only tenant. I went for the case I was preparing to take tomorrow. It housed an SRS-A2, a classy, lightweight sniper rifle. I chose it because it had less kickback on my tiny body frame. It was capable of one-thousand-yard grouping with minimum movement. It was compact and easy to assemble. I learned quite a bit while I was away.

After assembling my SRS, I crawled towards my hall closet, where there was no line of sight for anyone. I rummaged through it, looking for my binoculars. I grabbed them and crawled to my bedroom. There was a hatch where I could reach the roof of the building. I crawled across the top after climbing up the ladder. I got as close to the edge as I could so I could see who was watching me. I pulled the balled-up earpiece out of my pocket and plugged it into my phone. I lifted the binoculars and took a glance. In the first car, a red Monte Carlo with black underlining, was a big, muscular man. He looked like he could rip a steak in half with his teeth. I needed to see more of his face. He made the mistake of looking out the window, and I recognized who he was. It was baby brother, Brian, stalking my front door. In a black Buick on the opposite corner, it looked like Patty sweating in the front seat. I saw him wipe a towel across his face and look around as if he was nervous.

In my files, it listed Patty's phone number. I remembered it as part of knowing the target. I dialed it on my phone, and while waiting for an answer, I put myself in a position where I could see either brother from one spot. When I heard the line click, I put Patty in my scope. “Yea, what is it? I'm busy,” he said, with a snippy attitude.

“Yea, so about this angry guy,” I started, and I saw him squirming in his seat. He looked behind him, to the left, and to the right.

“How did you... You know what I don't want to know. Just do me a favor and don't come home.”

“Are you gonna tell me why I shouldn't just get in my car and drive home right now?”

“My brother and his friend will be answering that if you go.”

I moved my scope back to Brian and tried to adjust the lens. "Since you know who I am and what I'm supposed to do, why would you try to save me? Wouldn't it be just as great if you let your Hulk smash?" I asked, trying to buy time until I could get a bead on the friend.

"I never wanted to hurt people. I just wanted to make money. I wanted finer things in life. I liked doing the heist for the challenge of whether or not I could. The Group won't let me go. They won't let you go, either. You shouldn't even be here."

"Is that sympathy, Patty? How does a mob boss learn something like that?" I kept inching over to get a better line of sight. I saw movement from the Monte Carlo. I watched until I finally saw the friend. It looked like they were arguing over something, and the friend moved into the back seat. "Bad move, bro," I said under my breath.

"I don't want my brother hurt, but I can't control him anymore. He is a monster. And a problem for the Group and me. I want to keep my life. And I want to save you from this life," he confessed.

I was silent for a moment. I was trying to think of what to do. Whoever told him about me was obviously really close to him that they'd go against Mom. *Fuckers are crazy to think they could even.* "Fuck!" I exhaled loudly and said, "If you had a second chance, would you spend it thinking about what you lost in your old life? Or would you find a new reason to live?"

"I would leave and never come back. Live in a library and stay confined to my imagination. An angel would have to come down and stop you from coming home and allow us to..." His silence came from hearing two shots fired and they seemed to echo through my earpiece and outside his car. I moved my scope back to him and watched as he got out of the car and stared up the street. He sounded like he was hyperventilating. He dropped the phone and looked around. I stood up so he could see me on the roof. He picked up his phone and was sobbing again. "Why? Why? *Why?!*" he screamed.

"Luckily for you, I'm the only one who lives here. Luckily for you, I still have some humanity. Your brother was a monster, you said so yourself. Even if you somehow got away tonight, it wouldn't be long before he would make trouble for you again. And Mom would be all over your ass. You already said that you wouldn't be thinking about this place anymore. So, go. Leave the car, too. I'll take care of the rest. You have to tell me who told you about me, though. This won't work if I don't have that person. And if you don't, I'll have you shoot you right here and now. So, choose. Run or die." I turned the laser sight on the scope and aimed it at his chest so he could see. He backed up nervously, and I followed with the scope of my gun. I could hear his breathing get erratic as he moved and my scope with him.

When he stopped moving, he let out a sigh. "DiMarco," he said. "He was in the diner when you got the assignment. He held the counter up for you as you went to see Mom. He drives for Mom when he needs to do secret work."

"Thank you. Now get the fuck outta here."

"Wait! Go to my office. The safe. You go by yourself. Then tell Mom. Sixteen, twenty-three, four. I hope you know what you're doing kid," he said as he dropped the phone and took off running.

I let out a heavy breath as if I just got back from a jog. I bent over, dropped my rifle, and rested my hands on my knees as I tried to catch my breath. *I need to clean up this scene before anyone comes. I know that shot was heard.* I got to Patty's car as fast as I could. His car was running still, so I ran towards the Monte Carlo. I opened the back-seat door and dragged the friend out of the vehicle. I pulled him to Patty's car and shoved him in the front seat. I shot at the driver's window to make it look as if I shot through both vehicles. I drilled some more holes in both the cars and put the friend's foot on the gas pedal. I put the car in neutral and moved it in line with the Monte Carlo. I picked up the dead guy's leg and dropped his foot on the gas and jumped out of the way. I sat up in time to see the Buick ram right into the Monte Carlo. I ran away and took aim at the gas tanks, then I shot until the cars caught fire and blew up. I jumped back from the blast in excitement. Laughing, I ran back to my car and took off towards the Cleopatra.

When I arrived, I had a scratch on my head, I was covered in smoke and dirt, and I was still carrying my SRS. Walter, the bartender, caught wind of me and screamed for help. I suddenly got dizzy and couldn't stand on my own. My knees gave out, and I fell to the floor. Before my head could hit the tile, Walter caught me. I blinked, and everything got blurry. I could see Milton running my way. When he stood over me, I smiled and said, "I did it, Pa. I got 'em for you," and passed out. I could hear voices fading out as the room went dark around me.

When I came to, I was in a bed hooked up to hospital machines, but I wasn't in a hospital. I looked around to see if I recognized where I was. My head was so heavy. I tried to move my arms, but they were sore. My legs felt like sandpaper had been rubbed all up my thighs. I reached over to see if there was a light, and I guess I knocked over a cup. I could hear feet shuffling outside the door to the room I was in. The door flew open, and Milton came from the other side of it. "Thank God!" he exclaimed as he ran towards the bed. He put a hand on my head and wiped my forehead. It felt weird.

"What the fuck was that?" I asked. Milton laughed a stuffy laugh as if he was hiding another expression. When I looked up, he had tears in his eyes. I looked at him, confused, and asked another question. "Milton, are you crying?"

"Fuck, Doll. You had me worried. The way you showed up to the club. The mess outside your house. You been out for three days. I had to ask my badges to hold off investigating in front of your house until I found out what happened. They couldn't identify anyone in the car, so I said I'd see what you could tell me."

"That's right. The O'Rileys were coming for me. They knew where I lived. I saw them pulling up and got them before they could get out the car. I think the guy in the second car got hit first then ran into the first car, but I just kept shooting. Then, BOOM! I got in my car, but I don't remember where I went or was going. I guess in my subconscious, it was here."

"Damn. She took out both O'Rileys? Regular Mata Hari, like the boys said, huh, ain'cha Cher," said a musky voice from the corner. It was Ali. The first time I put eyes on him and the first time I realized he was jealous. "How you let this chil' run wit' us boss? She barely survived her first mission. She migh' make us look bad."

"Shut up, Ali!" Milton expressed. "No one questions her. I handpicked this one. Just as I did you. Now get the hell out."

"Oui, monsieur," he said, and bowed out of the room.

"Don't listen to him. He just wants to keep me safe. I trust that man with my life. I actually have something for you."

"Yea?" I said, wiping my eyes to help them adjust better. Milton turned on the light I was searching for in the dark and brought around a velvet box. It looked like jewelry, to which I got uneasy. I was feeling sick to my stomach. "Milton, what the hell is this? I hope you not proposing. I just don't think it'll work, grandpa," I said with a smirk.

"Shit. No! You and yo mouth woman! Fucking open it, ya brat!"

I opened the box, and it was a pendant. It was all silver with some rubies in the points. There was a symbol in the middle that I could clearly make out. It was an upside-down "G" and "T," and I guess it represented The Group. I saw symbols that looked to be a belt at the bottom of it, with a small shield in its open space background. The words engraved around the inner circle were written in fancy script, separated by a gold asterisk. "What's it say?" I asked and brought it closer to my face.

"Diseacht thar aon rud eile," he replied.

"Loyalty above all else. Huh! Not bad. Wait! Is that my name? What the hell is that?" I asked, confused.

"Ah!" he chuckled. "I got the idea from what Ali said. Mata Hari was the fiercest French assassin of her era. Suits you well, I think."

"Okay?" I said, raising an eyebrow. Milton moved to the side of my bed and sat in the empty space.

"For your first assignment, you did great kiddo. You got made and adjusted so well! This could have been a bigger mess than it was, and then you cleaned up like a real pro. I'm proud."

"You gonna make me blush. Stop it." I replied jokingly. "Serious, though?"

"Serious, dude," he replied mockingly. "I don't know anyone that would've handled that situation like you did. To be on their first time out, so young, and a woman at that!"

"Maybe you were right to embrace my gifts."

"The Pharaohs of Egypt would keep female bodyguards. They said having a strong woman at their back made for a strong leader. I'm embracing that logic."

"Is that because I'm Black?" I asked with a pout. He let out a big laugh, and it made him lean back at the deep parts.

"I love ya kid! I wan'cha to take up the Mata Hari mantle. Become one of my Rebels. Move up the ranks properly and you can be my number one."

"I dunno, Milt. I'm still processing shit from yesterday. I'm okay, but there is, like, shit about this that still needs to be settled. Like the motha' fuckah that set me up!"

"Quiet. I took care of it. We know already. And by the way, you been out for three days."

"WHAT THE FUCK, MILTON!" I screamed as I jumped up. My legs started to give out. Walter ran into the room to see what was going on. Milton put his hand up to stop him from advancing further. "Don't you think that you should lead off with the important bits!? Dude! Three goddamn days! Oh my God!"

"I'm sorry. You're right. There were moments when you seemed lucid and coherent, so I assumed you would remember those parts," he said, with some sadness in his voice. He cleared his throat and asked, "What's the last thing you remember, Doll?"

"Pulling up in front of the club and then waking up here. I don't even remember how the hell I got outta my car!" I inched closer to him. “Milton, what happened while I was out?”

“Well, you walked in the club on your own carrying the sniper I got you for your graduation. They called for me and I came running. When I got there, you told me you did it. And you called me ‘Pa,’.” He chuckled a bit.

“The blood was rushing everywhere at the same time, and I felt like my chest was gonna pop. I didn’t know what I was doing. My instincts just took over.”

“Good that you have it, so you come to me first. And between you and me, I think you’d make Ali jealous as fuck if you ranked to my number one.”

I sat there silent for a minute. He sighed and got up. He went to lean in to kiss me, and I gave him my forehead like any other time. There was hesitation from him before he kissed my forehead. When I looked up at him, he seemed to be disappointed, as if he expected something more. I was confused at first, and then Walter distracted me with a tray of food. I was starving. As Walter walked over, Milton walked out. He whispered something to Walter and then left the room, closing the door behind him. Something smelled foul. *What the fuck else happened while I out?*

I got better and mentioned to Mom about the safe Patty told me about. Accompanied by Ali and me, we checked out the safe. Inside, we found gold bars. It filled the safe with just enough room at the top for the briefcase he had stashed there also. I pulled it out as I let the men move the gold. It had a combination lock on it, but Patty only told me one set of numbers. *Could he be that stupid?* I put in the same combination for the safe, and it opened. I closed it immediately after a glimpse of what was inside. My heart was pounding as if someone was playing ball in the most hollowed-out room in the world. I didn't want them to hear me. I turned around, and they were busy counting the bars. I picked up the briefcase and box with some business crap in it and went out to the cars.

As I was closing my trunk, Ali dragged an old duffle bag across the gravel to his car. It looked like they took whatever out and put the gold in it. Milton came out with a bowling ball and gym bag. He gave me the bowling ball bag and said, “Keep it. Better your skills and self. Don’t blow it all, though. For I now know you have the means of your own.”

“Such freedoms, master. Are you sure?” I snickered. He smiled his granddad's smile and got in the car with Ali. There was no need for me anymore. I was paid for my service, and him going with Ali meant he had business to do after. I had considerable money betting that he would not be telling the Group heads about the gold. He’d chalk it up as profits from taking over the O’Riley territory. I went home and hid my gold but stared at that briefcase. *Patty is a dangerous man to piss off. He seems the kinder type, but I know now that he is vicious. I wonder where he is.* I asked myself if I would ever need to see the contents of that case again. After a long thought, I decided to hide it with my secrets. I went on being Mata Hari. I went on killing for a man that I was slowly realizing that I should never have let in close to me.

FINAL ENCOUNTER

Her

I stared off into the distance as I relived the worst moments of my life. It had me frozen in an alarming déjà vu. I was pulled out of it by a beeping noise from behind me. Snapping out of it, I turn around and see the grey box with the blinking light. Like fog lifting from the dusk of day, I started to remember where I was. I looked around the room. "That's right. I'm in trouble," I said to myself. I started to think about how much I didn't care about whatever trouble I was in. In the same moment, my heart sank into my feet, and tears swelled up in my eyes. I felt naked even though I was wearing clothes. I tried to hold the tears in as I stared into Keith's face. I tried to speak, but the words got caught in my throat. The more I choked on my embarrassment, the harder it was for me to hold back the tears. He looked at me, confused, and took a step towards me. I jumped off the desk I was sitting on and moved back. I closed my eyes tight to let the tears fall so I could see. I stood still for a minute and put my hand over my heart as I accepted that I could not stop crying. When I opened my eyes, Keith had moved closer, and he was face to face with me.

He raised a hand to my face and wiped the tears away. He lifted my chin so I could look him in the eye and said, "I meant what I said in the alley. You don't have to apologize. You know who you are and what you want. Never be sorry because you wanted a better life. What's real though, is that I know who you are, and have known before I even knew your story. I had my doubts when I saw you with that guy. I was shocked but I knew that there was something to it. I never thought I'd be caught in the middle of a real-life *Scarface* moment, but I have no regrets." I sniffed and looked down. He immediately raised my face again and kissed me, messy face and all.

"The battery," Walter said as he got up from his chair. He walked over to the corner, dug around, and pulled a small bag from the dark. He was rummaging through the pack when someone's phone started ringing. Everyone looked around, confused, until it stopped. The air was awkward, and everyone was still looking for the phone. It began to ring again. Finally, Fred settled confusion by crying out, "It's me!". He walked away to talk, and Walter returned to looking through his bag.

I turned back to Keith and walked towards him. I took his hands and looked him in the eyes. "I need to thank you," I began, "for everything. I also still need to apologize. I know you say you're choosing to be here, but if you get killed, I'll still feel a bit guilty. I don't know what I would have done if you hadn't come for me. I was afraid that you'd see me differently if you knew everything about me."

"Actually," he started with a high tone, "It kinda puts a lot of things I've witnessed into a much better perspective. Fills in a lot of holes and explains how you could always get away from me."

"See, one's gotta wonder if now is a good time to be cute."

"Is there a time not to be?"

"Ah, you didn't get the memo about appropriate moments."

"I think I was at a convention when that went out. Sorry." I laughed, and he said, "There it is. Thank you. And you're welcome."

Our seemingly first average couple moment was interrupted by Fred. He wore the look of one who already accepted his resolve and fate. He walked into the middle of the room and stood firm. He looked around at us all and said, "Lookouts say Mom is headed this way. The militia is moving into position. They are loading up the reserves just in case. He is coming deep, and he is many. We need to be prepared, Billy."

Billy let out a sad, heavy sigh, took his baseball cap off, and wiped the perspiration from his forehead. He walked around in a circle before turning back to us and putting on his hat again. "Well," he started shakily, "This is where we make the decision, kid. Now, I prefer that you weren't here for the blood bath. You can walk away right now. Never worry if Milton lived or died. Leave here with the faith that we did what we set out to do or gave our lives trying. You don't have to see any of this through. But if you're going, go now. There is time to get ready while you take a break." He stopped talking for about two minutes. We listened as more cars approached and feet shuffled on the stairs outside. He walked up to Zora and placed both hands on her shoulders like a loving father would, and asked, "Wha' 'sit gonna be? Are you Neveah or Mata Hari?"

I stared around the room as more cars and voices approached our hideout. *Can I just leave these people to clean up a mess I made? I know they have their reasons for this fight that I could never take away from them, but I wouldn't want anyone to die for me.* If I made a big speech about how this was my fight, I knew Walter, or Billy, would get all “elder uncle” on me and remind me that this fight was coming before I was born. *These people who joined his ranks all have something to prove and want or need to move on. I wouldn’t dare take that from anyone. I fought my entire life to get away and be free of this. I know how important it is to them and me.* There was only one person that worried me.

Keith stood there looking around and making small talk with Fred and other people... I watched him make jokes and laugh like he was at a company mixer, trying to keep his best hat on. *Whatever I decide will affect him, too.* I turned and looked at my case with my guns in it and started to wonder if I had the resolve to pick them up again. Amid my pondering, I heard yelling from outside. “HE'S HERE! THEY'RE COMING! PULLING IN AT THE GATE!” someone warned, and the room immediately got loud. I looked around, and instead of panic, I saw courage and concrete motions. No one was dying for me. They were there to get justice and prevail with honor. I saw people flock to Walter, asking what the plan was and calling him “chief.” I took a final look at Keith as he peered through the groups of people and set eyes on me. My heart was telling me what to do.

Before I could speak a word, a high-pitched tone from a bull horn echoed in the air. Someone was learning the buttons or how to use them. Either way, it pierced the ears of everyone there. A man's voice came through after, and I knew exactly who it was. “See, this isn't at all what I wanted,” Milton spoke. “I was thinking of a nice reunion, some explanations, and we just let bygones be bygones. But you had to join up with the merry men of the Canadian forest. This makes me think you joined the enemy. But I know that can’t it, we’re family, right? Family can work anything out. We can talk about how you’ll be punished. I won’t kill you. I’ll spare you and your flock, including Mr. "Last Cop Standing." I just want Neveah to come out. That's all. We can avoid the bloodshed if she surrenders and comes out to face me. My boys will leave and never come back, and I won't hold a grudge against anyone who is here. Scouts' honor!"

There was so much silence. I didn't know what to do, and words were nowhere near ready to come out. People were no longer looking to Walter. All eyes were on me, and my heart started pounding as the room seemed to spin. Gravity stopped on Keith. I stepped forward with something to say, but I couldn't find the words. I looked at the table with my guns and slowly walked over. I ran a finger down one of the barrels. The steel was freezing as if it had just been unearthed from a cold slumber. I picked one up, cocked the back open to see if it was loaded and clean. Saw two slug bucks loaded, cocked it shut, and aimed it.

I knew what I had to do. "Listen," I started, "I don't know most of you or what your story is. I spent my life running just to live. I've lied about who I was. I've killed and hurt many people. I am no different from the man you all hate. I was one of his top lieutenants, and one of my jobs might have been to take away the very person you're here to avenge. I don't want to take your justice from you. I won't even try to tell you not to fight. This man is a terror and needs to be put down. This town needs its freedom, and I know what peace feels like- to not have to look over your shoulder every day. I won't waste this opportunity that you are allowing me. With that said, if I know you or not, you guys will be with me in my heart as my family if I survive this night. In return, I will ask that if you also survive this night, please live. No matter what happens, or who may get away, please make this your last fight."

I looked around for Walter. Finally, I saw him squeezing through the crowd. When he reached me, I just hugged him. I squeezed tighter as if I never would see him again, and I think he felt that. "Hey now!" he said as he pulled me away. "None of that. I'm proud of you. And I'll be right here till the very end. Whether it be tonight, or years from now. I love ya, kid. Nothing will change that."

"I don't care what your name is," I started in a broken voice, almost succumbing to tears. "You'll always be my Walter."

"That's my girl!"

"I don't know what plan you have but do it quick. I'm going out there." I turned around to the table. I lifted the second gun out and removed the grey suede lining of the case. Beneath the lining were holsters for the firearms, leather-bound with black buckles. Out of the crowd, I heard him say, "But you can't!" I closed my eyes and sighed. This was the hard part. When people care, they interfere with what needs to be done. That's why I never managed. I wanted to turn around and tell him not to worry. That I knew exactly what I was doing. That everything will work out okay. But I knew I would just be lying to his face. *This is the part where I regret having him here. However, I am glad that I met him and experienced some level of what love could start off being.*

While I stood there trying to muster the courage to send Keith away, I felt his hands on my shoulders. He walked around, saw my disappointed face and said, "Now that looks like it could be disappointment in you or me. Either way, I have no regrets. But if you're going out there, so am I." Before I could rebut his request, Walter came out of nowhere and pushed Keith aside. "I appreciate that you came all this way. That knot in your stomach is telling you that this is love, but I refuse to watch her live her life depressed and sad- all because some greenhorn thought he'd show off about how noble he is." I chuckled a bit as Walter did his little hand of royalty as he spoke. "Neither one of you have to go," I said.

"I know we don't have to do squat!" Walter sassily remarked. "BUT!"

"You can't stop the people that love you to stop wanting to protect you," Keith finished. "I agree, though. Running out there and not knowing a fucking thing will get me shot. So, I will trust Walter to bring you back to me."

"I appreciate that you came all this way," I said as I genuinely blushed for the first time in my life. "I don't know how to be anything but what I've been. But I do have to say that you have made it very interesting, and fun. So, I'll try to come back and give whatever this is a try," I said as I approached Keith and pulled him closer. Without me telling or asking, he engulfed my soul in a kiss. It sang the song of longing and desire. I could feel the burning passion of not wanting to let go. After about three minutes, though, we had to let go. I walked to the staircase and stared up. *This is it. I will face him for the last time today. Today, I take my entire life back.*

Walter made sure he was at my side when I walked outside. I saw so many car headlights, I couldn't get an accurate count of heads out there. The collection of lights was almost too bright to see, but I saw him. Milton was standing there with the bull horn in his hands. His goons were blocking the gated entrance to the park. It looked like he was preparing to let no one leave. As ready as I was to face him, my heart raced, and my body filled with nervousness. I walked out in front of Milton to show I wasn't scared. I approached him, and he called for a goon to take the bull horn. I didn't get close, but I was close enough for us to speak without yelling. Without fear, I stared into his eyes, looked back at Walter, and clutched my guns in my holsters.

I said nothing while I stared him down. There was nothing for me to say, knowing he would never let me go. After an uncomfortable silence, he moved toward me, and I jumped back. "Oh, don't be like that," he said. "I just want to talk." I waved my hand for him to proceed. "I see," he said "I am the only one that has something to say. That's fine." He let out a heavy sigh and dropped his hands to his sides. "I missed you. I never had anyone watch my back like you. When you took off, I was mad at first because I thought you betrayed me. And the longer time went by, I thought you dead," he said sincerely. "I just don't understand why you would want to leave the life you had. You were feared by most and rivaled by no one. You were your own woman at such a young age, and I gave you that."

"Stop right there!" I exclaimed. "I was never my own woman. I was at your beck and call. You made it clear that you owned me. After the first meeting, you told me I owed you. And I believed that. As I got older, I got smarter. And I saw you for who you were, a monster. What you gave me was a life confined to death and destruction. And I wanted out."

"I gave you more than death. I let you have your life after killing my blood. Granted he deserved it, that's just how the world works. Even good deeds have consequences."

"This coming from the person that thinks he will never suffer consequences. You are hilarious, Mom. And the life you speak of, it wasn't given, nor did I ask for it! You forced it on me. So, I did what I had to do."

"But you chose to do the job. You chose the life."

"That is not what I mean, and you know it! Or would you like me to air your dirty secrets here in front of your men?" I sassed angrily as I spun to look at his goons, who all had blank expressions on their faces. "You have to pay for your needs as well. And I handed out the first blow by getting rid of the life you so-call 'gave' me."

"Wait, what do you mean you got rid of the life?" Milton asked with his grandfather's caring voice.

"Well, now," I chuckled, "I think you're a little old for me to explain how the whole birds and bees thing goes."

"You…" he stumbled, "You… what did you do?"

I let out the heartiest laugh and said, "So what did you think was going to happen, Daddy? That I would be okay with how you forced yourself on me? That I would thank you for making me a nineteen-year-old mother? That I'd love you? No, sir. I refused. That's why I ran. That's why I hate you!"

Milton's head was down. He stared at the ground and froze in his spot. He looked confused at first. Then, his face lost all its color, like he wasn't breathing. He was figuring it out. He never knew until now, and I tried to spare us both from it, but I guess you can't run fast or far enough from your past before it catches up with you.

I was expecting Milton to come up crying, and ready to tell his men to fire. I stood at the ready with hands on my guns, feet planted and looking for that last-minute confidence. I heard a whimper, and he slowly started to raise his head. He stopped after a second, maybe to catch his breath. The moment he began to raise his head again, I clutched my guns hard with fingers rightly off the trigger. His arm was rising too, as if he meant to shoot the moment he was up. *Showing the enemy your play is his rule. Is he that overcome with grief that he would give the upper hand like this?* I was confused. I had to watch his every move. He was up to something, and I knew it. I could feel it. I could feel something.

I felt cold, then warmth coming from what I thought was my shoulder. Something hard hit my knees. My head was so cloudy that I couldn't focus. I looked down to see what hit me. I saw red, and my hearing appeared to have gone out. Soon, I heard ringing and saw flashes of sparkling lights. Something hit my back, but before I could turn my head to look, the dirt hit my head. I felt the cold before I heard the sound. Or was it the other way around? I laid there on the ground, confused and aware. Aware that I was shot and fell to the ground but confused as to why and who. My hearing was coming back as screams and gunfire passed over my head. I could hear only anger and pain in the screams. Laying there bleeding out, the only thing I heard was the pain and sadness in Keith's cries while dwindling into shadow.

Him

Milton called for Zora to come out. I could see on her face that she was thinking about going out. I also knew she wouldn't let me go, but I didn't want her to go alone. I looked over at Billy, well Walter, as he talked to others in the group while listening to what Milton was saying. Zora moved over to the table with her guns and started putting them on. My body froze with fear. *Is she really going out there? What will happen? Will I lose her after coming all this way?*

Zora was making a speech to everyone. *I was right, she is going out there.* My body started to move on its own. I slowly moved through the crowd of people to reach her. When I heard her say she was going to confront Milton, I couldn't stop the words coming out of my mouth. "BUT YOU CAN'T!" I yelled. Zora stepped forward and tried to assure me this was for the best. I wanted to assure her that I'd never leave her. Suddenly, Walter pushed me out of nowhere, and I stumbled back. I looked at him, confused, but ultimately, I did not protest. The look he gave me made me feel confident in him, so I let Walter handle it.

Zora kissed me and took me towards the entrance. She hesitated before going up the winding stairs; I guess she wanted a minute to herself. Walter was finishing up giving orders to some of the militia people, and they took off out the back. Passing by me before joining Zora, he stopped to speak to me. "Listen," he started, putting a hand on my shoulder, "I will be with her. But I need you to keep cool. No matter what happens out there, I need you to listen to my guys. They already know what to do for any given situation. Even if it goes bad. I need you to be ready to do whatever they tell you. Zora will need you to be ready. Zora will need your strength. No. Matter. What. I don't care how much grief or happiness you happen to be overwhelmed with, just follow the others, protect yourself, and keep her safe if it comes to it, okay?"

I stood quietly for a minute. I didn't really know what was going on. *What is the plan? Why won't he tell me? Am I that much of a liability? Should I not have come?* I put my head down and let the doubt and shame hit me. I started to panic. I didn't know if I could protect Zora. I didn't even know if I could defend myself. I didn't know how to answer this conflict in my heart. *If I say 'okay' and something happens, I don't think I can forgive myself.* Walter must not have noticed my panicking, because he pulled a nine-millimeter coated in black steel, cocked the gun, and handed it to me. The moment the metal hit my hand; my attitude changed. *This means I have no choice but to fight. If I cannot find the courage for my life, I need to see it for Zora's sake.* I looked up at Walter with the sternest look I could muster. "I understand," I replied calmly. "I will do as you ask. If it means Zora lives and we get out of this mess, I'll do whatever it takes. Even if it costs me my life."

"That's what I needed to hear," Walter said, smiling as he walked away. He caught up to Zora, peered back at me, and they left up the stairs. I stared down at the gun, trying to visualize the things I might see and have to do when I got out there. I started walking around, watching the rest load gun magazines, put on bulletproof vests, and load up with the hardware for the fight. I was restless. Feeling useless, I started looking for an opening where I would be of some use. However, everyone looked more experienced, and they were in this war long before I stepped into the picture.

Suddenly, Fred called for people to start moving out. I watched as the room emptied, feeling stuck and not knowing where to go. “Just breathe,” a voice said from behind me. When I turned around, I saw a small, elderly lady carrying a double-barrel shotgun. She had a row of shells strapped to her chest. “We all lost someone or are trying to protect someone. That’s why we’re here. We are all in this together. Nothing ever goes according to plan. The world isn’t perfect. We do what we must when we must. Trust in your feelings. Dead or alive, as long as you stay true to those feelings, you’ll be fine,” the lady said. She then walked past me to the stairs, and headed up to the battlefield. *She is right. I came here, didn't I? I already declared that I would never leave Zora's side. I already promised Walter that I’m ready to do whatever it takes to keep Zora safe. I shouldn’t have any reason for staying behind. Zora needs me.* I walked towards the stairs with confidence in my heart.

With my chest poked out and my head held high, I approached the opening to the outside. The way I was feeling, I was ready to fire off on Milton if needed. Not paying attention, I was yanked back into the hallway with the stairs. It was Fred that had a grip on my arm. “We ‘ave uh place fah you, monsieur,” he said, pulling me away. “We need you in tha right place, no? We ‘ave a plan. But you must trust us, yes?”

“Plan?” I asked, out of breath. “Okay...so what am I supposed to do?”

As Fred pushed me through the halls, he checked the corners before pulling me out into the open. "Just go to your position. We know it's gonna be 'ard dealing with Neveah, but you have to understand that Billy cares about her too and wouldn' let not'ting get at 'er, yea? Trust we know what to do and do every'ting we say."

"What if I can't help it? What if I can't control my actions?" I asked, as I stopped to rethink what I was getting into.

"Not to worry, no? We thought of that, too. Trust, monsieur."

"Okay," I said, and succumbed. "No matter what, I'll do what you say. For Neveah." That name sounded funny coming out of my mouth. I knew her as Zora. *No matter what she did or where she came from, she will always be Zora to me.*

Fred walked me to another side of the park. Other militias were in place, watching the spotlight where Zora, Walter, and Milton stood. I tried to watch where I was walking and kept an eye on them. I was led to a spot not too far from them. From the position they led me to, and the fact Walter pushed me away from joining Zora, I concluded they meant for me to escape. *I wonder how they will do it, especially if I'm supposed to take her with me.* My mind was racing. *I do not know what the plan is, but the more I watch that spot, the more I am ready to do whatever it takes to make sure we get out.*

Looking over the gun Billy gave me; I was feeling out of place. *Will I have to actually fire this thing? I've shot a gun before, but only at a range. Shooting at people is different, especially with the intent to kill.* I wasn't sure I was ready to kill anyone, even for love. I tried to see if I could hear anything from Zora and Milton's conversation, but I wasn't close enough. I caught Milton moving close and looking distraught, while Zora's emotions were getting hostile. I turned around to look back towards the road at the back gate, still wondering how we would get out of this bullshit. "That's not what I meant, and you know it!" I heard Zora yell across the dead amusement park and turned to see what was happening. Zora looked pissed! Her body language had me worried, and without realizing it, my body was making its way towards her. I couldn't stop myself! I panicked over not getting there in time, going against the plan, and if I was in the line of anyone's fire. However, all that didn't matter to me. I just wanted to get to Zora, before....

I heard it, but it didn't stop me. I saw it, and I didn't care. My body took off in a sprint, and at the top of my lungs, I was screaming, "NO!" I couldn't process it all at the same time, no time to think straight. I didn't care that bullet were whizzing past my literal ass; I needed to get to her. I didn't care about the bodies that dropped around me; I needed her. I saw nothing, no one else, just Zora...on the ground and bleeding out. I felt like *"The Flash"*, running so fast that everything around me stood still, and the world paused for me. I wish it did. I would've been able to save her.

However, I was no superhero, and time did not stop. I saw Billy pull Zora to cover, and I immediately changed direction to where they were. When I got there, Zora was unconscious, blood everywhere, and Billy was shooting from behind cover. I couldn't hear the multiple gunshots over the sound of my own heart. My heart was playing "*The Hardest Button to Button*" by White Stripes, and I was the only one who heard it. I didn't know what to do. I wanted to touch her, but I didn't know if I should. Tears welling up in my eyes, I yelled at Billy, "What do we do?" Tears were already falling down my face.

"Nothing right now," he said, as he returned fire from behind our cover. "I know this is upsetting, but I need you to focus! Remember the promise you made!"

"Is she... Is... she?" I tried to ask through my crying.

"Don't think about that now!"

"I need to know, damnit!"

Billy sighed and came back behind total cover. "Kid. Neveah is gone. But regardless, we have to get her out of here. I need you to respect her final wishes. If you can't keep your promise, then I'll shoot you now! You'll just be a liability! So, what the fuck ar' ya gonna do?! Sit here crying like a pussy!? Or are you gonna protect her like you said!?"

Stuck between offended and shocked, I stopped crying. I felt this build up in me that started from my feet and hit my heart, and anger slammed me. "I did promise. I said I wouldn't leave her," I said in a frustrated voice. "And I'm not a liar!" Wiping the tears from my face, I looked Billy in the eye and asked, "What's the plan?"

"Good lad. Good lad," Billy said, as we turned to return fire. He fired off a few shots and turned back to me. "Listen, you need to go back to the spot where Fred led you. If Fred is not found or dead, anyone else over in that spot will assist. They know the plan," he said, out of breath. He seemed tired, more so than usual. Without arguing, I positioned myself next to Zora's body to have a good grip on her before I tried to run. Turning to Billy to make some motion that we were going and needed cover fire, I saw it.

Billy had been hit numerous times. He was holding his wounds like I couldn't see the blood spilling out from under his fingers. I moved an inch in his direction and he put his hand up, and just shook his head. He took his hand away from a gunshot wound in his stomach. It didn't look that bad, until he turned to show the one in his side and the two in his leg. “I can't go any further, kid,” he said calmly. “I was never gonna get out of this alive. Either Mom was gonna get rid of me, or I’d die trying to put him down. I couldn’t ask for any other way out. I got this far. I saw her grow into a wonderful woman. I saw her get out. And that’s all I ever wanted.” By the time he looked back in my direction, my eyes were welling up again. “Don't do that, son,” he said, chuckling. “I need you to take her. You promised. You ain’ dead yet. So go! I’ll lay cover. Go now!” I didn’t hesitate. I took off back to the spot Fred led me to. I couldn’t look back. Feeling like I already let Zora down, I refused to let anyone else down. *I will get her out, Billy. I promise.*

I didn't see Fred anywhere. The people that were back here were barely standing. Everyone looked so involved that I didn't know who to approach. Thoughts were going in and out of my head so fast, it made me feel like I was spinning. Looking around for an answer, I saw the whole park spin around me in my heightened anxiety. I felt heavy, and it wasn’t because I was carrying Zora. I was feeling the weight of the situation so heavily, I dropped to my knees in the dirt. My breathing became erratic, and I was lost. I closed my eyes tight to accept whatever fate would come.

Just as I was ready to join Billy and Zora, I felt a hand on my shoulder. It was Fred! I gave myself no time to feel grateful. Immediately, I grabbed Zora and asked, “What the fuck are we doing?” He snatched me up without a word, and pushed me to the back gate. As we ran, he laid cover fire. My body was moving off pure adrenaline, and I couldn't stop thinking about Walter now. Fred caught up with me, and out of breath, he said, “The blue car in the front. Go!” Now I knew where I was going; there was no stopping me.

Carrying the body of the woman I loved had me so far in my feelings, I couldn't tell what I was feeling. People were dropping right in front of me as I ran past the gunfight. When I got to the gate, I slowed down. I made sure I couldn't see anyone and tried to put an eye on the car. It seemed clear, so I took off. Before I could go through the gate, however, I noticed a body on the ground. It was the old woman who gave me the advice about tonight. I started to feel sad, then confused, and finally, fear. I haven’t been in this long, but I was catching on quickly. *Something is off; she shouldn't be here. I saw where her original post was.* Looking around, I saw other muddy footprints on the ground. *She came here with other people.* Blood was still seeping from under her body as I approached with caution. *Wait! She was killed back here!*

The moment I figured it out, two of Milton’s goons came out of the shadows. Without hesitation, Fred started firing. At the same time, I ran as fast I could with Zora and through the gate. I saw the blue car. It was just ahead. “We made it,” I said to myself. Suddenly, I felt a pinch, and my left leg wasn’t moving correctly. I kept moving; I couldn’t afford to stop. Looking down to see what the issue was, I saw a trail of blood behind me. When I looked behind me, I saw one of Milton's henchmen on the ground, and so was Fred. Right on my ass, the wounded second henchmen were closing in. *Someone really thought this plan out.* I saw one of the doors was open when we got closer to the car. Even with my injured leg, I was still faster. I sort of tossed Zora on the passenger's seat, and without thinking of where it was, I pulled the nine Billy gave me from my pocket, turned, and let off four shots.

I then froze in my spot and looked around. I looked around. I was ready to shoot if anyone approached. When I calmed down and realized no one else was back here, I ran back to Fred. He was still alive. “Good job, no?” he said.

“Yea,” I replied, “She’s in the car.”

“Oui,” he coughed. Reaching in his vest, he handed me a syringe. I looked confused at him, and he explained. I listened to him tell me everything as his body and soul gave out. “Now you know. Take the car. Go!” he said in a raspy voice. Blood was spilling from the corners of his mouth. I patted him on his chest and said, “I don’t know you, but I appreciate you. Saved my life. I’ll never forget it. Thank you, Fred.” He didn't hear me, though. He was dead by the time I said thank you. I stood up and looked at the battlefield. I had no clue if Milton bit the bullet; however, I don't think I cared. I lost enough tonight, and I was ready to get back to my life. I was prepared to get out of this life.

I tore a piece of my sleeve and used it as a tourniquet on my leg. The gunfire had all but stopped. It was starting to get quiet. That gave me some peace that this was almost over. I made my way back to the car. Sloppily and not paying attention, someone stumbled upon me. The fear that crept up on me was worse than anything I felt before. Earlier, I was ready to die, but being this close to home, I was now petrified. “You... You're not gonna leave without saying goodbye are ya?” Milton asked mockingly, with a gun pointed right at me. “Hell, boy, I dunno who the fuck you even are, or what this has to do with you!”

“She has everything to do with me!” I said, nodding to the car where I placed Zora.

"HA!" he laughed. "Son, you have no idea who the fuck you are dealing with."

"Oh, I know," I responded, with surprising confidence. "All I need to know is you took the person that meant everything to me. And that's all I need to know to hate you."

"Hate me? Why? I groomed her perfectly. You're actually welcome. You know dick about her. Color me curious, though. Why are you here?"

I inched closer to my impending death and said, "I told you. I'm here for her. I don't need to explain anything to you. Especially you. You are cold and empty. You could never understand…"

"Oh..." he interrupted. "Love?"

"That word is poison on your lips. You don't get to use that word here. Not for her!"

"Son, you do realize I have a gun pointed at your head, right? But I like you. You got spunk!"

"Spare me the "come join me" speech. I have no desire to live this life. And you took her from me already."

He looked through the back window of the car at Zora. "So, if she is already dead, then why are you still trying to run away?"

"I'm not running!" I screamed. He was pissing me off. I didn't have time for this. "Unlike you, I am a man of my word. All I'm doing is trying to keep it. Now you're starting to piss me off, Guido," I said insultingly. I moved closer to him, and he moved to the side of the car. "You're right. I know nothing. About you or your shitty operation. I don't care. I don't wanna know. I did my job. If I die right now, I wouldn't regret a thing."

"Whoa now, let's not…"

"LET'S NOT WHAT, MILTON?!" I yelled. "WHAT COULD YOU POSSIBLY DO TO ME NOW? WHAT MORE CAN

YOU TAKE FROM ME? MY LIFE? TAKE IT! IT WAS NOTHING BEFORE SHE CAME!" I was livid at this point. Dying meant nothing. I moved closer, but this time he didn't move. *Just as I thought.*

"Now, son hold on. No need to keep spilling blood. You can walk away. No more damage than you already have there."

"Yea? You're gonna let me go? Just like that?

Milton let out a horrendous laugh "No. Not just like that. I know you're smarter than that."

"No. Kill me. Because that's the only way you're getting her. Dead or not, you can't have her!"

Not moved by my conviction, he moved closer to me. He was close enough now to put the barrel to my temple. "You do have spunk. In the face of death, you remain defiant. I like you, kid. I really do. Such a shame I gotta waste you."

"Milton, you know what your problem is? Huh?"

Again, he laughed. "Seeing as how you don't look like a killer, and are highly green to this life, I'll let you have your last words. So, tell me, Sir, as you Americans say."

"You don't know how to love because you don't know people."

"Son, my entire business is people!"

"That's just my point. You don't look at the people, even those close to you, as extensions of you. They're your property. Something for you to throw away when you're done with them, or when they've outlived their purpose."

"Man, I really like you!" He chuckled. "It's just too bad I gotta shoot ya." I stared down the barrel as he raised it to my face. Taking in as much air as I could, I puffed my chest out like I was Superman when he first steps out of the phone booth. Closing my eyes, I accepted my fate. Hearing the gun cock stilled my heart. I was ready, though. I just wish I could've held Zora one more time.

I felt nothing when the gun went off. There was no pain. I didn't even feel the bullet. *Was I still standing?* I began to wonder what happened. I opened my eyes and felt a shock throughout my entire being. Standing there, smoking nine in hand, was Billy! I looked down, and saw Milton's body fall over, sliding down the car's side door. Shaking from head to toe, Billy stumbled over to me. He said no words as he reached me and grabbed hold of my shoulders. He pulled himself up, raised his blood-soaked hand, and patted me on my face like "Atta boy." His eyes were rolling as he sunk into my arms. We fell to the cold concrete, and he smiled while blood spilled from his lips. He was gone.

Empathetic, I dragged Billy to the car and used all my might to put him in the back seat. Closing the door, I just stood there, leaning against it. The gunfire was so quiet now, it sounded like fireworks. As soon as I let out a sigh of relief, I could feel the pain in my leg. Dragging the almost-dead limb, I made my way to the driver's side and got in the car. The keys were already in the ignition. A box was on the floor in front of the passenger seat, and I hadn't noticed when I put Zora in the car. I stared at her face as she slumped in the passenger's seat. I leaned over and hugged her. She still felt warm to me. Without warning, tears came flowing out of my eyes. I let out a loud scream as I sat there and bawled like a baby.

As the light hit my red, burning eyes, I lifted my head from the steering wheel. The sun was coming up, and I was all cried out. *I have a promise to keep.* I started the car and took my time shifting it in gear. Finally, I put my foot on the gas and drove away.

REVEALING ENCOUNTER

The sound of sharp but disorienting splashes was the first thing I noticed. Focusing on that sound, I realized it was water dripping from a faucet. It took me all of two minutes to learn the darkness I woke up in was from my own eyelids. They felt heavy As I struggled to open my eyes, I tried to let my other senses tell me something of what was going on. Whatever I was laying on was soft, but not a bed. I could smell coffee and cedar burning. When I finally got my eyes open, the objects in front of me were still hard to see. My head felt instantly groggy when the light hit my eyes. I needed to focus.

After what felt like an eternity of pinching my eyes closed, my vision improved, but not completely. I confirmed what my other senses found. I was laid out on a stretcher with a plastic mat in front of a fireplace. Still unable to move, I used my eyes to look around to see what I could. The wooden frame and moss growing on the windows told me I was in a cabin in somebody's woods. There was a small kitchen area where someone made coffee. Different food ingredients were scattered, as if someone was getting ready to cook something. I could see corn, green beans, and some flour in a bowl. There was a door next to the kitchen too small to be the main entrance. In the middle of the top half of the door was a window that let in the light from outside. I couldn't see much but the wooden beams for the porch and some plants sitting on the ledge. I tried to move, but my muscles wouldn't respond. Even moving my head around was a task. I tried to listen more to figure out if I could hear someone or something that would give me an idea of where I was.

Suddenly, I heard a door open, and footsteps approaching. Their clunking boots sounded heavy and mean. I started to panic and tried to inch myself towards the edge of the stretcher. Maybe if I fell off this thing, I could roll somewhere. The footsteps stopped, and I froze. *Should I close my eyes and pretend I'm still out? Should I just take my chances on the roll?* The walking started again, but slowly. The closer they got, the more my heart sank into my stomach. I didn't know who was around that corner, and I'd never been so scared. I closed my eyes when I saw the toe part of the boots come into view. Laying there, trembling, I could feel whoever it was, was getting close to me. I was thinking of biting them if they got close enough. I was preparing my mind for the worst. My fear was immediately demolished when I felt a warm hand on my face and my name off his lips. "Zora?" he asked. I opened my eyes and saw Keith standing over me with tears in his eyes. "Oh my God, woman!" he exclaimed as he reached in to hug me. "I thought you'd never wake up!"

"Keith?" I said, confused. "How...?" Before I could ask, he put a finger over my mouth.

"You need to regain your strength. Your muscles need time to reacclimate. They feel pretty heavy now, right? I'll tell you everything. Just lay there and rest, please."

"Well, can you at least move me off this thing?" I chuckled. "I could roll off and I kinda wanna sit up."

Keith helped me sit up and swung my legs over one of his arms. With the other, he raised the rest of me up and carried me over to a small couch in front of the fireplace. After setting me down, he grabbed a green blanket covered in pictures of colorful leaves. He then wrapped it around my shoulders. Bringing me It was tea. He knew, and it made me smile. He stood in front of the mantle and started fidgeting with his hands. “I’m not really sure where to start.” He nervously chuckled.

“How ‘bout whether or not Milton is dead?" I responded, taking a sip of the tea.

“Oh yeah, no worries. He is dead. But it wasn’t Milton’s men that shot you.”

Spitting out some of the tea I just drank, I asked, "Excuse me, Sir!?"

“See, Walter knew Milton wasn’t gonna be satisfied with nothing but your death. So, he had one of his people shoot you with a special bullet. Yes, it wounded you, but it also put a drug in your bloodstream that was designed to make you seem dead. It slowed your heartbeat enough to give the appearance of death. Fred gave me the antidote to wake you up. Told me to give it a couple days. There was this box in the car they had for us. It told me how to dress your wound and where to go. This is a cabin from Walter. He said no one knows about this place, so we should be safe for a week or two. If people are alive from the gun fight and looking, then we should keep moving till we get back to the states. They won’t follow us back there. Walter said if Milton is dead, along with most of the people he brought with him, no one will come that far. They’ll most likely be glad and start over the way they want without him. But it won’t be safe if we stay in Canada.”

I had finished my tea by the time he was done telling me everything. The tears that were falling from my face had replaced the tea in the cup. *I am free! No more Milton! No more looking over my shoulder! My life was mine.* I smiled as the tears fell into the cup. I almost started to laugh. Keith stared at me, I'm guessing, to make sure I didn't crack. Using the blanket to dry my tears, I looked up at Keith and said, “I’m fine. I’m simply happy.” He nodded with a joyous smile, and made his way back to the kitchen, repeating “Happy” to himself.

My legs started tingling like they were waking up. I could wiggle my toes freely, and my arms didn't feel heavy anymore. I tried to get up, but it was a struggle. When I made it to my feet, I followed Keith and the smell of good food. I wobbled my way to the kitchen area and looked around. There were red beans and rice with ground beef mixed in, and a bowl of green beans and corn set out on the table. On the counter, there was a colander bowl with paper towels hanging out. I got closer and saw some fried chicken nesting on the paper towels. I looked back towards the stove, and Keith was taking out a fresh pan of cornbread that smelled like heaven! I took a big whiff, closed my eyes, and said, "Damn. Is this what a Black American household smells like on those Sunday dinner days I hear so much about?”

He smiled, and I saw all thirty-two of his teeth. He placed the hot pan on another towel and turned to look at me. "That's right," he said as he wiped the sweat from his forehead. "You never really got close to anyone to show you around a kitchen proper, huh?"

“I am always up for learning new things. Think you can teach me?”

"Only if you stick around," he joked. But I knew he was serious. The room got silent, too silent. *I knew what question was coming. I wasn't sure how to answer.* I studied Keith so I could interrupt his next thought. And right when he was about to speak, I asked, "So, we've been here three days already, don't ask me how I know. That means we have to leave in a day or two. How we gettin’ back to the states?”

“Uh. Oh, there was money and passports in the box. The car is legal and registered to your American name. I’m using my real info to get back. There is no record of me coming so I won’t be an easy target. We can drive right over the border.”

“Yea, they ask questions though," I replied, throwing the blanket back to the couch. I moved around to the counter to help Keith move food to the table. "Do we have a cover story?"

“Yea, that’s what I was working on while you were out. I got some pics of us at the convention. And the couple we met in Colorado, the wife, De’Borah, sent me some pics of their visit to Niagara Falls to clean up for her. So, I made copies and photoshopped us in so we could say we were there. The box already had receipts from hotels and gas stations, so I put everything together to see what kind of story I could make. Good thing I brought my camera.”

"Wow," I said while helping set the table. “I am impressed. You amaze me. And that takes quite a lot of skill to do.”

“Good. I got more surprises to come,” he replied, as he cut into the cornbread.

I smiled and turned to look for plates. As I turned back to the table, I asked, "How did you know about the tea, if I may?"

“Oh...uh," he started, "Walter said to give it to you when you woke up. Said it would help calm you. You don't like waking up not knowing where you are. Anxiety, right?"

“Yea," I said blankly, staring off into the distance at nothing at all. *That’s right. Walter’s not here. Which means he didn’t make it.* I think I stayed silent longer than I should have.

“Don't worry," Keith said, finally breaking the silence. "I didn’t leave him behind. For obvious reasons I couldn’t wait for you to wake up to bury him, but we can say goodbye before we leave. This was his place. So, it only seemed right.”

As he talked, I felt a warmth in my center that I never felt before. The tears in my eyes would not stop. They kept coming, like a naturally flowing stream. In place of my usual frown, was a smile that made me feel at peace. Frozen in place, I cried silently as if Keith couldn’t see. I closed my eyes tight and just let the tears fall. In the midst of my grieving, I felt Keith put his arms around me and pull me in close. I hugged him back and let out a sob of a cry. The sound from my cry came deep within my chest. The way it came out sounded like a cough one was trying to hold in. Walter was gone; it hurt me more than I realized.

Keith made us plates, and we sat down at the table to eat. He told me about college and his two friends I met at the business meeting in Chicago. He told stories of his childhood and growing up with a single mom, his crazy adolescence, and his embarrassing teen girlfriends. It was like he didn't mind talking. Like he knew that I didn't have any stories like his. He already knew my life story. He didn’t even ask if I wanted to talk, and I think he did that for me. He just watched me tell my story to a room full of strangers. I appreciated him for being so kind. Laughing, eating, and just enjoying this whole encounter made me feel normal. He made me feel normal.

Since Keith cooked, it only felt right that I clean up. My muscles were loose enough for that, at least. He complied and went off to straighten up the rest of the cabin. While I washed dishes, wiped the counter, and straightened up the table, he got rid of the stretcher I was on and the bloody mess and bandages from dressing my wound. There was somber music playing from what I assumed was Keith's phone, and the atmosphere felt so peaceful. I couldn't help but wonder if this was what life had in store for me now. These normal peaceful moments without wondering if someone will crash through the front door, wanting to eliminate me, gave me butterflies. It felt nice and welcoming, like it was where I belonged.

After drying and putting away the dishes, I went looking for Keith. I hadn't seen him in an hour or so. Walking around into the living room area, I could hear water running in the back of the house. I followed the sound until I found Keith bending over a steamy tub with candles lit around the bathroom. Without turning around, he spoke. "A nice bath will get your body back to its old self again."

I leaned in the doorway and folded my arms. "Is that an order, Sir?" I asked with a smile.

"Sir?" he asked, standing to face me.

"I mean...you been in charge for so long and doing good."

"Well, in that case, yes, it is, Miss. Nothing but rest."

"Well hopefully not just rest," I said, approaching the steaming tub and removing my clothes. Naked, I sauntered past him and brushed a hand across his face. He had great restraint. Looking down, I saw his dick at half a chug. He was really holding back. He took my hand and helped me down into the sudsy water. Letting my body disappear beneath the bubbles, I watched him walk out of the bathroom and close the door. After about five minutes, I sank under the water to let it wash away my worries, fears, and tears of the past.

I dried off, oiled down, and put on the pajamas Keith left out for me. He was really something and had me surprised at every turn. Leaving the bathroom, I turned to turn off the lights and close the door. It felt like there was no time at all from when the door closed to when I felt his hands on my arms. His hands were on fire. The warmth was comforting to my body, so much that my heart sped up with Keith's every move. The impeccable urge to touch me was pouring out of every breath that I felt on my skin. I was craving him just as much as he was craving me. It had been quite some time since we were intimate. However, this time would be different. This time, I wasn't going anywhere, and I think he knew it.

Like a heroin addict needing a fix, we were all over each other. We scrambled over one other, trying to assist in unclothing the other while getting in some fiery kisses. *I have been ready to receive my newly appointed king. I have waited a long time for someone to love me, as myself.* We managed to reach the bed, kissing and tearing clothes off. Hitting the bed seemed to bring things down to a slower pace. He stepped back and proceeded to remove his belt. I bit my lip as I watched him undo his pants and let them and his boxers fall to the floor. Without hesitation or strain, his dick just popped out and stood straight, so hard and ready. I got turned on just from the form it took. When he was confident, he was massive. I could tell from where I was that he was aching for my warmth.

His solidity twitched and jumped as he approached me apprehensively. I was ready to bend over and let Keith take me, but I couldn't resist when I saw it, that clear nectar, starting to seep from his protruding flesh. There was so much precum dripping from him, my mouth watered. I acted without thinking. I dropped to my knees as he got closer, and with no guide or assistance, his throbbing penis found its way to my lips. He tasted sweeter than honey on fresh biscuits. I licked the side of his shaft, and when reaching the top, I engulfed all of him in my mouth. Making sure he hit the back of my throat with every thrust, I grabbed him and twisted my hand as I moved up and down. Slurping the spit I left behind, I made more at the same time. I moaned to the pleasure that he got from my skills as a proud dick sucker.

After letting me have control for a while, Keith let out a moan that was closer to a low growl and grabbed a handful of my hair. He started moving on his own. I opened my lips wider to let him have full access. He moved slowly in and out of my mouth until more slob started to drip out the sides of my lips. Keith put his free hand on the back of my head and moved me himself. He face-fucked me good. Shoving it down my throat, he held it there until tears swelled in my eyes. He yanked away to let me catch my breath. I coughed and closed my eyes tight to pinch off the tears.

I think I took three good breaths before I felt his hands in my hair and on the back of my head again. His dick throbbing in my face, and getting closer, I opened my mouth to receive him. He shoved it back in my mouth and started at a fast pace. The way he moved in and out of my mouth made it water all over again. When Keith realized this, he slowed down some. He moved his hips in a circle. I let my tongue massage every part of his penis I could reach. With every new motion, he was moaning, and I started to get wet from his sounds. I moved my hand up his thigh, stopping when I reached his bare hanging balls. I massaged them as he fucked my mouth slowly. His moans boosted when he felt my touch. He let out a mess of statements like, "Oh damn,"

"Shit," and some of the usual sounds. It was when he threw his head back and said, "Oh my God, woman!" that made my pussy throb from excitement. I wanted him to take me.

I told myself that he knew exactly what I wanted when he stopped, picked me up and pushed me to the bed. This felt familiar. *I see.* My turn to scoot back and watch the hungry hunter come for his prey; I did just that. I laid back and waited for him to mount me, but I got a different sensation instead. I could feel his hands slowly caressing my freshly bathed and oiled legs. He ran his hands all the way up to my wet and sticky pussy. That whole aggressive ordeal had me dripping and ready for dick. It would seem, however, that Keith wanted to take his time.

Rubbing my clit with his thumb, he got closer to me. I twitched and moaned from his warm hands on my body. When he stuck his fingers in me, I moaned louder, and my pussy grabbed his fingers. "Oooo," he let out and removed his fingers. Keith then brought his face to my clit and started eating my leaking box. I couldn't help it. I couldn't take getting head now; I was too anxious. I think he knew this as he let slip some moans while smacking on my lower lips. I let out aggressive moans that said I was trying to fight him off. I didn't want to cum yet. I wanted to feel him. But my anxiousness would tell more than I realized.

As I rubbed his head in pleasure, he flicked his tongue on my clit and licked the juices I was leaking. He stuck his tongue in and out, dragging his tongue to my clit over and over. I tried to hold my reaction, but it was too much. "Damn! No. I don't want to," I whispered. He lifted his head from between my legs and replaced his tongue with his thumb, rubbing my climax button. "Don't want to, what?" he asked back and returned to lick my throbbing pussy. I was going to have an orgasm, and he knew it. He started to get aggressive and ravaged my pussy. I squeezed his head with my legs as I approached my heightened climax. I tried not to squeeze hard as I hit cloud nine, and my body was overcome with what felt like an overdose of adrenaline. Tingles started inward and moved throughout my body, and my moans sounded like a cry of surrender.

Wasting no time at all, he lifted up and climbed on top. I wasn't even finished having convulsions from the orgasm he just gave me. Again, I felt his solid member fill my walls. My pussy grabbed ahold of his dick, and he sighed in pleasure. He started off slow-moving his hips in a circle, being kind to my being sensitive. Every move he made intensified the eruption in my body. It was like a domino effect of cummings and orgasms. He started going a little bit faster, thrusting more. That set me on fire, making my pussy leak with every motion. His movement in and out of my juicy pussy, the feeling of his dick hitting that spot all the way in the back, and his warm breath on my neck were enough to trigger a massive orgasm. My legs started shaking, and he noticed. He lifted up some more and picked up the pace.

As I moaned in ecstasy, I lifted my shaking legs and wrapped them around him. Giving in to me, he laid back on me, and his movements got harder. I wrapped my arms around his head to get a better hold as the bed started to rock with our bodies. He moaned in my ear as he felt the throbbing in my pussy increase. "Cum on this dick!" he whispered in my ear. *Damnit. He was so on to me.* There was no hiding my expressions from him, so I let it all out. I gave in and let the orgasms take me. "Oh damn," I moaned when I reached the point of climax again. This time was different. Behind this orgasm, I was cumming, and with that was a flood gate of juices. I could feel it when he moved out, and I thought I would gush all over him. Instead, it was held for this. As I came, the warm liquid was released and flowed down his dick. He short pumped me for about five minutes to make more leak out as he pressed against my twitching clitoris. My eyes rolled to the back of my head as I moaned and let him make me squirt all over his chocolate-skinned dick. I was getting sensitive, and I started to claw at his back. I could feel his dick throbbing as he slowed down and moved in and out to tease me. I could tell he was close to cumming. I wanted to return the many favors he just gave me.

Moving my hips below him and in rhythm, he got the impression I was ready for more. But he rolled over and let me have the top. *Excellent. Just what I wanted him to do.* I positioned myself so I had proper leverage to bounce on my own, and he could move with ease below me if he wanted. I wasn't going to take it slow or easy. I grabbed the headboard with both hands and started at a moderate pace. Keith moved his hands up and down my body while I rolled on his lap, making his dick go in and out. I turned my feet in and started bouncing my ass on his lap. His grip on my waist tightened and loosened when I came down on his dick. I bounced up and down and moaned in his ear until he started to get more verbal. I came up until it was just the tip of his dick in my pussy and stayed there to let my juices drip as I throbbed on his tip. I came down slowly, and his body jerked into mine. I released my feet and rocked my hips from left to right. I pushed off my thighs and moved my ass up and down as I rolled my hips front to back. His moans got louder, and the pulsing inside me got stronger. *This is it. He is going to cum for me.*

Keith surprised me when he held off. He flipped me off him and rolled me over on my stomach. He put my legs together and arched my ass up some. He slid inside my sticky pussy with ease. He grabbed onto my waist and pounded the shit out of my ass. At the pace he was going, the consistency of him hitting that back spot was making me feel a fiery eruption throughout my body. As my moans got stronger, his pace got faster. He was fucking me harder and harder, and I got closer to exploding. Right before I was about to cum, his moans started to match mine. I wanted to cum with him, but I couldn't hold it. I let out a cry of pleasure as I came on his now firmly hard dick, and juices squirted out of my box as he kept fucking me. My moans didn't stop after I came, and neither did his thrusting. He moaned with me, and I kept leaking with every glide inside me. He grabbed me tighter as he was about to cum. Out of nowhere, he took a hand and grabbed my throat as he pumped harder on my ass. This excited me enough to make my clit twitch as he fucked me hard. "Damn! I love being in this pussy," he whispered. "Got this pussy dripping," he said as he used his other hand and grabbed my hair.

I couldn't resist giving into the scene. I didn't even think about what I was supposed to say. I just responded with, "That good dick make this pussy leak."

"That makes this my pussy then?"

"Yes."

"Yes, what?"

"MMMM," I moaned instead of answering directly. *I'm not sure what it is about that word, but it just makes me act so defiant.* I didn't want to just say it. I wanted him to make me. But he knew that, which is why he wore me out first, and it wouldn't take much.

He repositioned himself over me and let my legs go. He pulled my ass up more in the air, and I complied. He pushed the middle of my back down, so I laid at an arch. With no warning, he shoved his throbbing member in my dripping pulsating pussy. I moaned off the first entry, and he did not go slow. He fucked me rough and fast like he was trying to prove a point. I screamed and moaned as I tried to fight off more orgasms. He grabbed my hair and pulled me into him. I lifted up, and he immediately grabbed my throat again and squeezed a little. As he fucked me, more juices started to leak out of me and down both our legs. Feeling his breath on my ear, he whispered, "That pussy still leaking and starting to cream. Why you doing that?"

Oh, he was a cheeky bastard, but I liked it, and I responded with, "Cause this dick good."

"So, it's mine, right?" he asked.

"Yes."

"Yes.... WHAT!" he said in a demanding yet low voice.

I couldn't deny him anymore. I was about to have another orgasm, and he felt my pussy get tight around his dick. With a hand on my throat and my hair tangled in his fingers, I let out my final cry of passion as the flood gates below opened and a wellspring of nectar came flowing out of my pussy and down our thighs. He moaned deep and hard as I responded, "Yes, Daddy!" With that, he came and felt his hot fluid shoot into me. My pussy was having convulsions as we succumbed to our emotions as we fell on the bed. Tired and breathing heavy, we came together and ended up in the spooning position. I didn't need to stay alert to wait until he fell asleep. I let the exhaustion take me and fell asleep in his arms.

The next morning, I woke up before Keith and started the coffee. There were brand new boots by the back door that looked to be my size. I put them on and went out back. I walked straight for about three minutes before I saw it. There was an irregular dirt heap in the middle of the woods, next to the tallest tree in the area. It looked as if someone had dug the dirt up there. I figured it was where Keith had buried Walter. I half expected a headstone or something, but we were on the run. They would think we killed him. I wouldn't want that for Keith. I stopped before the heap and stood there. I thought I was all cried out until I saw that dusty old baseball cap of his resting right on top. *Yeah, I am going to miss him. He loved me like a real daughter and looked out for me.*

I heard a twig snap behind me and turned sharply. It was Keith with two cups, one of piping hot coffee and the other hot tea. He handed me the tea and put his arm on my shoulder. He said nothing for a while. He finally broke the silence with, "Walter was the one who shot Milton, ya know."

"Shut up!" I exclaimed. I didn't hear that part of the story.

"Yea," he said, as he walked closer to the large aspen tree. "I was cornered and thought Milton was gonna shoot me, right. I closed my eyes, and I heard a gun go off, but I wasn't dead. I opened them, and Walter was there, barrel smoking and all. I thought I was a goner for real."

"Shit! That's intense!"

"Yea. Before that, though, after you were shot, he was too. And he helped me get away from the crowd, and I lost him for a long while before he showed up to shoot Milton."

"Damn. That's comic book worthy. Sounds like him, though. Always saving the day in one way or another."

"Tough S.O.B., that's for sure."

"Nobody like him at all. I'm really gonna miss him. Thank you for bringing him here. Allowing me to say goodbye.

Nothing you did, you had to. And I know you keep saying not to thank you, but I wouldn't feel right if I didn't."

Keith approached me and threw his remaining coffee out. He grabbed my neck and drew me in close. He let out a heavy sigh and said, "Stupid. You thank me just from smiling." With that statement, I cried more, and we went back to the cabin.

Over the next few days, we managed to leave the cabin. We headed across the border and made it back into the states. Our cover story worked. I think it was because we got a patrolman who had his honeymoon at Niagara Falls, and the pictures Keith fabricated made him nostalgic. He didn't want to give a newly wedded couple a hard time, so he let us go after stamping our passports. We drove for days, only stopping to get gas, food, and sleep at some roadside motel. When we reached the middle of Idaho, I had to ask.

"Keith?" I inquired, while he was surfing the horrible T.V. channels at the latest dive we stopped at.

"Yea, babe?" he responded.

"Um. Where are we going?"

"Oh. Um, I travel where I need to for work. I mean, I have an apartment in Seattle, but I figured you'd want to check in with the hotel and whatnot."

"FUCK!" I shouted as I jumped off the bed. "I didn't even think of that. I don't even know what I'm going to tell them. I have nothing to say as to why I was gone so long."

"You remember Walter said your assistant was one of his?" Keith asked as he sat up and turned off the T.V.

"Vaguely," I responded, looking bewildered.

"Ok so, Ciera was placed there by Walter. He never lost you. He just didn't tell Milton. And sent him on some wrong trails when Milton got close. Unfortunately, Ciera was compromised."

"Yea, I figured when Ali showed up in Colorado."

"So, Walter had access to everything she did- including your schedule at the hotel. He made it so you were on numerous business travels to, quote on quote, "ascertain" other locations after the deal we made in Chicago. Your bosses won't know anything. You can go back when you want. I just figured your life was there so we can go get your stuff or check in. Whatever you want to do."

"And how do you know all this?" Again, I was asking with bewilderment.

Keith got up and went outside. I stood there wondering what the hell just happened. In no time at all, he came back with a medium-sized box. It was metal, and looked dense from the way he was carrying it. He set it down, and I closed the door behind him. "In this box was everything we needed to get out. Walter left it. There was a note. Not sealed or addressed to anyone. It had some details we were missing, like the cabin, your job, shit like that." I grabbed the letter and sat down to read. It was carefully detailed with everything, just like Keith said. Before I could reach the middle of the first page, a joint appeared in my face. I chuckled and took it from Keith. I smoked while I read. Everything was laid out for Keith. He had to do a lot while I was knocked out. This made me appreciate him even more.

As we passed the joint between us, I learned some things. The letter told me how to get out of Canada, where the cabin was, and even told me the location of a safe house in Chicago if I wanted to go back. *I could start there and check everything out before I show my face.* The house was in the name of my birth mother, so nobody would ever find it.

I didn't even know it until I read the letter. I was curious how Walter knew, but I remembered that he was an undercover cop and let it go. I now knew about the money, the safe house, and there was something else. *If I went to my mother's house, I could know the truth about everything the letter says. I could just walk away and start over with this money. Any normal person wouldn't hesitate.* However, I was curious.

I told Keith I wanted to go to my mother's house, and we mapped out a route from the motel. In a week, we were standing outside a red brick house in Rockford, Illinois. The name on the mailbox said Humphreys, like the last name I was using. I got confused. I pulled the letter out and read about the house again. *It says my mother's name was Anitra Watson. But Humphreys is on the mailbox.* I read the address and checked the house number. I was in the right place. The letter said it would be a red-bricked house that sat on the corner. The corner was on a hill, so it was like the house was pushed back further than the others. *There should be a spare key in a fake rock sitting under the first step to the porch.*

Keith took my hand and walked me to the house. When we reached the porch steps, I looked for a fake rock. The only problem was, they all looked like real rocks. *It will look weird if we started chucking rocks across the lawn...* Keith tapped me on the shoulder and handed me a pen. "Genius!" I said excitedly. *The fake will be hollow!* I tapped all the rocks until I found the one, I was looking for. I was scared when I put the key in the keyhole. I looked at Keith and turned the key, and without looking, I opened the door.

After being pushed inside, I looked around. It was a normal house. Fall themed living room with warm brown and orange colors in the wallpaper. The couch was also brown with small leaf pillows, and there was a small end table and no T.V. There were stairs off to the left of the entrance, and I went up while Keith explored the rest of downstairs. The stairs went up for about eight steps, then veered off to the right. I saw a bathroom and hall closet coming up the last stair. I walked down the long hallway, peeking into each of the rooms. There were three rooms upstairs, and all were plainly decorated. There were just bed frames with white sheets and no comforters. The pillows were white, but dusty like nobody ever used them. There were no dressers, ottomans at the foot of the bed, or any other bedroom decorations.

One room in the back, though, had an old chest sitting in the middle. After checking all the rooms, I stood in the doorway, staring at this chest. I could hear Keith roaming around, and eventually he made his way upstairs. When he approached me, I turned to look at him. "Did the letter say anything about this?" I asked, pointing at the chest.

“Uh... I don’t think so," he said, peering around to look at the chest. “The only box Walter mentioned was the one in the car.” Keith walked around me and up to the chest. He observed, walked around it, and kicked it. He squatted behind it and said, “There is no lock. If you want me to open it, you can stay there.”

I thought for a while, nervously rubbing my hands over each other. I finally told him yes and walked into the room. When Keith opened the chest, dust flew off the top when it fell back. There was another box inside, and a cream-colored envelope. When Keith handed me the envelope, I saw I was mistaken, and it was not cream; it was just really old. There was some old clothing, toys, and dingy old photos alongside the box in the chest. Keith and I took turns turning everything over and examining things. The photos were really dusty, dirty, and barely visible. The one good photo we found was of a man and a woman. They looked like they were at Mom's club back in the day. The curtains in the background had Milton written all over them. The guy was white, slender, and full-haired. He had a strong, square jawline and eyes that seemed familiar. The woman was black, a foot shorter than the man, and I had never seen her before. I flipped the picture over and saw written, "*Billy and Ani, 1986*".

I was getting captivated by the discovery of this chest in my supposed mother's house. Photos of an old, mixed racial couple made me wonder who they were. Every now and then, I looked up from them to see Keith reading what looked to be an old leather-bound diary. I assumed the lady was my birth mom, with the house being hers. The photos gave me a way of knowing her. I grew up in foster homes and the streets until Milton took me in, so I never got a chance to know who she was. She looked happy, and like she was having fun in all the photos. I could tell. Her smile lit up a room, it seemed. As happy as I was to see she had a good life, I was getting just as sad, wondering why she didn't keep me.

Keith had stopped reading whatever it was he was reading and made his way in front of me. The toes of his shoes hit my leg, and I looked up, annoyed. *There are just some things you do not do when you know that a person can kill you eighteen different ways,* I thought to myself.

"Sorry," he said, after realizing what happened. "Zora, did you read the letter yet?"

"I forgot really," I laughed. "Got caught up like a nerd in a library."

"I think you should read the letter. I'll leave all this here. Sit on the bed; it looks like we'll be here for a while. And technically you're still healing. I'll go get food and drinks. And something tells me beer is needed." Keith dug around in his pocket for a tiny, red, clear tube. Even from where I was, I could tell there was a joint in there. "I'll leave this here for you. And bring back more. I'll just... go," he said, placing the joint on the bed. I thanked him, watched him leave, and grabbed the leather-bound book and the letter.

I looked at both the diary and the letter like foreign objects until I reached the bed. Picking up the joint Keith left me, I flopped down on the bed as I lit it. Opening the diary, I realized it was not a diary at all. It was a report book given to undercover cops. They could document every detail of their case without always having to report in. Knowing that and recognizing the handwriting, I felt at ease figuring out that it belonged to Walter. I instantly remembered that Walter told us his real name was Billy. My mind then wandered to the words I read minutes before; "*Billy and Ani.*" ...*Was Walter into my mom?*

Taking a small puff off the still-lit joint, I got even more curious and stared at the letter. *Was this from Walter, well, Billy?* My mind couldn't keep up with what my heart was trying to process. I put down the book and tapped the ashes off the end of the joint. I picked up the envelope, and it felt like something hard was in it. Pulling out the letter, a small golden key fell out. I sat the key on the pillow, and I got comfortable to take in what I might read. Kicking off my slip-on shoes,, I climbed further back into the bed, took long drags off the joint, picked my feet up, and read.

Dear Zora,

If you're reading this, it means Milton is dead, and so am I. I'm happy you found your way to the house. It's yours if you want. Before you decide, I feel that I must tell you the truth.

My real name is William "Billy" Browne. You probably know me by now as Walter. If you made it this far, you now know I was a cop. I knew your mom, your real mom. Her name was Anitra Humphreys, and she was my firefly in the darkest of nights. Her father was a big-time gangster way back when named Tommy Wilson, so she used that name to get in and out of places she wanted. She was wild and untamable, and everybody loved her. But she chose to love me. I loved her in secret for a long time. And when she got pregnant, people just thought it was one of her many suitors.

Milton was one of those men after her. He was furious that she wouldn't tell anyone who the father was. Milton was a monster, but he wasn't evil. He wouldn't harm your mother while she was pregnant. I was on the force but not a detective yet, so I had truly little power to protect her. After you were born, she tried to have a life with you, but the constant violent visits from a jealous Milton would make anyone nervous. We decided to give you up. We didn't know the system would fall apart and betray you like it did. I tried to use my authority to keep tabs on you, but I lost you after age ten.

I was happy and pissed off when Milton started bringing you around. I was worried about his plans for you. When it was revealed that he would make you part of THE GROUP, I wasn't angry but grateful that he would teach you everything I couldn't so you could escape. I stayed as close as I could and watched out when I could. I'm sorry I had to keep everything from you until the end.

I set this stuff in motion after you came to me that night. I wanted to kill him dead with my own hands, but I was too far undercover. That's why I helped you get away. It was going to be my gift to you for abandoning you. The things you asked me to hold are in the small chest. The key can be found in the envelope with this letter. All are accounted for, and I put some things of my own in. Leave you some things of your mom and me to help you get to know us better.

About your name, if you look in the report book, you'll find your real birth certificate. Your mom has family there in the states, and they helped hide your mom when she got sick and left. They helped me keep you hidden, and to get this house. All these things were set in motion when you left, so there may be some papers and whatnot to sign depending on how long it's been. There are some names and numbers in the report book if you get curious about where you come from. Please believe me when I say that your mother and I never wanted to do this. we never wanted you struggling to live. we just loved you so much that we wanted you to live. Even if it meant away from us.

I gotta tell ya, kiddo, if your mom could see you! She'd be proud of the woman you became–the first woman on the elite squad. Enough to make old Ali tremble. Man, Ani would of gloated! You would of loved her.

I'm sorry again how things turned out. Don't be sad for an old man like me. If I am dead, I'm with Ani once again. I love you. Always have, always will. Don't forget that.

Love,

Your Dad

By the time I was finished reading the letter, I had soaked the pages with my tears. I didn't know what to think or say. "All this time," I sobbed. "Yeah, toughest S.O.B. around." I picked up the report book and flipped through the pages. I noticed the names and partial phone numbers in my dad's handwriting that were wiped away by erosion. I smiled when I came across random photos hidden in the pages. While I was flipping, I heard Keith coming back. I thought about wiping my tears away and making it look like I wasn't crying. That was out of habit. I knew there was no need for that. Keith would be happy for me, and I didn't need to hide anything from him.

I listened to his footsteps climb the stairs. Relighting the joint that I let go out, I prepared to hand it to him as he entered the room. I could smell the food in the hall and knew it was polishes and fries. Tears still staining my face, I watched him as he walked in with a mouth full of fries. He stopped at the joint, took it, and laid the food down on the bed where I sat. The smile he had on his face went away when he saw mine. He approached me with a worried look and wiped the remaining tears off my face. I didn't say a word, I just smiled at him. The look he returned said he needed answers. So, without saying anything, I handed him my birth certificate.

Keith paces when he is conflicted. When the pacing stopped, he looked up and smiled. "So, your name really is Zora?" he asked.

"Yep. That's what it says,", I responded, sniffling the last of my tears away.

“So, Walter- I mean Billy...suggested you use this name when you left?”

“Yea. I told him I was planning to leave, and he said he would take care of the paperwork and I.D.s. I didn’t think twice about where the info came from.”

“He set you up. Good. You have been using your real name and United States social security number for a while. Do you know what that means?" he asked with stars in his eyes.

"Yea," I chuckled, "I am me! And I have never been anybody else.”

“Hot damn! I was worried about how we were going to keep you hidden from bad guys and the government. One less worry. Now you just need a nest egg to start over in a new light.”

"I might have a solution to that," I said as I slid off the bed. I picked up the little golden key and went to the chest. Once the lid was pulled off the box, a small safe was revealed. Keith got intrigued, took a long drag off the joint, and got closer to see. I showed him the key before inserting it into the safe’s lock. I turned the key slowly until we both heard a sharp “click”. The safe had a top lid, so when it unlocked, the lid lifted just a little. Slowly raising it, I showed Keith what I had suspected was in there this whole time. With the sun beaming through the window, it added an extra dramatic effect of twinkling. There, in the safe, was a stack of gold bars. “Holy fuck!” Keith screamed. “How? When did you...? WHAT!?” He was hysterical. I could tell I had to give him an explanation.

"I'm gonna make this short," I said, picking up a bar. I rubbed the cold gold once over and handed it to Keith. "So…." I started, "Do you remember my first job I told you guys about?” I waited for him to acknowledge that before I kept going. “I let the guy go. In return, he led me to a safe in his hideout.”

“But I thought you turned that over to Milton," he interrupted.

I stood up to stretch my legs, grabbed the joint, and toked. "Yes," I said as I exhaled the smoke in my lungs. "You don’t bite the hand that feeds you. I took Milton to the safe and gave him the gold. But not all of it. I went to the safe the same night and took shit out for me. I even took some old files he had on Milton and his goonies for insurance purposes if I needed an out. I was gonna use it back at the amusement park. I guess Billy took care of that, too.”

“Well, we wouldn’t need the files anymore, would we?” he asked.

“Not so fast, Hop-A-Long. It’s not that simple. It wasn’t just stuff on Mom. It was the whole Group. Right now, I don’t see anyone coming after me. There were so many people that wanted Mom out, and not just the outside people suffering from his semi-rule. There were common, decent, innocent folks that wanted him gone, too. From inside the club, people wanted better treatment and respect. Without Mom, free reign for a whole new regime. Now if someone under Milton took over and had something to say, the only person that would be is Ali. And I doubt he made it out that lot. But if he did, I could take him and if I couldn't, the files would definitely come in handy."

"So not out of the woods yet?"

"Big yes, little no. No, because we don't have any eyes back there to tell us what's going on. At the same time, big yes- because anyone who knows me, and my name wouldn't dare come after us or won't want to bother with an old headache. For now, we are fine. No need to worry at all. Breathe easy." When I was done talking and stood still to look him in the face, I got the impression he really didn't hear me. His reaction to the gold bar was almost cartoonish, like drooling over a coveted item. We ate food and drank beers, talked about the next moves to be made, and spent the night in the house cozied up together with no worries.

The next day, I woke up and just stood in the living room staring out the wall-sized window. This day was different. For the first time in my life, I had nothing to do and nowhere to go. There was no one to run from or look out for. I watched school-aged children board their busses; moms and nannies waved them goodbye. I just soaked up all the normality I was witnessing and was happy to try to be a part of.

"Penny?" I heard Keith say from behind me. I jumped as I heard it. I must have been so deep in my daydreaming that I didn't hear him coming. I sighed with relief and smiled. He walked toward me, gave me a hug, and kissed my forehead. "Liking the scenery, are we?" he asked.

"Yes," I said, with another sigh. "We are, actually."

"Does that mean we have decided on what we're going to do with our lives?"

I hesitated and pulled back from Keith. He looked worried, and it made me more nervous. "I love it here," I responded. "I have this whole new, sort of old, me to figure out. People I have to learn about and meet. I don't know anything about leading a non-assassin life." Keith looked distraught and flopped down on the couch. I walked up to him and kneeled at his feet. "I don't know what any of this means for me. And I can't think of anyone else I'd rather have by my side on this journey than you."

Keith's look of astonishment was comedy. It could have been that I was happy to see him happy and unworried. *Is this what people do when they really care about someone? Their happiness makes you happy? This is a different kind of happy. It has a mixture of hope in it.* The air I was breathing got fresher and clearer somehow. The light from the window got brighter, and the smile on his face got bigger. I didn't know what it was about that day. But whatever it was, it made me hopeful and ready to face any new encounter coming my way.

Miss Me

This has been on my mind all day. Ever since that one night, your touch is all I want. I'm catching myself daydream about how electric your hands feel when they're on me. If I close my eyes long enough and put a finger to my lip, I can feel you kiss me.

2:45pm. Fifteen minutes left. I've been texting you all day telling you how I want you to taste me. Responses like "make you flow like Niagara Falls" gets me juicy between the legs.

At 3pm, I'm doing my last check over on work before i leave. I say "Bye" to my secretary and head towards the elevator. My mind is racing with thoughts of you me feel like a real woman. I get to my car and my phone vibrates. The message says, "Don't move". All of a sudden, a wrap is placed over my eyes. My heart skips a beat. I hear you whisper, "Don't worry. I will take care of you."

I am moved to the passenger seat. I hear the car start and feel us move. There is silence. My excitement level is so far beyond what I'm used to that I cannot control the wetness from below. I move my hand to my thighs. I'm feeling my legs slowly moving my hand between my legs. I want to release some of this excitement. I get my fingers up my skirt. Easy access seeing how I don't like underwear.

I move my fingers to my lower lips and feel the moistness and it turns me on. I play in the mess i have made before I take a finger and gently rub. After about five minutes I add a finger to go inside of me. You hear me let out a small moan and reach over to help me. I feel you warm masculine hands move mine out the way. No hesitation and you slide 2 fingers into my now dripping woman hood. The moan that escapes my lips fills the car with better music than if the radio was on. I can't see it, but I know there is a smile on your face.

I move my hips as to help you explore inside of me. As the temperature gets higher so does my level of excitement. I'm ready to explode all over your fingers. You feel my muscles contract and you know I'm about leak. You stop before I climax and say, "Not yet." I feel the car come to a halt and I get nervous.

With the wrap still over my eyes you lead me out of the car and into someplace warm. I am led to the middle of the room and left there for a while. I can hear your footsteps moving around me and then closer to me. I let out a sigh of anticipation as I can feel you in front of me. You start with my shirt and unbutton it. It is slid off my shoulders and hits the floor. My skirt is next. The zip on the side makes it easy for you to remove it and it too slides to the floor.

Now in front of you stands a caramelized morsel with nectar flowing downing my leg. With the blind fold still on you get on your knees and spread my legs. Your hand caresses its way up to my glory spot and plays before moving your lips to mine. Nirvana.

Heaven. Valhalla. I'm feeling all of these as your tongue flicks in me and your fingers explore my box. Still, you don't let me orgasm. You stop and stand up to push me down on my knees and put a hand on my face. You rub your finger with my juice all over them across my lips almost asking me to taste it. I stick out my tongue and wrap it around your fingers. I taste the candied liquid that I left behind.

Your member pulsates from excitement, and you take your fingers from me and replace it with something stronger. I feel the tip hit my lips and I open more to receive you. I let my tongue slide down the shaft as it enters. Once you hit the back of my throat my lips curve around you to a perfect fit. You thrust in and out while moving your hands to my head. As my mouth gets wetter, the tempo picks up. You hear me slurp and moan as u move in and out. I force my throat on you to take you deeper inside. Your head falls back and you let out pleasuring moans as you slide inside my throat. I hold it there until you can't take it anymore and pull away from me. You pull me up by my arms and thrust your tongue in my mouth. The passionate kisses are just a distraction. You walk with me until my back hits a wall.

The kisses stop and you turn me around with force and bend me over. My hands try to find a spot where I can brace myself know all too well what is coming next. You approach me throbbing and rub the tip across my clit before entering. My moan is a mitigation of anticipation. There is no grace period. You immediately begin to pound me as if never been with a woman before. My hand flies free from the wall and I reach behind me to feel for you. You grab my arm and fold it behind my back to use for leverage. Speed picks up tremendously and can't control my outcry. A melody of "Woo! ".. "Yes!" ... "Oh, my gawd! ".. comes singing from my lips.

My muscles start to squeeze around you, and you pick up speed again. You know I'm about to climax and you want me to this time. You love me harder as I reach my orgasm. You pull out fast to watch me squirt all over floor. You take the blind fold off and kiss me like you never have before. We walk over to the couch and you sit down. I straddle you and slide down on your rock like member. You don't hold back on moaning and showing me how good I make you feel. Your hands manly grab my back as I rock back and forth. You wrap your arms around me and sit up close when i change pace and start to bounce.

You bite me in the ear and whisper "You like this don't you"? I wrap an arm around your neck and one around your head. I get close in whisper "Yes Daddy". The sound of my voice sends tingles up your spine. You wrap your arms around me and hug tight as I bounce faster. You help me go up and down, and you cry out in ecstasy as you reach your climax. I start scratching at your back and you release a sound so befitting to my ears that it makes me smile. I start my climax and you hug tighter. As we both let out a chorus of pleasurable moans, we both hit our orgasms. I leak juices all over your thighs while panting and trying to catch my breathe.

After we catch our breath, slow heart rates, and calm down. You kiss me and say........ "Hi"

Final Thoughts and Honorable Mentions

Blind Encounters came from something me, and my ex-husband tried to do. He was a writer too, and at the time, we worked different hours and barely got to see each other. The story got to the middle of the first chapter and our marriage started to fall apart. I wanted to keep going with the story, so I changed some things, gave the characters names, and ended up adding seven chapters to it. I wasn't looking for closure or anything like that. I just had so many ideas for a story I thought would never be told.

Some of the things in the book were based off some true events. The closing of the amusement park is true. There really was a park in Canada that closed that way. No one still knows what brought the police to the park. The museum being robbed by Irish brothers, and the fire being set as a distraction, also real. I didn't use ant real names, just the situations. There is a club in Canada called the Cleopatra. Hopefully, they do not hate me for choosing them for my mob base. (HAHA) I chose Zora as a name for my character because I really admire Zora Neale Hurston. Not a lot of people even know who she is/was. She was a big inspiration growing up. Her work was intriguing, and the stories were damn good!

It took me almost six years to finish this book. I was in some very dark moments in my life. It kept me from being creative. But the moment I said fuck everything that wasn't under my roof, I started to gain clarity. It took someone close to me to snap me out of my dark days and to them, I say thank you! I was feeling like I had nothing and no one but he stayed by my side, even during the worst of times. I was homeless at one point, and no one would take in a woman with five children. And still that person stayed by my side.

This book was my way of getting out of my own way and not wasting years of talent in depression. The work and effort I put in on this book took everything in me. When you are depressed, you just let everything fall apart. But, with this book, it was like medicine for my soul. I knew I didn't want to leave it unfinished.

I chose erotica for my genre because I am sexually comfortable, confident woman. I don't mind telling people what I like and what I'm into. I don't mind having a serious, mature conversations about things that would make most people uncomfortable. There was a meme going around for a while that said, "If you don't masturbate, I can't fuck with you. Cuz, clearly you don't fuck with you". I felt that to my core. You can't expect someone to know you if you don't know yourself, in and out. Some women don't know what they like, or they hide it because they think they will be judged. I like getting it out there upfront, so I am not disappointed. If you don't think you can keep up with me, then don't try.

I'd like to break that narrative that only guys care about sex or only guys like talking about sex. Sex is a perfectly natural thing. I also want to get rid of the narrative that any woman who likes sex just as much or more than a man is hoe. No, we're not. My five children were the result of my one marriage, and they have the same father. I am very respected in my circle and in my private social groups, where we discuss various sexual concepts. I am often praised about how open and confident I present myself in the situation. We are all human. There is no reason why any one group should be singled out for anything. If nymphomaniacs were a race, we'd be suffering from hellacious racism to the public. At the same time, those same people would be trying to join us privately.

Be who are, do not be ashamed, and love the skin you are in. You never know what you have to offer the world, or what it has to offer you. There can be some hurdles and maybe some halts in your progress, but never stop. Keep going until you are satisfied that you have given it your all.

To some people I did not forget:

Katrice Brevard, I love you! You took me in when I was down in my worst. I appreciate this woman so much. I probably wouldn't have gotten better or thought about my future if she didn't help me when I needed.

Ari Gibson, my first editor, set up my blog for me, and whom without my story wouldn't have been told. I appreciate the early work you did for me and being one of those to recognize my talents.

Desiree Joyce and Everette Jones, while things got rocky, I still appreciate everything you guys did for me. Desiree, if you didn't invite me to a new city, new surroundings, I don't know where I'd be. I appreciate you both!

If you feel as though I left you out, I do apologize. Just know I appreciate everyone who was there for me in my life when I really needed and helped me get through my first project!

"Diseacht thar aon rud eile"

"Loyalty above all else"